GW00367576

POWERS

Close to Dublin's Ormond Gate, on ground formerly known as the Friary Gardens of St John, stood a hostelry from which the mail coaches started their journeys north and west. In 1791, the proprietor – one James Power – converted the establishment into a small distillery. And so began the history of one of Ireland's most famous whiskeys – Powers Gold Label.

The venture prospered and James Power presided over continuous expansion until his death in 1817. The business then passed to the founder's son, John Power, who in 1821 took his son James into partnership. Henceforth the firm traded as John Power & Son – a style still to be found on the label of every bottle.

At the time of its first centenary the firm was exporting its product around the globe. John Power & Son was among the first distillers in the world to bottle its own product – thus ensuring that the whiskey reached its final destination in perfect condition. Powers also pioneered the miniature bottle – still known today as a 'Baby Power'.

As the twentieth century progressed, Powers John's Lane Distillery remained a landmark of Ireland's capital. Through all the momentous events of successive decades, the production of whiskey was never interrupted, as the city, the nation and the world enjoyed its Powers Whiskey.

In the spirit of its founder, Powers responded to the rapidly changing times. In 1966 the firm joined with the other great whiskey houses of Ireland to form the Irish Distillers Group.

Powers is produced at Midleton in County Cork, with the skill for which it has always been renowned and with the pure, natural ingredients that are available only in Ireland.

As ever, Powers Gold Label Irish Whiskey is distilled from a mixture of malted and unmalted barley, the malt being dried in closed kilns to preserve its smooth taste. The result is a subtly developed flavour with clear malt undertones and Powers Gold Label remains the Number One whiskey in Ireland.

THE PUBLISHERS ACKNOWLEDGE WITH GRATITUDE
THE SPONSORSHIP OF
POWERS GOLD LABEL IRISH WHISKEY

WRITERS' WEEK
AWARD-WINNING SHORT STORIES
1973–1994

WRITERS' WEEK
AWARD-WINNING SHORT STORIES
1973–1994

EDITED BY DAVID MARCUS

First published in 1995 by
Marino Books
An imprint of Mercier Press
16 Hume Street Dublin 2

Trade enquiries to Mercier Press
PO Box 5, 5 French Church Street,
Cork

A Marino Original

Foreword © David Marcus 1995
All works © their respective authors
1995

ISBN 1 86023 017 2

10 9 8 7 6 5 4 3 2 1

A CIP record for this title is available
from the British Library

Cover design by Niamh Sharkey
Set by Richard Parfrey in
Caslon 10/15
Printed in Ireland by ColourBooks,
Baldoyle Industrial Estate, Dublin 13

This book is sold subject to the
condition that it shall not, by way
of trade or otherwise, be lent,
resold, hired out or otherwise
circulated without the publisher's
prior consent in any form of
binding or cover other than that
in which it is published and
without a similar condition
including this condition being
imposed on the subsequent
purchaser.

No part of this publication may
be reproduced or transmitted in
any form or by any means,
electronic or mechanical,
including photocopying,
recording or any information or
retrieval system, without the prior
permission of the publisher in
writing.

The Publishers acknowledge with
gratitude the sponsorship of
Powers Gold Label Irish Whiskey.

CONTENTS

FOREWORD

The publication of *Writers' Week Award-Winning Short Stories* on this, the twenty-fifth anniversary of the festival, is a matter of great satisfaction for everyone involved in Writers' Week.

There is hardly a successful writer in Ireland who has not been associated with Writers' Week, and this anthology clearly indicates the influence which the festival has had on Irish letters over the past quarter of a century.

On behalf of the festival committee, I would like to thank David Marcus for initiating the publication, and for all his support down through the years. We are very grateful also to our valued sponsor, Irish Distillers plc, especially to Deirdre Farrell, who has been a great friend to Writers' Week for many years, and to Marino Books, the publishers of this anthology.

I trust that these award-winning stories will give great pleasure to their readers. Who knows: we might have a second collection on the occasion of our fiftieth anniversary in 2021!

Madeleine O'Sullivan
Chairperson, Writers' Week

INTRODUCTION

There was a period, not all that long ago, when some critics and reviewers were confidently predicting the imminent death of the novel. Not surprisingly, they were wrong – most prophets *are* wrong most of the time, which is just as well for the quality of life. That the novel refused to die, but in fact burgeoned into rude and lusty health, was due to a variety of factors, not least the establishment, both in Ireland and in Britain, of a number of well-endowed, highly publicised annual awards for the genre.

The short story, on the other hand, was not marked down by the aforementioned Cassandras for an early death simply because it was considered to have been dead for many a day. While that may have been largely true for Britain, it was not true for Ireland. Since Joyce's *Dubliners* in the 20s, Ireland has produced a disproportionate number of this century's great short story writers – Somerville and Ross, Frank O'Connor, Sean O'Faolain, Mary Lavin, Elizabeth Bowen, Bryan MacMahon, Benedict Kiely, Edna O'Brien and William Trevor, among others – and the attraction of the form for our aspiring writers was nursed throughout the 30s and 40s by a clutch of periodicals, joined in subsequent decades by women's magazines and by national and regional newspapers. To all these print-media accoucheurs must be added the introduction of short story competitions.

Over the years there have been many such ventures – some one-off, others short-lived – but unquestionably the most important is the annual Powers Gold Label Short Story Award, organised by Writers' Week and now in its twenty-third year.

In a country as small as Ireland such an attractive, open competition draws entries from the most widely scattered areas, north and south. Winning the Powers Gold Label Short Story Award is a national accolade – quite apart from the financial reward – and its consistently high standard is attested by the subsequent success of so many of its winners, as the biographical notes of the contributors to this collection record.

On many occasions I have been appointed by Writers' Week to adjudicate the Powers Gold Label competition. It is a task in which I delight, not only because for so long the short story has been my special love and concern, but also because to be enabled in this way to keep in touch with the Irish short story's development and thematic shifts, and to read so much high quality work by, for the most part, previously unpublished writers, is hugely gratifying and unfailingly thrilling.

Writers' Week is to be saluted for recognising in its very early years the importance to Irish writers and to contemporary Irish literature of a national short story competition, and Powers Gold Label is owed an incalculable debt of gratitude for sponsoring the competition from its outset – and still counting. So what could be more fitting than that the 25th anniversary of Writers' Week should be celebrated with the publication of an anthology of all the winners of the Powers Gold Label Award? I am confident that the following pages will provide not only inspiration and encouragement for a host of our as yet unpublished writers, but will also be an enduring source of pleasure and pride for anyone interested in contemporary Irish writing.

So, Reader, charge your glass, settle back and read on.

David Marcus

O LORD, DELIVER US!

DAMIEN ENRIGHT

'Gerrup!' shouts Macauley, like he's been kicked by a cow. Silence fell, instantly, over the classroom.

'Get up, boy,' said Friel, 'and bring me my chalk . . . '

In the back row, by the wall, Barry and Kierney, Micheleen Hearst and Phil Gannon, frozen unnaturally in mid-movement, tried to thaw. They could feel Friel's eyes.

Macauley rose slowly beside Barry, his left ear glowing from the sting of the chalk. 'It wasn't me, Father,' he said. 'It was Barry, so it was, and . . . ' bleat, he continued, bleat, like a bloody sheep.

Silence. Barry stared at the book before him as if it were the Doomsday Book and the page bore his name. Silence: then a short hack, like the hammer of a gun.

'Barry, stand up . . . '

Summer shone outside, white on the school-yard, where sparrows played. And Father Friel didn't have a cold.

Macauley sat down, prissy as an altar boy, folding his hands on his knees. The flush of righteousness spread from his inflamed ear across his round face; dawn reddening a newly awakened planet. Maybe also it was dawning on him what he'd be facing after school.

Barry rose. Kierney, beside him, tipped his leg; for courage and luck, Barry thought. Or maybe because it was Kierney, in the first place, who dropped the egg.

'Pick up the chalk, boy!'

It lay by the speckled umber of the sea-gull's egg, red yolk spattered on the worn, board floor.

'Bring it to me, now! Quick march!'

Barry raised his eyes. Friel stood by the rostrum, broad and black, like a *préacán dubh*, a black crow or a sharp, black scaffold. Only his lips moved, tightening white and loosening, in short spasms. There was froth at the corners, white bubbles like cuckoo-spits against the big, pitted face. Barry felt his stomach sink, like diarrhoea. He had a sudden, awful urge to go to the jacks. Chalk in hand, bending, he made his way past Charles Macauley, who drew back his knees like a girl ('Mammy wants Charles to be a priest . . .' they said). Suddenly, Barry felt a very small boy . . .

As he walked up the aisle between the long, dark benches, his feet seemed to miss the floor, like that time he put on Micheleen Hearst's thick glasses. His face burned, prickling at the scalp of his head. It wasn't the first time he'd gone up to Friel. But Friel had said next time he wouldn't be responsible for what he'd do.

As he approached the master, Barry again raised his eyes. Friel stood in front of him. He lowered his throwing arm and extended it, palm up. The open palm . . . Barry's hand shook as he placed the chalk. It touched Friel's fingertips. And fell. It echoed on the floor.

Friel said nothing. His quick eyes darted to meet Barry's,

returned again to focus on a point above his head. His arm remained outstretched, the palm open. Barry knew well what he had to do.

Friel's shoes, black and cracked and shiny, like his eyes. Chalk dust on the toecaps, the chalk between, sitting there, a small stub.

Keep out of the way of the boots!

Barry, on his haunches, reached out. He could feel the blow on his unprotected head. Feeling it, expecting it.

But, suddenly, he was upright again. It hadn't happened. Friel hadn't hit him. He hadn't moved. His hand was still open. Barry placed the chalk there. The hand, like a sprung trap, closed on his.

'No, Father . . . !' said Barry sickly, jerked into rage. Friel's blow caught him on the side of the head, knocked him off the iron radiator on the wall.

When Barry stood up, his nose was bleeding.

'Back to your seat, you scut!'

Friel, I hate you! But you shouldn't ever hate anybody. God, I can't bear you, Friel!

The long walk back to the end of the room now. The slow, tense torture. The class swam, then righted itself. Again, he felt he had no legs. The class raised hands before faces, bridging fingers over the bridge of the nose. Like attitudes of prayer to protect themselves. The blackboard duster! Friel had picked it up . . .

Could he take it, the half-pound teak duster cracking off his skull? He wanted to raise his hand, behind him. But Friel wouldn't let him do that, he knew. *Friel had malaria on the*

Missions and smallpox – you can still see the marks on his cheek and neck, black hairs growing out of them. He speaks five African languages. He has to shave two times a day. They sent him home to Ireland because he was mad . . .

'Stop! No. Barry, don't turn . . . '

Silence. Then, behind him, the sudden, violent swish of the shiny old soutane. His shoulders hunched.

No duster whistled across the silent room. No sudden, searing red; no crack, no pain. Just silence.

He stood, facing the class, his courage almost gone.

'Did you wear your knickers today, Barry?' Friel gently asked.

'No, Father,' he answered, lowering his eyes. His face reddened but he bit back his tears. One day, long ago, he had turned up on the football field wearing camogie shorts – he didn't know the difference and his mother hadn't said. They had belonged to an elder sister, were, like most things he wore, hand-me-down. He was seven years old then. But Friel wouldn't forget.

'Speak up, boy!' he said. 'What didn't you do?'

'I didn't wear my knickers, Father.' Barry raised his eyes. Macauley moistened his lips, smiled, shifting in his seat.

'You didn't *wet* your knickers, Barry? Didn't you now? I'd take a bet . . . ' Friel paused. 'Lift your head like a man and go back to your seat.'

'I'll kill you,' Barry wanted to say. 'I'll kill you!' As he sat down, the blood, like a red cloud, rushed up at him; he covered his eyes. He was trembling and his breath seemed to break. Looking between his fingers, he saw Friel take the duster from behind his back, hand it to a 'pet' in the front row. The pet minced up and cleaned the board.

Friel wrote . . .

From the terror of the Vikings, O Lord, deliver us!

The class repeated it, like a litany, over and over again.

Up and down the aisle of his classroom Friel walked, everyone therein now hanging on his every word. He spoke of the Vikings (savages like himself, Barry thought) sailing up the rivers, destroying everything in their path. They murdered the people and burned the monasteries, melted the sacred chalices for gold. Near their own town, at Áit na Coille, a famous abbey once stood, a seat of learning known throughout the world. The Vikings razed it, burned the books and stole everything, it was said, except the ancient bell. The monks rolled it down the slope, into the river. When the Vikings came, they slaughtered the priests for the pleasure of it, disembowelled every one.

'What happened to the bell, Father?' asked Barry quietly, raising his hand. He wasn't sucking up to Friel. He wanted to know. Dates didn't interest him; this did. It was a picture in his mind. Let him not take it as a sign of weakness! Friel didn't do that.

He looked up. 'Ah! Little Miss Barry,' he said. 'Always interested in the fairies' tales.'

The front row tittered. Barry turned away his face. It made him feel sick. Friel's disease, whatever it was, the way he turned everything around. It made him want to vomit suddenly, like earlier, when Friel drew him close to smash him off the wall. He smelled the sour-sweat, the sick, the stale sanctity . . .

'If you were a Viking what would you do to him, Barry?' Kierney asked, as they wheeled their bikes out of the school yard.

'I'd murder him, for sure I would! But it would be a sin to hit a priest . . . '

Next morning, when Barry woke, he began dressing automatically. But his movements slowed . . . He remembered: that afternoon, the class had Friel. He couldn't face it. Nothing he did or didn't do would change how Friel looked at him, what Friel saw. It nauseated him all over again; he shook to cast it off. Also it frightened him and filled him with despair. Not the beatings. The four years yet during which he would be Friel's creature three hours of every day . . .

The priest's shadow lowered over the room and his smell seemed suddenly to pervade it. Outside the sun shone in a blue sky, at eight o'clock in the morning already splitting the stones.

When he left the house, Barry, instead of hurrying past the church with the quick sign of the cross and the running genuflection, dodged inside and said three fast Hail Marys and a few Glory Bes. The nine o'clock bell rang for school; the last scurrying footsteps echoed past. In no time, Barry lay by the river bank, contentedly on the flat of his back. We must be mad altogether, he thought, going to school on a grand day like this! And amn't I learning anyway?

The mayflies were hatching on the river and he began counting how many survived. As soon as they rose off the water on bright new wings, wagtails and chaffinches would swoop down on them from the trees, nip in the bud their one short day of life. Seven out of ten were taken; three survived to flutter high enough on their unsteady wings to catch the wind and shimmer off for the day. Barry was appalled. Respect for nature or no respect for nature, these mayflies were being slaughtered, outright! To redress the balance, he pulled out his catapult and found a nice, round stone. 'Now,' he said, addressing the wagtails, 'one of ye as much as move and we'll see who picks off who on the wing!'

Friel was, for the present, forgotten. It was Saturday tomorrow and then Sunday. No school for three full days. Happy at the thought, he contented himself lobbing a few stones into the trees. The marauders shrieked and fled . . .

At noontime, he sat down at Áit na Coille and munched blackberries at the foot of a wall. The old abbey was now no more than a few stones on stones, abandoned but for jackdaws and cows. But it had a feeling about it, as if the air was sanctified, held out of time, still. Within the walls, as though the bones of the monks long buried had charged the soil, the grass grew stronger and greener and the wild blackberries sweeter than anywhere around. It was Barry's favourite spot. But it too, now, contained Friel. Thinking of him, he kicked out viciously at a rock. It rolled down the slope and splashed into the river, like the bell.

When school was over, Barry went home for tea. After the Rosary, he left the house. He called on the lads first but they were all out. Then he remembered the couple of Wild Woodbines Jimmy Houlihan had given him when he arrived back from England to nurse his leg. He took them out of the chimney where he had hidden them and went off down to the bridge for a quiet smoke.

By and by, Kierney appeared, grinning grimly, walking along the wall. His hands were stuck deep in his pockets and he was wearing that kind of face on him that told Barry he was on the cadge.

'Christ, Barry,' he announced, 'I have a terrible thirst on me for a smoke!'

'Have you, now?' said Barry. 'And what are you wasting your time here for, then?'

'Because,' said Kierney, staring into the river like an ould fella, then making up his mind, 'because I'm looking for bats!'

Bats? Had they mad Kelly, the science teacher, for class instead of Friel? He sometimes sent people looking for things. But why Kierney? He was a small 'maneen' of a fella, shrivelled from late nights, much given to showing off the invective he learned in his mother's bar. The only interest he had in nature was in human nature and that strictly from the point of view of where he could cadge the next fag. Maybe Barry should have gone to school after all!

'What,' he said to Seanín, 'would you want with bats?'

'Ah now . . . ' said Kierney, considering. 'Alright. I'll tell you if you give us a drag of a fag.'

Right, thought Barry, it's worth it! He handed over the butt, watched while Kierney sucked it and savoured it and blew a few rings.

'Now,' he said, 'what about the bats?'

'Bats? Bats?' shouted Kierney. 'Yerra, bats, Barry, you must be bats yourself!'

And he was away under Barry's arm before he could grab him, yelling 'Bats Barry!' and draining the last dregs of the butt.

When Barry caught up with him, he began to twist Kierney's arm.

'You louser, Barry! Let me go, you louser!' he yelled.

'I'm going to throw you into the river at Áit na Coille. Into the haunted pool!'

'No,' said Seanín. 'Seriously, Barry, seriously! I have wicked bad news for you. That was why I came.'

'Go on.' Barry still held his arm.

'It's Friel. On Monday he says he's going to put you across his knee.'

'He can't. He never did that to anyone.'

'He says he's going to do it to you.'

Across Friel's knee. In front of the whole class . . .

'I'll tell my father!'

'He won't let you leave school.'

Would Friel try to take his trousers down!

'I'd sooner go back to England with Jimmy Houlihan!' Barry said.

'Yerra, don't be codding yourself! Friel doesn't matter. You shouldn't be minding him, Barry. Anyway, where would you get the five pounds for the fare?'

Yes, thought Barry, where? Not that I want to go to England anyway. Yet Jimmy says it's a great place. Father Dinan calls it, from the pulpit, 'The Cesspool of Camden Town'. Women by the dozen, according to Jimmy, that was how he got his gammy leg. Acrobatics with a Lady of the Realm in her Rolls

Royce. I wonder what it's like, all that stuff? I suppose you'd have to go over to find out.

Barry took the second Woodbine from the packet.

'C'mon and we'll walk up to Áit na Coille,' he said.

Kierney looked at him. At night, Áit na Coille was haunted. But there wasn't much Kierney wouldn't do for the sake of a fag.

As they approached the black bulk of the hill, rising against the sky, Kierney said, 'Must have made a great splash altogether. Probably drowned a coupla monks.'

It was the right tack, he decided, make a joke of the whole thing. Barry wouldn't seriously think of going in.

'Probably,' Barry answered, shortly. Kierney began to get a worried look.

'Sure, didn't Friel say them were fairy tales?'

'Do you believe Friel?' Barry looked at him. It was a confrontation.

'No. No.'

'He knows nothin'! Nothin'!'

Barry seemed older than his years.

'I wouldn't piss against him for shelter if I had to run to China for a bush!' declared Seanín, staying on the right side. But he had to talk sense to Barry. The pool was haunted! Everyone knew that.

'But the Vikings pulled it out,' he said, definitively. 'To make brass swords and spears out of it. That's certain sure!'

'Brass swords and spears! Christ, Seanín, you're even greener than you're cabbage-lookin'! Brass swords and spears!'

'Well, brass breastplates, brass dog-collars, brass knuckles!

How would I know? Maybe they banged their balls off it and said Glory Be's . . . ' He laughed but Barry didn't. 'Anyway, they'd have taken it, that's all I know.'

'They'd have known where it was, eh? How? They killed all the monks!'

'They'd have tortured one before they killed him! And anyway, 'twould have rusted away – under the water three or four hundred years!'

'Three or four hundred years? Ten fourteen, boy, Brian Boru bate the Vikings out of Ireland! The sea around Clontarf ran red with Viking blood!'

'Aye, and Olaf the One Eye ran into Brian's tent and split his head with a hatchet! And . . . '

But Barry wasn't listening. They had arrived under Áit na Coille.

'Brass doesn't rust, Seanín . . . '

He stared into the river, dark below.

People had seen Him, it was said. Sometimes He foraged on land, came out of the pool. Cows were taken at night, heard screaming in the dark.

But always He waited there beneath the still, dark waters for a swimmer's body, to clutch it and take it down, sucking the life breath out of it, to give Him life. And when He released it – the pool was bottomless – the body would sink and sink . . .

The classroom. Monday. 'And what were you doing not at school on Friday, Miss Barry?' Friel would ask. 'Getting the bell out of the river, Father. The one you said was fairies' tales . . . ' Friel could hit him and hit him. It would never be the same again.

Barry began to take off his clothes. He thought about his

family. His mother's heart. And his ingratitude, pride. Not caring about them. They were saying the Rosary. The Five Sorrowful Mysteries. They offered them for him . . .

The water closed over him, gripped him. He sank more than he meant to but then shot to the surface and started lashing out. No! No, dog-paddle a bit. Plain water. It eased his fear. Float.

The moon above, staring back at him. Below the surface his back, hung there, iridescent. Exposed. A discorporate mass rising, winding; the long, hopeless descent into the dark!

Hold on to yourself, Barry!

'Seanín.'

'Are you alright?"

Kierney was still there, a glow in the darkness. Lighting the butt.

'I'm going down, Seanín . . . '

Down, keeping his mind closed tightly as his lips. His eyes open though, feeling the water as he divided it. Rub against God-knows-what, waiting in the depths. Touch His head, maybe . . . kick Him by mistake! Down, down and down. Darkness. An image of his body swimming to outdistance a shadow; couldn't outdistance it, couldn't evade . . . Lungs bursting; black with red splashes in it. Black on black. And then, as if there, right close beside him, a loud whisper.

'Which way is up?'

He swung and his hand touched! Before he could swerve, he was on top of it, a dark, spongy mass. His shoulder hit as he spun, frantic, twisting like an eel, for dear life upward-swimming, knees tight against his chest, pursued by the awful vision that he was caught in Its hair . . .

Darkness. Pitch black. No shape or outlines; only air. (The moon behind a cloud, hidden . . .)Was it not air? Was it not the world? Could he not see!

'Seanín, Seanín?' he called, timorously.

A match flared.

'Come out,' Kierney said.

Then, suddenly, his eyes were shot with quicksilver as the moon bared and the river leaped into ripples, shimmering as it spread. He was shoulder-high in a seething plain of silver; air felt real, tasted richer as he gulped it. Life!

But, God, between his fingers . . . Strands of Its hair! He panicked and ploughed for the bank.

He lay on the grass, his body all chest, burning, sucking at the sky as if to inhale the stars, fire to fire, and perish. When the earth calmed and the moon no longer shook, his bones turned slowly into water, coursed warmly through the channels of his flesh. He closed his eyes for an aeon and when he opened them Seanín was standing above, a question on his face. It seemed not to matter, the question; it was a long way to words. He looked up past him, into the enormous sky, the stars so near, pinpricks in the dome of his skull, the spaces between them tangible. The space he moved in warm, heavy-scented, the summer night. His fingers explored the texture of the strands.

He giggled. An overpowering joy!

He raised them, stiffarmed, against the moon. There, a handful of fibres hung. He giggled. He sat up. Kierney leant over his shoulder.

'You found the bottom, Barry, didn't you?'

'I did, Seanín, I did!'

The strands lay wet and glistening across his fingers, in the moonlight drained of colour, a drowned man's hair . . . They stared at them in silence. Seanín reached for a match. Before he lit it, Barry told him. In the match light, it was river weed.

'Seanín,' he said, 'c'mon! Come in the river with me.'

Kierney looked up. He eyed Barry for a minute, sharply. He began to undo his tie. A few quick drags on the Woodbine. Kierney, with a ferocious scream, was in! Barry, after him, surged to mid-river in a long, racing dive. There he treaded water.

'Kierney, lookout, lookout! He's after you!' he shouted suddenly, manufacturing hysteria, slapping the water with the palms of his hands.

'Yerra, go on outa that,' said Kierney, quietly, dog-paddling away.

Barry had the right man! He watched Seanín as he swam closer, calmly, his black head bobbing, his breath short gasps. For all that he was wizened and crabby, Kierney could stay afloat as well as the best of them; Kierney'd be the last man to drown!

And then Seanín disappeared . . .

The next Barry knew of him, Kierney had him by the leg, climbing up him, rising over him, his arms wide like a ghost, shouting a huge shout.

In minutes, the spectres of centuries were laid, laughed out of existence, scuttled, sunk.

'Are you game?'

'Game for what?' Kierney asked, his eyes narrowed to slits.

'Y'know. The bell . . . '

Kierney said nothing for a while.

'There's no monster anyway,' Barry said.

'Aye, and no bell.'

'They'd put our names on brass plaques in the museum in Dublin, like Josie Shaughnessy that found the guns.'

'Put our names on tombstones too, wouldn't they?'

'You dropped the egg . . . '

'Aye,' said Kierney, 'and I'm sufferin' for it! Take the belt off your trousers. Each of us will hold one end.'

After the first few dives, the absence of fear swelled their diaphragms, left more room for air. The trouble wasn't getting down but staying down, crawling along with one hand. They abandoned the belt idea as courage gained. The bell might be standing bolt upright while they wasted time. Backwards and forwards they went, bank to bank, quartering the riverbed, covering ten feet of the bottom in each long dive.

'I'm freezing,' said Kierney at last.

'Alright, we'll build a fire.'

Up to Áit na Coille, like walking into the stars. Soon a fire, brambles and bracken crackling, bats squeaking overhead, moths dying their death in the flames. The idea took shape in the fire; raising into the moonlight that which had lain so long in the cold, dank waters, encircling it, in awe, as it stood glistening high on the bank. And the mind's eye returning to what once might have been, the monks long ago praying over it, maybe, on a night like this, before, mourning, they cast it and all its offices into the dark. '*Ní chluinfear a cling go brath* . . . '

and the bells don't ring any more, like the old poem says. They, Barry and Kierney, would raise it again into the light!

'Another dozen dives then, Seanín, before we go home?'

'Aye. Might as well be hung for a sheep as a lamb.' Seanín was gripped now too.

Down the slope and in . . .

A dozen didn't do it. But Barry wouldn't leave off. The more he found nothing, the more determined he became. 'Will ye come out, Barry! Yer clothes are dry and the fire is dead and the dew is fallin' on them and we'll be slaughtered when we go home!' But before Kierney had even finished, down Barry went again, scrabbling along the bottom. And there, beneath the mud, he felt something hard.

A stone, could it be? Stones lay everywhere, parts of Áit na Coille, rolled down the hill by generations of small boys, just for the splash. Deeper down, there were hundreds, maybe, all the walls of the monastery. If you raised them all you could put the whole place together again.

But this was no stone. No; sharp, circular, regular, this thing. He said nothing to Kierney when he surfaced, only dived directly again. Bracing his legs against the bottom, he pulled at it. It gave. His arm slid through a corroded metal ring. Pull at it as he might, it wouldn't give further. He was yelling before he reached the surface. And Seanín came back in.

They pulled together. It was anchored in the mud. No amount of heaving would move it; they'd have to dig down. Tomorrow. If it was there ten centuries, it wasn't liable to walk away. They marked it with stones. Happy, they went home.

Tomorrow, they'd be pulling it out, what Friel said was fairies' tales! And let him do his worst then, thought Barry – it won't matter! Everyone in the whole class will know.

'But let ye not count your chickens before they're hatched now, Barry!' Kierney said.

'Listen!' answered Barry, 'that ring's attached to the bell!'

'From the terror of the Vikings, O Lord, deliver us!' Thinking of it, Barry giggled like a fool. Indeed an' he'd fix Friel . . . !

Next morning, Seanín's whistle from the yard woke him and he reached the window in one jump from the bed.

'Get up, get up!' called Seanín. 'The river's in flood!'

In consternation, he looked at the locks of waters, catching the sun in the yard. He dashed downstairs in panic. Would the bell be shifted? Would the rocks and the ring be covered in mud?! He galloped his breakfast as a matter of form.

'You've a train to catch?' stated his father, a cocked eyebrow over the newspaper, full of wit and wisdom, Saturday, the morning off.

'Mumble,' answered Barry, his mouth full of brown bread.

'What's the hurry on you?'

'Fishing,' he gurgled. 'The river's in flood.'

'Mind you don't fall in,' said his mother.

'I won't fall in, Mam.'

'We only ever see you at breakfast,' she said, as he bolted out the door.

Down to Áit na Coille with Kierney, quick march.

'Oh, I had a good job and I left . . . '

'You're right!'

'My baby was there when I . . . Listen, Seanín, how high is she? How high?'

'Two feet up the bridge blocks and rising!'

'Jesus! I left . . . '

'You're right!'

Out onto the road, Kierney panting alongside him, hands deep in his pockets, skipping to keep up. Over the ditch and across to Áit na Coille at a gallop; surveying the black pool from a height. A state of emergency altogether. Brown river water spilled out into the field, the river, like a dun humpbacked whale, riding by.

'Currents,' said Kierney. 'And whirlpools!'

'Below the surface, it won't be so strong.'

'If you ever get below the surface without being drowned first!'

'An inner-tube and a rope! We'll drift down and tie it! A marker and a float!'

Off, so, to Michael Murphy at the garage, quick march, left-right!

'Loan of an inner, Michael?"

'Any chance of an old piece of rope?'

'Oh, yerra, fishin', fishin'.'

Back to the river and in!

Riding the back of it, down-river hurtling, under and down! Surge is less near the bottom but the inner-tube pulling away on top. The stones, last night's markers, scattered right and left. Groping, groping. Ah, here it is! Got ya, me ould ring of the bell!

Flood doesn't matter now. The tube secure, anchored to

the bottom, something to hang onto and catch your breath. Hand over hand up and down the rope. Meeting sometimes half-way, eerie in the ochre, surface half-light, a slap and a push. Digging away at the bottom, like a couple of badgers! And the flood, friendly, carrying the mud away. They felt the rough curvature of a dome!

But, six hours later, their hands white and wrinkled and sore, they had uncovered only a foot of it. Impossible, it seemed, to dig down far enough to uncover the whole thing. How far would they have to dig, anyway? And nothing was visible at the bottom; it was all by touch. For certain, 'twas the bell; what else could it be? Now that they'd found it they had to get it out but they couldn't lift it themselves, that was the thing! They could, of course, go to Friel.

'But, but that wouldn't be the same at all, at all! No. He'd take charge and his, it would be, not ours, the bell we found. He'd bloody lord it as usual!'

'And as well,' said Seanín, 'supposin' it was a piece of an ould car?'

'Christ, Seanín,' said Barry, staring at him, 'don't you know?'

They fell into silence again, sitting on the slope, right out of energy. And only the one last ditch, too, to cross.

'A horse? We could steal a horse!'

'Twould need a team of horses,' said Kierney, and he was right.

A team of cows, then? Somehow, they had to get it out themselves, by hook or by crook!

'Jimmy Houlihan! The tractor of Willie Joe's!'

'You're right, Barry!' said Kierney. 'Bejesus, you're right!'

Jimmy used to drive a tractor before he went to England, working with his uncle, Willie Joe Houlihan, pulling in old cars. And all the better too, if it was Jimmy; he was the next best thing to one of the lads!

So, to the widow's pub, to lay hands on the bould Jimmy. Go in or call him out? Go in.

Eyes lift as they sidle, hands in pockets, through the door. A break in the conversation. The widow looks up.

'The Butt Houlihan here, missus, please?'

She eyes them, takes it all in. A glance directs sideways, to the inner sanctum. The widow sniffs and goes back to filling a pint.

'Isn't he the changed man, though?' said Barry, afterwards.

It was a slow, long-drawn-out midsummer dusk, with swallows flying low over the river and myriads of midges swarming beneath the trees.

'How d'ye mean changed?' Kierney asked.

'Yerra, the slip-on shoes, the new suit, everything. You know, all the ould chat about women. Nothin' else seems to interest him at all.'

'Except the porter. Still, sure isn't he well off, having women to support him? Hasn't he the cushy life?'

'Sure, you wouldn't know . . . '

The brown water curled over the stones. A swallow whipped through the bridge arch, over their heads, twittering softly as it passed. The shadows were drawing in, gathering over the shallows. It would soon be dark.

'He said if ever we went across to England he'd introduce us.'

'Aye,' said Barry, tossing a stone. '"How's tricks," says he, like we're a couple of acrobats! Sure, if we knew tricks, we wouldn't be sittin' here waitin' for the tractor.'

'Give the man a chance, Barry! Isn't he willing to steal the thing, in spite of Willie Joe? Sure, Willie won't lend it to nobody since he was caught stripping the lead off the Protestant church! He has to keep to the law!'

'Aye, but I wish Willie Joe'd go off to Benediction if he's goin', and I wish Jimmy'd hurry up. And I wish it was Monday morning so I could see the black look on the face of Friel!'

Saturday evening: the West of Ireland. A mad clatter of bells sending the crows cawing mad over the town and then a dead hush over the streets, hardly a dog or cat moving, a single echo of footsteps over the bridge, someone hurrying to church. The Oblates preaching a mission; inside, soft bells, soft voices, a gleam of soft candlelight on brass, the swinging censers, the smoke, haze and afterglow. Tenebrae to follow Benediction. It would be dark before the church got out.

They heard the tractor start up half-a-mile away.

'He's got it!' Barry said.

Out from under the bridge and onto the trailer, giggling as they clambered aboard.

'Good-on-you, Jimmy! I wouldn't doubt you!' yelled Seanín.

He turned in the high seat where he was perched, preened as a bantam cock. 'All right, lads?' he smirked.

Away they went, Jimmy, the ne'er do well fag-end of the Houlihans, God's-gift-to-women, driving the old Massey-Ferguson as if it was a coach and four!

'Dive in now and tell me how much is showin' of it,' said

he, like a ganger, on the bank.

'Yerra go in yourself!' said Kierney.

'Me go in? Are you daft? Me, with me legs!'

'Give me the rope,' Barry said.

But the rope broke under the strain and Jimmy had to go to Willie Joe's to get a hawser. He was more subdued when he got back.

'How do ye know 'tis a bell?' he said.

'It feels like one.'

'Can ye see the brass?'

'You can see nothin',' said Kierney. 'Nothin'. You might as well be blind as a bloody bat.'

Jimmy took a comb from his back pocket and began smarming his hair. It looked like damp Woodbine tobacco glued to his head. The exercise helped him think.

'Must weigh half a ton,' he said, putting the finishing touches. 'If I break this cable for nothing, I'll be shot!'

He gunned up the hill and, when the cable tightened, almost up-ended the tractor on himself. No stir out of the bell. Maybe the monster was sitting inside it trying to hold it down! Jimmy took it from another angle. With a huge plop of eleventh century air, it came!

'Easy now, Jimmy, easy! We've got it. Jesus, we've got it!'

Clapping one another and dancing by the wheels, Barry and Kierney watched as slowly it ascended the bank and came to rest. Lying on its side, you could stoop within it. It didn't look much. The clapper was gone, probably still on the bottom. The sides were broad as your hand, black as a kettle, covered in thick, chalky stuff and weed. It was bigger than a tar-barrel, nearly twice the size. Down one side ran a long crack; they knocked away at it with rocks until a slab of the overgrowth fell off. Beneath it, dark green, pitted metal. Scrape away to the detail. A Celtic cross. A square faced, bandy-legged saint or something, with a mallet in his hand. A fish and some class of a cow. Jimmy rubbed and rubbed at it, scraped at it with his penknife. The cross took on a dull gleam by the light of the moon.

Jimmy lorded it in the bar; it was he who insisted on going for a drink afterwards. When one of the locals asked him where he was going with the tractor, Jimmy gave Barry and Kierney the quick wink. 'What would we be doin',' he whispered, 'informin' the likes of them?'

It was the first time Barry ever drank alcohol. Two glasses of cider and he was on his ear. Kierney, though he drank as if to the manner born, was likewise. No fit state to go home in, for sure. But who wanted to go home? Weren't they with Jimmy? They were in good hands. If he said 'Good Luck!' they said 'Good Luck!' If he chinked glasses, they chinked glasses. If he spat, they spat.

They staggered aboard the tractor at eleven, because they had no money left. Jimmy bought a bottle of cider 'to keep us topped up'.

Kierney fell off twice on the way back, and when Jimmy steered into the field, he took half the gate with him. But he didn't give a damn . . . !

There she stood, where they'd left her, on the trailer in among the trees! Kierney, mad drunk, embraced her, and kissed her while Jimmy sang solemn snatches of Plain Chant. Barry, all but incapable of standing, lay on the flat of his back in the dew and laughed. At last, they hitched up the trailer and, passing Willie Joe's house, seeing there were no lights on, drove into the yard. They parked the trailer behind the wreck of an old car.

'Willie Joe won't mind, now that we have something to show for it,' said Jimmy. 'Better to leave her here than on the side of the street.'

'In case your man of the pool might come and try to take it!' said Kierney.

'Not if He met up with Willie Joe!'

On the way home, Kierney mimicked Friel until he had Barry in stitches. He was giggling like a madman when he weaved indoors. His parents weren't home yet, luckily. Thanking the stars, he crept up to bed. Soon he was dreaming wild dreams about the bandy-legged saint with his round mouth wide open, like a cow looking over a gate. He woke up smiling when the startled saint became Friel . . .

It was Sunday morning and the church bells were ringing fit to bore holes in his head.

'Hurry up! Your father will kill you if you're late for Mass!' His mother added to the clamour from the foot of the stairs. His father! He rushed out of the house without stopping, for fear they'd smell last night on his breath.

'And where were you on Friday, little Miss Barry?'—the image loomed up at him during the Offertory of the Mass. Friel. On Monday! Twenty-four hours away . . .

I'll provoke him, that's what I'll do! I won't answer outright. I'll get him to not believe me first.

But if he forgets, forgets about Friday? He wouldn't. Not Friel. But, just in case, I'll come late to class. Park the trailer outside and cover the bell with a few sacks. Yes. Then lead Friel on. Rope to hang himself with! Leave the trailer there all day for the whole school to see! If they try to move it, let down one of the wheels!

The bells of the Consecration roused him. He was committing a sin. 'Vengeance is Mine,' says the Lord. He bowed his head.

God present on the altar in the bread and wine. The transubstantiation. He began to pray . . .

When Mass was over, he waited around the door, looking for Jimmy Houlihan or Seanín. Maybe they'd clean up the bell, take the weed off it; it would be a grand way altogether to spend the day. No sign of Jimmy or Seanín, but he met Marie Hearst. They walked out the road together, she on her way home, he on his way to Willie Joe's. He dodged into a shop and emerged, offering her a sweet, she smiling sweetly as she took one. She was a nice girl. They walked on. What a happy day it was, strolling along, people greeting them as they hurried past to Mass. Barry felt proud of himself. He decided to tell her about the bell; he trusted Marie. She said she admired him for standing up to Friel. She was looking forward to hearing the result when they met again.

As he entered the yard, Willie Joe was turning the tractor. He was a big, thickset lump of a man, wearing an ass's belly-band for a belt and a handkerchief knotted around his throat, like the tinkers wear. He had on his working clothes and Wellington boots and there was an ould cap stuck on his head.

He waved with more than usual cordiality, but Barry was ready to turn and run, afraid he might be bucking over the tractor and be after his blood. He wasn't though.

'Let you stay there now and not be destroying your good shoes,' he shouted and, giving one of the mangy dogs a boot, went into the house to get Jimmy. Jimmy appeared, a broad sly grin pasted across his face. He sidled past Barry with a sideways nod of his head.

'C'mon . . .'

Barry followed him. He led him into the back of the forge.

'What's up?' he asked Jimmy, shadowy in the firelight.

'Hold out your hand.'

Barry did so and felt something hard, wrapped in paper, slip into it. He unfolded it. Five pound notes! And, inside them, a thick disc of metal, yellow metal, catching the light of the forge fire . . .

Jimmy put his arm around his shoulder and winked at him.

'A souvenir,' he said. 'And, sure, ye have the fare to England. Isn't that better than any ould lump of brass . . . ?'

THE WEIGHT OF THE WORLD

MAURA TREACY

She sat brooding in the corner of the deep windowsill, her bare arms wound around her legs, her chin resting dejectedly on her knees. There were marigolds in a jug on the windowsill too; she had pushed them over to the far corner and now she stared at them in their vibrant colours of orange and gold as if she might divine their secret of resilient life, but even as she watched, their mystery seemed to darken them and her sullen eyes slid away.

Milo crossed the yard, carrying the lid of a churn and singing. When he saw her inside the window he tossed the heavy lid and balancing it on the flat of his hand, held it near his shoulder; he threw out his other arm in a gesture of Latin abandon and releasing all the yeasty passion of his soul into his song, he swooned about the yard and bellowed: 'It's now or never, my love won't wait'; and with a side-long leer he passed by.

She made no response. His good humour, infrequent, and, when it did come, extravagant and hardly ever for an obvious reason, put her teeth on edge. A thousand times he had brutishly trampled her own enthusiasm. Since they had both grown up it hardly ever happened that their good moods coincided, and if they did, it never ended well.

She eyed the door as she heard her mother's footsteps outside and when they passed by she relaxed grimly. You didn't want your mother pursuing you around the house, you didn't want her talking at you all the time, hounding you out when you wanted to be alone and blurting everything out to you. Once you even asked her why she didn't say all that to your father and she said, 'All what?' as if it were nothing, instead of all the worries that occupied her mind, and anyway, she said, he had enough to do and wouldn't want to be bothered; which, you knew, wasn't true. You saw how it saddened him, irritated him, the way she avoided talking to him. And he loved talking to people but not to her. She had been brought up to behave with abject deference to men but in the first years of their marriage her husband had squandered all they had and she had realised that even men were not to be relied on and all her understanding had been confused and thereafter she couldn't even listen to him with respect or without an embarrassed awareness that the source of wisdom and authority was itself a flawed vessel.

The door opened anyway.

'Is that where you are? I thought you'd have come out and said good-bye to them.'

'I waved. I don't think they saw me.'

'It's as well then they didn't. I said you were likely gone up the road to Peggy. I had to make some excuse. Are you not as great with her as you were, or what?'

'Why?'

'I thought maybe since you went away to school and all . . . '

'You think she's jealous because she hasn't a fairy godmother too and only goes down the road to school?'

'Well, I hope you know the chance you're getting and make the most of it. There's no obligation on your aunt to spend her money on you.'

You turned it over in your mind; it seemed like a good time to tell her that you weren't going back. But you knew very well that just now you were the least of her concerns and you couldn't humiliate yourself by playing for her attention when she was preoccupied.

'You're a handful, everyone of you. Martin, too; fancy him bringing the girl here on a Saturday. It's easy seen,' she said with brusque pride, 'that fella's turning out to be a real city man. He must think I'm Lady Ormond that I can be ready for visitors any hour of the day.'

You wished she'd stop pretending to be annoyed with him.

'Still, we have a lot to be thankful for. Miriam's a very nice class of a girl, didn't you think so? No put on airs about her, or anything.' She said it with faint surprise and seemed ready to reassess herself because Miriam had spoken to her with respect. 'And sure, like that again, I suppose they wouldn't be all that much better off than ourselves, just their circumstances were different.'

Your Circumstances were a variable measure, the sly foot tipping the scales so that you weren't outweighed.

And as she went on, expanding complacently on what the future could be expected to offer, you turned away. All the while your thumbnail had been chipping away at the indented edge of the cap of the tiny bottle in your hand. You looked down at your right hand now; she couldn't see it – and you held out the brown bottle so that the light filtered weakly through it, making a smoky amber stain on your fleshless fingers. You thought you looked like a corpse already. There were nearly thirty tablets in the bottle. Your mother took two every night to help her to sleep and for months you had been stealing them one at a time. One night you had made her go to bed early and you had brought her her glass of milk and two tablets; only they were Aspirin which you had painstakingly chipped down to the right size. They looked peculiar but you told her your fingers had been wet; anyone else's mother would have screamed and sent for the priest, doctor, Guards and coroner, but she was so overwhelmed by your attentiveness that she swallowed them without a question. You were probably doing her a world of good but you could just as easily have been giving her arsenic. Her unawareness could drive you mad at times.

'Himself's in high good humour,' she said indulgently, as Milo, still singing, crossed the yard again. 'Have you any idea who he's going with these times?'

'This one, and that one.' She couldn't expect two triumphs in the one day.

'He was all pie to Miriam, chatting her up as nice as you like.'

You knew; you'd seen it all; it was always an exercise in scepticism for you to watch Milo making himself agreeable.

'I wouldn't mind but I thought he wasn't gong to put in an appearance at all and I was trying to cover up for him. That's another thing I meant to say to you –' she was reproachful now – 'I thought you'd have put on a nice little dress when they came instead of them bits of things you wear. Wasn't that a grand dress Miriam had? I'd say it must have been very expensive, there was a lovely cut to it. And yourself and Milo! Tearing like mad things around the yard; that was the time for you to wear your jeans, it might have saved a lot of embarrassment. And the roars out of you! I was mortified in front of Miriam and I'm sure Martin must have been ashamed of his life after bringing her here.'

'I'll be quieter the next time.'

After dinner you had washed some clothes and taken them out to dry. You were hanging them on the line; your mother wouldn't let you hang out your underclothes at all if she thought there were any men about, and even when she did, she insisted that you arrange them so that their nature wasn't obtrusively recognisable. You thought that there was no end to her obsessions. As you were hanging up your slip, something shot by your ear and whipped the peg out of your hand. It was an onion. There were hundreds of them laid out on the gently sloping roof of the hen-house. There was Milo sitting cross-legged on the roof, smoking a butt, his outlandish wide straw hat making him look like a Mexican layabout. He knew the house-rule as well as you did and was tipping you off not to make a Peeping Tom of him; you picked up the onion and pelted it at him; it tipped his hat as he ducked; it was a mistake anyway, all the ammunition was at his side. As you darted around picking them up to throw back at him, you stumbled over the hose, snaking down from the tap at the backdoor; you hauled it up and turned it on him. He jumped up and, crouching, lumbered towards you across the roof, avoiding the water as best he could. At the edge he paused and took something out of his pocket; you couldn't see what it was; he opened his hand slightly, shielding it with his other hand. Something moved, you wavered, the hose in your hand; he knew you detested frogs; you braved it out for a minute; he didn't love them either but often brought in one to make your life scary. Then you dropped the hose and ran and he slid off the roof and came after you, and as you ran yelling past the door your mother came out to see who was going to strangle you, and you crashed open the gate of the haggart and the escaping hens got under his feet and you broke into the garden and he chased you across drills of cabbage and the wet leaves that were probably full of snails brushed your legs and you lifted your knees higher as you ran and you went through the potatoes and was it your imagination or did the blue spray on their leaves sting you; and you launched yourself through the wire fence and into the hayfield that ran around the side and front of the house and there was nothing to hinder you; he couldn't run as fast as you and you had trams of hay to dodge behind, so you rested. Your breath was rasping and your lungs felt like cinders and you put your hands on your knees and staggered around, laughing at his wide trousers and torn check shirt and he said, 'Do you see the cut of your own legs, smartie?' And you were plastered with clay up to your knees and you laughed and shouted at each other as you bounded around and he tried to jump over a tram and scattered the top off it and went sprawling through the remains. It took you back years, back to where you had been before they had got the notion and the money to do something about you and have you educated and civilised. And you sat down together and he gave you a cigarette to smoke but when he saw how you took to it he said they'd be bad for you and he took it from you and when you tried to snap it back, he ran off and you went after him and the chase was on again. He led you back towards the house and when he jumped the fence, you took a short cut and sprinted over the wall, your legs and clothes in disarray, your blood-curdling war-whoop lassoing the silence, and there they were.

You stared at the big clean car; you remembered hearing a car but had thought it was your father's.

'Hello, kid,' Martin said. He was smiling; if he wanted to he could make them accept you as a likeable tomboy; but you knew he was surprised, maybe disappointed and annoyed with you.

'Nally!' your mother was bereft of a plausible excuse.

And that was Miriam.

You all went in and your mother apologised for the state of the house and said the room should have been done up this year but it wasn't worth while now that you were going to build the new bungalow down near the main road. And instead of sitting down and looking as if she were in her own house, she rushed around straightening cushions, hiding newspapers and trying to rub finger marks off the table-top with the corner of her apron. And all the time she kept looking over her shoulder, thinking that Milo, who had disappeared without a trace, was going to walk in with muddy boots smelling of silage and she was wondering how she'd manage to hunt him out without provoking him to roar at her as he often did and how she'd cover up for his manners. The last time Martin was home he had hit Milo for shouting at her and Martin had ended up across the hearth, his head saved – except that for a minute he didn't recognise his mother – by falling among the sods of turf in the corner; and your mother, unaccustomed to chivalry, asked Martin what he had done that for; and you knew that the trouble with Martin was that he thought that civility and a decent suit should achieve anything and hide everything. With your mother, you wondered where he'd got such an idea. Milo, in his stubborn raggedness, unimproved speech and manners, was twice as arrogant.

You escaped to clean yourself up and you took your time about it.

But you had to go back, and because Martin was watching out anxiously for you, you sat beside Miriam and when she admired your nail-varnish, you admired her shoes. But then your mother, having no notion of the difference between reality and pretence where two unequally favoured women were being civil to each other, leaned over and asked you to agree with her but wasn't that a lovely brooch Miriam was wearing.

'And your ring matches it!' your mother said in the wistful, breathless way she did when she wanted to flatter someone, but the ring was no more like the brooch than the back of a bus and you felt the weight of hopelessness leaning on your mind again and you wanted to escape.

Sometimes when they were fighting, you used to think how nice it would be to have a polite, gracious family who'd sit around making pleasant, unwounding conversation with visitors.

Martin glanced at you with deliberate suddenness and caught the sorrowful look on your face. You could have kicked yourself. You tried to smile but he knew you too well, better than anyone, and he gave a sort of wry smile as much as to say why had you ever thought life would be any different. But you didn't; he was the one who saw the possibility of change and strove for it even though he must have known already that it wasn't going to make him any happier than he had been. For yourself there was only the enervating conviction that if your life began in misery, that was how it was meant to go on, and that belief, almost physically a part of you, undermined every spurt of optimism or ambition that ever visited you and that wasn't much.

You dipped a ginger biscuit in your tea and swayed it back and forth.

'Nally, what are you doing with your tea!'

It was the only way your mother took notice of you when anybody was there, drawing attention to your flaws and in the process only highlighting the inadequacy of every one of you; in spite of yourself you jumped and the sodden biscuit fell away and disintegrated in your tea. You began futilely to gather it up on your spoon, your mind screaming hatred at them all for watching you, and Miriam who had helped your mother to make the tea said: 'I'll get you another cup.'

Martin laughed but there wasn't much amusement in it. 'Begor, Nal, we wouldn't have turned up our noses at it, many a cold morning we faced out to school with less.'

And besides your shame, you felt what he felt always, the depression of remembering, seeing your mother as she used to be on Monday mornings, stooping over the fire of wet sticks that you had helped her gather in the ditches, melting dripping in a pan and giving you a piece of bread each to dip in it. That was the way your mind was too, always slipping and sliding from the expanding comfort of the present to the squalid past.

But in his eyes where there should have been sympathy, there was only tired cold impatience with you because you wouldn't let the memory go and neither of you could as long as you both lived and a glance at each other was enough to reduce everything around you to a mirage that blinded you for a while to the humiliation and poverty that were your real surroundings, because when you were born into it it became part of you, and anything else, anything better, was only temporary scenery. And he was looking at you and suffering maybe; his head tilted back, he was looking down his nose at you and thinking maybe that this was where you parted because you couldn't bear to follow him into the sphere he was entering and what was worse, he was trailing himself into it and now he would always make the story of his humble origins his party piece and you hadn't the pride, or the humility, for that.

And Miriam was smiling at you, the smile of a missionary nun among uncivilised people, that forgave what she had never experienced and could only vaguely understand.

When your father came in, Martin went out with him; he still owned some cattle and it was he who had started restocking the farm. People said wasn't it great the way you'd got it all back into the family and your father looked serene as he went about his work but you didn't see how, when he had had such a love for gambling and the life that went with it, he could be happy without it and be content to stay at home and read the racing news. To you he seemed wraith-like, but then you all did – living differently to the way you had lived before, living better anyone would have said but to you it didn't seem real. And when Martin came home you noticed him noticing the small signs of re-emerging prosperity, and he thought you all took it for granted after all it had cost him but he felt no resentment only an edgy, half amused awareness of his own redundancy.

Your mother and Miriam made fresh tea and just when you thought you could slide back into oblivion, your mother mentioned that your holidays were nearly over and you'd be going back to school. It was as if she wanted it to be known that though you were uncouth now, something was being done about it and they could look forward to an improvement. And Miriam said that since you were in that school you must know this other girl who was her friend's sister. You knew her, a horrible little snob, a tell-tale and at the back of it all a nose-picker which was something even you didn't do. You hated Miriam to think you were breaking your neck to be as good as her and her friends, and you thought it might be as good a time as any to tell them to stuff their fancy school, that you weren't going back, but then Miriam would know that it was because the other girls, ones like her, made you feel like a charity case. But now you felt they had used you enough so you confined yourself to 'yes' and 'no' and mostly, 'I don't know' and gradually they forgot about you, you slid out of the conversation and by-and-by, out of the room.

This time you stayed out.

From the windowsill you watched them when they said good-bye; with your mother it was a protracted ceremony; you saw Martin only half listening to her as he glanced around and you knew he was looking out for you and you saw the strong bleak outline of his face and for a moment you thought you could get up and go down to him but the others were there dealing in bland agreeable talk and you were remembering the first time he had gone away; you couldn't see then how the rest of you were going to survive without collapsing on each other and for a day and a night you had hidden out in a shed; and so you pressed your fists to your temples and you didn't see or hear anything till they had gone.

You heard your father shout, 'Hup!' as he slapped the last of the cows on the flank as he let them out into the field after milking. The cattle were quiet now; they were new stock, some of them that had been bought at the mart on Friday and all through the night and Saturday morning you heard their lonesome bawling at the gate and the sound could get inside your head until it seemed that the whole world was crying. Now they walked dumbly where they were driven and you were half relieved but sad too as if their resignation had infected you.

Evening wore on; the light changed and the clamour of the yard work took on a different sound, hollow and isolated, as the enveloping noises of the day fell away, one by one.

1975

ARTIFACTS

GILLMAN NOONAN

Wake up! said bony knee.

'Go away,' said Pat, pressing her legs into the corner. It was no use. The knee pursued her, jigging her, an agent of reproach for her indifference. It belonged to a skinny man who was eating peanuts from a crinkly bag. His wife was on the opposite seat talking to the priest. Above the noise of the train, amplified by the open windows, Pat heard her groaning about the cost of living. She kept her eyes shut. Indeed, she had had them so tightly shut for a while, as though dreading that they were going to force themselves to remain open, that she thought the priest and the woman would be nudging each other, silently remarking on it. So she had tried to relax them, and now one of the lids had peevishly started a quiver.

On her lap Pat held the evening paper and a new book on stave houses. It had a smooth shiny cover that was beginning to sweat against her palms. She had seen the priest, an ascetic looking man of about forty with intense eyes, looking at it before she resolutely closed her eyes when the train pulled out. A few minutes later he would have been saying, do you like archaeology, tell me? Or, aren't they digging up old Viking remains near Christ Church?

She didn't want to talk about archaeology, or anything. She knew, once started, that she would be dreadfully coherent and interesting, dreadfully for her because that part of her mind would be operating that for weeks seemed to have taken over, like an automatic worked by remote control, to sustain an articulate flow of thought to satisfy the world. Beneath the flow she would lie still as a skate, loth to make any movement that would disturb the sand and betray her presence, clouding her vision that was not vision but a mere instinctive recording of the teeming life around. Things that belonged to the earth drifted down to her in this strange element, and indeed she did record them, as she had been doing for two years on the dig, every morning preparing her books and pens to enter and sometimes draw the finds that came to light under the men's patient trowels. But now she wrote on air, or in invisible ink, registering not the nature, size, shape and location of the find but criminally unscientific words like 'large artifact,' 'small artifact'. As on the day the skeleton was found she had written in her diary: 'Skeleton found in square IV, in good condition', and had felt that that was all that needed to be said. A diary was not a scientific record.

Even on the morning when the report came in on the find she could not recall having experienced any dramatic change of attitude. A warm April day. She had arrived earlier than usual and had the hut to herself. Outside, the men were collecting their trays and things. Joe, the surveyor, was setting up his planning board. Black Jack, the dig's watchdog Alsatian, was frisking with the little terrier that always managed to slip into the site despite Joe's attentions. A spring morning so sunny and warm even at that hour that she hadn't thought of lighting the oil stove. The report was on the table. It was technical but what it amounted to was that the skeleton was of a young woman who had met with a violent death while in childbirth. The infant's bones were partly through the pelvic girdle. She had received a blow on the skull and another on the jaw, this one apparently while in a kneeling position. Laboratory tests showed that she had eaten gruel and eels.

A significant find, dramatic too in its suggestion of sudden violence and flight, the body of a young woman abandoned to rot in a cess pit. Did she stumble in? Was she thrown in? Who could say now? It was a find, a tragic find, one could say, but one to be registered like any other. More would come to the surface beneath the trowels of the men scraping away the crust of centuries to reveal the rotten stumps of staves still defiantly clinging together, wattle walls, stone hearths, wooden culverts, pathways, other cess pits: the habitats of small swarms of people who had come to Ireland's shores a-viking, some to remain and become merchants, the true founders of the city, scattering about them the materials of their trade, bits of bone and leather and pottery; others predatory, snatching their booty and departing in their longboats, leaving behind few traces of their habitation. And at some point in these fitful comings and goings a young woman was struck down. A Viking girl most probably with a name like Rannveig, or something gentler perhaps, like the lap of water against the bank, Halla. And a husband or master with a name like the bite of an axe into wood, Thorstein or Thord.

Wake up! said bony knee again.

In vain, Pat pressed her thighs together. She slipped the sweating book under the newspaper.

Of course, when Kitty and the other girls arrived, they had all speculated about what could have happened. She had taken their remarks home with her to Ray. It had suddenly made it all very real, she had told him. She argued, unconvincingly, the perversity of its coming almost as a relief sometimes to come upon evidence of human passion, even brutality. One always suspected its presence, as in contemporary life. And while sherds of pottery, bronze pins, gaming pieces and the like were interesting in themselves, they could never transport one back into the scene as vividly as the remains of someone who had been a victim of the times.

'True,' he said, bending over his drawings of the new estate, 'and you felt a particular empathy, I suppose, being a young woman yourself and pregnant to boot.'

Which was perfectly true and something she had felt from the moment she had picked up the report. It was a natural feeling, as natural as the sympathy she had felt for a neighbour who had been knocked down by a car some days previously. She had also been pregnant. Which is what surprised her later when she thought about it, and still thought about it now with her eyes closed and her face tilted up to the phenomenally warm stream of summer air coming through the window: this lack of any apparent shift at the time in her natural responses to human catastrophe. She had gone about her work as ever, enjoying the warm weather that even allowed her to sit out at times on the site with her lists and cartons of finds. She had visited her doctor and told him about the skeleton and he had been very interested, saying what a pity it was that (as he had read) so many interesting skeletons that had turned up in excavations throughout the country in previous years had not been examined *in situ* because expert anatomists were not available to examine them. A pity, indeed. And so the subject had drifted back into its proper sphere of relevance, that of being an artifact more or less revealing than others. A week later a splendidly preserved sword with a silver inlaid pommel was discovered in another part of the dig, and they all had a new topic of discussion.

Yet something must have happened in her because one morning she realised that she had stopped making porridge. That is, she had stopped doing so a couple of days before she was fully aware of it. One morning something had stayed her hand as it reached for the bag of oaten meal and directed it instead to the bread and honey. Also, she had begun to dream about the Viking girl. But once recognised as perhaps delayed reactions, these happenings too were immediately rationalised into their proper place. It was natural that one should be affected by life's more dramatic artifacts, which is undoubtedly what the skeleton was. And it was natural that one should dream about them. One was affected by them, but one learnt to take them in one's stride, as she came increasingly to define it to herself. Anyway, there seemed so little to say. Telling your friends that you had given up eating porridge in the morning would merely lead to a conversation about breakfast foods. And even her dreams contained so few of the bizarre or frightful elements which usually justified inflicting them on others that she refrained altogether from mentioning them. But it did surprise her that it wasn't of flashing axes and splitting skulls she dreamt but of domestic scenes such as men in leather jerkins and tight fitting trousers coming and going with tools, and women making bread in small pans. The young woman who was doomed was always there but obscured by the movements, sitting in a corner at her warp-weighted loom, showing only a little of her profile. Her skin was very fair, as was evident sometimes when she raised her head and turned slightly, revealing one of the large oval brooches that fastened the straps of her smockline dress, as though listening for something; and usually at these moments the river became audible, slopping against the longboats, slipping like a sigh through the rushes and flats of what would become a big city, down to the sea.

Yet, as though the moment of terror and flight and death were just a breath away, and her unconscious mind were refusing to experience it, she often awoke from one of these dreams in a sweat, her heart beating, reaching for Ray. It worried her, just as it worried her one evening coming home from work to find herself petrified on the pavement outside the GPO unable to decide when to cross the street. People around her were flitting across between the passing cars, but even when the gaps were big enough to allow her to stroll across at her ease she remained rooted to the spot. Still, that again was nothing. Weren't people always talking about taking their lives in their hands when they crossed the streets of Dublin? Drivers were so careless. And she was three months pregnant and wasn't going to take any chances. No, she wasn't becoming obsessed with personal safety.

But when a few evenings later on Westmoreland Street she

found herself transfixed, as before, on the pavement, afraid to cross, and then resolutely stepped out, together with a man carrying an umbrella, gaining the middle line, she had come to a halt, unable to follow the man who nipped across before an oncoming bus, waiting for the bus to pass and then for a car, and yet another, and then becoming helpless with panic as her eyes suddenly misted over with tears through which everything was blurred and menacing – waiting, quietly sobbing, for what seemed an eternity until a whole line of cars built up around her before groping her way to the other pavement. She fought it. One had to fight nerves. Give them their way and they would take advantage, splitting off into ever-finer strands of neurotic obsession. This was how people had nervous breakdowns, they became obsessed with things, and they ended up in clinics participating in group therapy sessions or being given some dreadful treatment like electric shocks.

She fought it and seemed to be winning. She forced herself to stay away from the safety of numbers that now seemed to draw her as her only refuge; to stroll by herself for an hour in the most deserted corner of the park (as though warring with some kind of agoraphobia. Ridiculous! Who ever heard of anyone having agoraphobia in Dublin!) She forced herself to have a coffee in large empty lounges on her way home from work and not to seek the crush of the bar where she could expect to meet people she knew. She forced herself to cross streets in heavy traffic, saying go on Pat, go on, follow that man, that car will stop, they're not all fools. And she forced herself to be lively and good-spirited, even while the menace, the unknown horror just a breath away, was pinging in her like the mysterious sounds in a telegraph pole; and that's what she was becoming, a rigid pole that walked and talked just like a human. It was such a good show that she thought it had them all fooled, even herself at times; though Ray occasionally looked at her curiously as though doubting her too consistent air of bounciness; and she felt that Kitty was not fooled one night when Ray was down the country and she had rung to ask if she could come and spend the night because a marathon party in the flat below was bound to make sleep impossible.

But when inevitably it came to the point when she knew she couldn't sustain her act any longer, when one evening it seemed inevitable that she would collapse into Ray's arms in a fit of helpless weeping, she provided herself with an alibi for any amount of neurotic behaviour and everyone else with every kind of excuse for her. It was about a month after the finding of the skeleton. She had wandered about the city after work like a zombie plotting her every move (I will look at the books on that stand, then I will cross and get a 13, no an 11) until, reaching the top of O'Connell Street she saw, an instant before being flung back against a stationary car, several objects, including distinctly, a pram, flying high in the air in a lot of dust. She came to almost immediately, sprawled in the gutter, and even while she was focusing on the confusion around her, only half aware of the screams of the injured and of the man with the big thick glasses bending over her, she remembered— yes, it was a distinct feeling!—this great sense of relief that it had happened to her at last, that the menace that had stalked her footsteps for weeks had at last materialised in the shape of some awful catastrophe of which she was one of the victims.

It was a perverse feeling, one of utter selfishness, and she clung to it as though it were something physical that encircled her like a lifebelt, different altogether from the actual feel of people's arms around her, different from the cloudy waves of shock that cushioned her from the scene of horror making her feel so detached from it all, so disembodied almost. It was a prayer she knew she had begun even then to say subconsciously, even while she was being driven away in the ambulance, a monstrous prayer of thanks to God for having sent this thing, this explosion on the street that had given bloody and violent shape to some deeper and more awful despair that had been closing in on her like a trap, a formless trap of no apparent substance that had yet lived in the air all around like some intimation of eclipse about to blot out the sun for ever. Relief, yes, an almost protopathic relief, all her nerve cells reverting to primal structures buffeting on mere sensations of survival, blindly accepting any loss for the sake of survival, even the life she carried in her womb which, staring stricken into the eyes of the young doctor in the ambulance, she suddenly felt slipping from her beneath the blankets as though her bowels had opened. Even then, in some tiny voice that drowned the scream of the siren, praying thank you, thank you . . .

But it was an alibi. That was the harsh reality, harsher than the real dismay and revulsion that set in when the facts of the outrage were made known to her, the numbers killed and maimed; harsher than the real and bitter sorrow at losing her baby. She fed on it while she fought it, telling herself over and over that it sufficed, that it was a real confrontation with tragedy, that she had survived much more fortunately than many others who had lost limbs or eyesight, women who could not have another baby even if they wanted. She fed on it while she tried to persuade herself that if what she had been looking for was something with which personally to indict the menacing world, then surely she had found it in this. Like a little girl she could tearfully scream: I told you so! I told you so! But now she must pull herself together and get on with it. She fed on it while she got on with it, returning every morning to the site to arrange her lists and cartons, going home in crowded buses, telling people whenever the subject arose that she had been there, bowled over, saved by a miracle. Fed on it, laughing, relating incidents; sucked on it greedily as though it were the very nipple of reality that walled in her garden, her peace, from whatever jungle she had felt creeping up on it. But it was food, comfort, that slipped through her without nourishing her. It was like hiding behind layers of colourful muslin a face whose ugliness was mental, something in the eyes or the twist of the mouth. But how to explain this? To Ray, to her parents and friends, she was being a brave girl who was showing true grit while to herself she had become a more abject coward than ever. Because now she had an excuse to seek the comfort of the crowd, to give vent to petulance inviting understanding and sympathy, to *demand* love. And she had sought and given vent and demanded with an indulgence that shocked her, even carrying over (consciously, it seemed to her) this indulgence into her dreams in which the doomed Viking woman recurred, now holding her baby in her arms, shielding it from the others as though it were deformed and in danger of being exposed to die, but the baby was Pat herself, dead already, and no one knew it but this mysterious and beautiful young mother . . .

Wake up! said bony knee, jigging with great insistence as the train flew over points.

This time she opened her eyes. The countryside was darkening under the approaching thunderstorms. All down the carriage people were closing the windows as drops spattered in. She smiled as the skinny man apologised for leaning across her to close theirs, and then refused with another smile his offer of peanuts. She opened her evening paper and pretended to read, but her mind was suddenly full of thralls, the Viking class that virtually belonged to their masters from birth, having no legal rights. A free woman who had a child by a thrall degraded herself to the father's level. She was thinking of the Viking woman becoming 'enthralled' and liked the thought, liked the idea of her secretly meeting a bondman somewhere along the Liffey, perhaps not far from Heuston Station where she had boarded the train. Perhaps she was already a Christian and didn't believe in having thralls, so she says, damn the family name, I'm becoming one myself. On the other hand, she would hardly be a Christian at that time. Still, it was a nice thought, the nicest she had had all day, she was going to dwell on it, on what the woman would wear going to meet her lover, on what they would say . . .

'Bad thing that in Italy,' said the skinny man, looking into her paper.

'Yes,' said Pat.

'Contaminated water. But sure we have enough of that ourselves.'

'Indeed.'

'*Man jumps from tenth storey,*' he read on. 'By God, that was a fair old jump.'

'Yes . . . '

'God help us, there wouldn't be much of you left after you hit the pavement from the tenth storey.'

Thralls, thought Pat. Did the word have any connection with troll?

'Oh, now, Father,' the woman was saying, 'you know the trouble we were having with itinerants.'

'I know, Mrs Gaffney,' the priest said, 'I know, but one must be very patient with these people.'

'Patient!'

'Patient!' echoed the knee with a jerk.

'What patience can you have with a man who beats his wife into pulp and then smashes everything in the caravan, everything, the caravan we, the town, provided for him?'

'Everything, indeed,' said the knee, champing on a nut, 'down to a garden, a garden, mind you, that I carted up in buckets to the site, earth from my own garden, I must have laid down a half-foot of it, enough to grow anything.'

You are my thrall .. You . . . are . . . my . . . thrall . . . I . . . am . . . enthralled . . . with you . . .

'Drink,' said the priest, 'God help us.'

'God help us, indeed,' said the woman. 'I thought we were doing a great thing for these people and look at the thanks you get.'

'Bucket for bucket,' said the knee. 'And cabbage plants and seeds, I gave 'em, and advice too. And the ruffian looking at me and smiling slyly and seeming to take it all in, and the poor wife saying God bless you sir, and looking at her buck of a man wanting him to say a word of thanks but would he? Would he, aroo. Pubs, drink, that's what he was thinking of.'

Are . . . you . . . enthralled . . . with me?

'Ah, now, Father,' said the woman, 'Christian charity, fine, but there's a limit. It's sad to say but . . . '

'Bucket for bucket,' said the knee. 'But bucket for bucket I carted it back again when we got them out of it. Good earth . . . '

I am . . . deeply . . . deeply enthralled . . . with you.

'And then,' continued the knee, 'having beaten the wife to a pulp the lout had the audacity . . . the audacity, there's no other word for it, the audacity to come to me and ask me for money . . . for the children, he said . . . *he* said . . . '

'I've got Jim to bore a hole in the door,' the woman put in.

'Oh, you can't be too careful,' said the priest.

'A peep hole, you get me,' said knee.

'I just wouldn't open the door now for anyone unless I knew . . . '

Pat rose and stumbled down the aisle. The two toilets were engaged. A few heads had turned looking at her, she hid from them in the passage to the door, hanging on to the vertical bars, wondering if she should attempt to go one carriage further and deciding she couldn't. She swallowed, keeping it down, staring at the writhing lines of steel as a small station flew past. It could be anywhere, she had no sense of place or time, no sense of how long she had been in the train, nothing but an overpowering feeling of being catapulted through space along knotting and unravelling cords of steel that tightened and relaxed on her stomach in regular heaves that brought gushes of saliva into her mouth. It's not nerves, she thought, I'm suicidal, that's what it is, and her soul swooned out into the kaleidoscope of forms wriggling at her feet to be ensnared by them, snapped off and flung into the ditch and mistaken by someone looking through the rain-streaked window for a bundle of rags. But she could not do it, she was too much of a coward.

She heard one toilet door opening but she couldn't seem to get her limbs working, she was in slow motion while everything about her flew past. By the time she had negotiated the corner the door was closing again on a large woman who didn't hear her call out. She was about to hammer on the door when the door to the other toilet opened and a little boy came out. She rushed in, almost knocking him down, blindly slamming home the bolt and throwing herself across the toilet bowl. But the more she tried to get it all up the less anything came, and she knew at once that she really hadn't expected it to, hadn't expected relief in this way. Again it wasn't anything physical, anything in her stomach that was causing her mouth to fill with saliva, it was the movement of the skate come alone now on the seabed, churning up the sand with abandon, seeking a way out of the ever-thickening drift of senseless objects around, the bits of bones and combs, bronze pins and antler tines, and pink eels that weren't eels at all but rolls of toilet paper that wrapped themselves fitfully round her stomach as though seeking a way in, while she flapped about drawing objects in her wake, plastic cups and bits of twisted tin and contraceptives, bloated things with open mouths that followed her like absurd pilot fish. But there was no way through them because they were locked in with her in a slow spin contained by vague figures circling outside, and it was over these she began to weep because they were loved ones and suddenly just as senseless as the other objects floating around. Nerves, nerves, she kept telling herself, but she knew it wasn't only that because they *were* senseless, they were really no different from the other smashed and mutilated artifacts around, only they didn't want to admit it, no one wanted to admit that he was a mere artifact no more interesting in the long run than the bones of the Viking skeleton, they all hid it behind tags of heaven or happiness or getting on with it. But could there be any getting on with it when one saw them for what they really were? Round they circled, her parents, Ray, the girls in the hut, her friends, and the Viking woman with her baby, all smiling at her through the murk, but their smiles passing through her as though she were a bottomless bucket that could harbour for an instant any amount of life but hold none, and that was what she wanted to do, to hold life, to gulp it down, selfishly, cruelly, as something that was her very own. Her ears sang with the violent effort of weeping, she gulped and swallowed and for a second, in her agitation, hardly realised that a hand had been laid on her shoulder. Then, startled, she looked up. It was the priest, bending over her solicitously where she sat on the bowl. How had he got in? Past his outstretched arm she saw then that the bolt of the lock had slid past the bracket. She stood up, helpless, muttering apologies, groping for the handkerchief she had tucked into her sleeve.

'My poor child,' he said, 'can I help you?'

'I'm sorry, Father.' She found the piece of cloth and wiped her face. 'I was just feeling a bit sick . . . '

He was standing close to her, inside the unlocked door. The train began to slow down, jolting a little.

'Can I help you in any way?'

'No, thank you, Father. I'm fine now.'

She almost lost her balance and held on to him. His strong hands gripped her. Outside people could be heard moving towards the doors.

'This is my station,' he said. 'Otherwise we could talk . . . but I hope you'll be all right now.'

He didn't sound very convinced, and perhaps it was this uncertainty in his voice that made her exclaim, out of all reason, 'Please, don't go, Father!'

Not showing much surprise at this, the priest made more comforting noises, still supporting her with one hand and awkwardly patting her with the other. But his mouth tightened with anxiety as the train continued to slow down.

'Don't go!' she said again and, unnerved suddenly at the thought of the train stopping, of doors banging and people departing, her mood reeling, she leant forward and planted a rough, wet kiss on the priest's lips. Shocked, he let go of her arm and all but fell back against the door which, at that moment, someone was trying to press in from outside. The woman's voice said, 'Are you in there, Father?'

'No!' cried Pat, and even as she uttered the word her hands flew to her lips. Ruefully, in a boyish way that touched her, the priest braced himself against the wall, dabbing his mouth to his sleeve as though he had been struck and not kissed.

Outside the woman was saying, 'Jim, go down into the next carriage and look for him, he'll miss his stop.'

'I'm sorry,' whispered Pat, aware that every second that elapsed without the priest declaring himself was critical.

'Try the other toilet first,' the woman shouted. 'I'll wait here anyway and no train will move off before he's found.'

Still the priest said nothing, and a few seconds later it was irrelevant. The shock and revulsion – it had been that, she thought–in his expression was giving way to genuine curiosity. Clearly, it wasn't every day he was kissed by hysterical young women, or any other kind, in train toilets.

'Why did you . . . ' He hesitated. 'What were you crying about?'

Pat caught a glimpse of herself in the mirror and touched her hair. Like a child who had had her tantrums she was feeling strangely glib. 'I don't know, really.'

'You don't know?'

'No.' She suppressed dreadful laughter.

'No sign of him,' said the returning Jim outside.

'Well,' said the woman, 'I won't budge from here until he's found. I only hope the fool hasn't fallen out.'

'Everything . . . and nothing,' Pat said vaguely to her reflection. It was like speaking in a noisy air bubble, throwing out callously provocative sops of information to creatures outside. The train was coming to a halt. The priest looked at her in some disappointment, thinking perhaps that it hadn't been worth the inevitable embarrassment. But what unheard-of dilemma could she have revealed in a matter of seconds?

From her pitch of eerie detachment she said, 'What are

you going to do?'

'Go out, I suppose.' Now he was looking definitely rueful.

'Will they misunderstand?'

'Maybe.'

The train jolted to a halt. It was like a cue, and indeed as Pat moved a memory of almost being flung on to the stage by an impatient nun came to her. She went out, closing the door behind her. The woman eyed her coldly. She had planted herself between the doors and from her expression it was obvious that when the time came she would resist the efforts of a regiment of stationmasters to allow the train to move out. People were beginning to get off and as Pat edged past the woman to find a way through she suddenly buckled at the knees. Grasping her for support, she almost pulled her down with her among the suitcases and parcels. How easy it is really to act, she thought, aware of the confusion she was causing as some people, thinking perhaps that she was going to have a fit, shouted to each other to make room for her, while others, including the woman, were trying to help her to her feet. In the background she saw the priest appear. No one seemed to notice him. Immediately she recovered, apologising, saying it had been a dizzy spell, and kindly refused the offer of an elderly gentleman to accompany her back to her seat. The priest followed her to collect his things but departed without a word. He was probably disgusted with her, thinking her a frivolous, hysterical thing. Through the dirty window she saw his face turn towards her as he passed outside, and she wondered if he would keep the incident to himself or relate it — and perhaps invite ragging — at the presbytery table. It was a matter of supreme indifference to her, as the train moved out. She was indeed an actress, cool and drained now as though she had just come off the stage after a strenuous scene. She was probably schizophrenic, hopelessly fragmented into a thousand such bit parts. Touch a nerve and she would become any one of them. It would go on like that until one day the game became too silly and she really would throw herself from a train or from the tenth storey of some building. That's what suicides were, people who hadn't the strength to remain themselves, who had outgrown them-selves indulgently into a plethora of people, becoming bits of pottery that could belong to any jug and not wanting, not being able to care.

In this frame of mind, an hour later, she listened to her mother talk about the farm and the crops and what a belting everyone had taken that year before the weather had changed, as her father drove slowly through the dim fields that were like shot silk after the rain. Mildly reproved by her husband with interjections of a more positive nature, she yet sustained her litany of woes as though convinced, looking back occasionally to her daughter whose pale thin face and puffed eyes had shocked her at the station, that this was the only remedy for the girl's more critical state. Pat said little. She was too tired and empty not to indulge herself again in her one reliable alibi of painful recovery from the traumas of bomb blast and mis-carriage. It seemed an inescapable excuse now since all her efforts to find a truth, or something resembling one, even an attitude of some psychological validity, to replace it had failed. They had merely led to bouts of phantom sickness and incred-ible outbursts of emotion with strangers in the most

71

compromising circumstances. So she said little, let it all wash over her, thankful that in her case classification was so easy, that the designations and labels for her plight in the eyes of the world, the bits and pieces of her that still remained intact, were so readily at hand.

The car slowed as they splashed through a stretch of waterlogged road.

'I wonder are we going to make it,' the father said. 'I think it's risen since we went through it on the way in.'

Rounding a sharp bend, they now saw that other cars with their lights on had pulled up on the verge of the flooded area. They weren't going to make it. The car suddenly coughed and spluttered and came to a standstill. The engine had died even before the father had switched off the ignition.

'Sweet Infant . . . ' the mother began, but the father brusquely cut her short.

'It's nothing,' he said. 'We're nearly there. I'll come down with Timmy and the tractor and get her out. We'll just have to wade a bit, that's all.'

So they waded, father and daughter in underpants with their shoes and trousers in their hands, mother with hitched-up skirt revealing frilly thighlong bloomers.

'I only hope there's no one there that we know,' she said.

'Don't be silly,' said Pat. 'Pants are pants.'

She was enjoying it. Like being let out to play, escaping not only from the confinement of space but also of self. Against her thighs the flow of near tepid water was almost sensual. In the lights of the cars their bodies threw fantastic shadows like those of monstrous beasts lumbering out of some vast pluvial belt. Improbably reminded of Pascal crying Fire! in his vision of god, Pat exclaimed, more pertinently, 'Water!'

'There's enough of that anyway,' said her mother, drily.

Pat had no vision of anything, yet as though compelled in incantation of some ancient memory that possessed her she again cried, 'Water!'

They emerged on to dry road, hailing people they knew. To cover his embarrassment, her father did a little dance, a rising laughter as he stumbled over his trousers trying to get them on, while she slipped on hers, aware of male eyes on her. Then she linked her parents and barefoot they padded off down the road.

For a long time afterwards Pat liked to think that that had been the experience that mattered, that in those seconds something elusive had happened to her, like a mysterious bone slipping back into place. But she knew that walking away with her parents she was aware of nothing like that. It had sufficed that for the first time in many weeks things seemed as extra-ordinary as they should be.

WATCH OUT FOR PARADISE LOST

MICHAEL COADY

No man can taste the whole wine? By God, old Donne went
for it anyway. Sermons and seduction. Body and soul. God in
woman. Up and at it with a metaphysical will.

Full nakedness! All joyes are due to thee
As souls unbodied, bodies uncloth'd must be
To taste whole joyes . . .

He stretched his legs down in the bed and adjusted the
book on his chest.

'John.'

'Hmm?'

'John!'

He turned his head and looked across the room. She was
sitting in her slip at the dressing-table, smearing something
around her eyes.

'What is it?"

She unscrewed the lid from another jar.

'Talk to me.'

'Just hold on a minute. I'm in the middle of something.
The Dean of St Paul's trying to get his mistress into bed.'

To teach thee, I am naked first; why then
What needst thou have more covering than a man?

Some boyo.

'John, will you put away the book and listen to me?'

'Hmm?'

'You never listen.'

He put the book down and blinked across at her. 'Alice, are you going to spend the night out there? Come to bed and stop fussing.' He moved over and turned the clothes back at her side. Page lost again.

She opened a drawer. 'I looked into Patrick's room. His mouth was open and he had half the bedclothes out on the floor.'

He searched for the page. 'He's all right. I put him to bed at eight o'clock and he was asleep halfway through the King's New Clothes. What would you do if you had a houseful, instead of one and a bit?'

The page. Love's War.

Here let me war; in these arms let me lie
Here let me parlie, batter, bleed and die.

A cold draught of air sneaked under the bedclothes. What the hell was she doing? 'Alice! Are you going to stay out there all night?' He sat up and faced towards her. 'What's the matter with you?'

Twitch of the shoulders. After eight years you knew the signs. Trough of low pressure approaching. Sometimes he came in to find her crying her eyes out over some old film full of rose-covered studio cottages, idyllic weekends, sobbing violas and Ronald Colman saying good-bye in foggy railway stations. And, oh my God, the night he brought her to Jane Eyre. Half the cinema turning around in their seats to look at her in the floods. As delicately tuned as a bloody fiddle.

'John!' Tears ran down her cheeks and plopped on to a framed photograph which she held in her hands. His mouth opened in astonishment. She made a sudden dive for the bed and buried herself against him, heaving with great sobs and covering his chest hair in a mixture of tears and skin conditioner. Oh God, oh John Donne.

'Alice, will you for goodness sake tell me what's the matter?'

Something was digging painfully into his gut. The photograph. He patted her on the back and drew the clothes around her. 'Come on. Talk to me about it. And take that picture away before you do me an injury.'

She relaxed a little. He felt a tear run down all the way to his navel. After a while the talk would come. And probably go on for hours. What would Donne have done?

'Aw now Alice . . . Did I say something? Did I do something?'

Under his neck she shook her head, disentangled an arm and held out the photograph, then turned on her back, her eyes half closed, their lids awash.

It was a picture of herself. He remembered taking it one day in the woods, before they were married. Her face framed in fresh-green branches. Whitethorn blossom he had confettied in her hair. Smiling; a girl. Sweet lovers at their play.

He studied it for a while, remembering, then leaned over and stroked her wet cheek. 'Alice . . . There's no doubt about it. You were the Queen of the May.'

She sobbed.

'And listen to me – you're the same girl now as you were

that day.' Dammit, it was true. Put her in a gymslip and she was seventeen again.

'You're,' she swallowed, looking up at him in bitterness, 'you're only trying to pacify me. I was a girl then. I'm a woman now. Twenty-nine. With stretch marks. And little wrinkles coming around my eyes.'

'Stretch marks? What in God's name are you talking about? You were always a woman. And you'll always be a girl. Nothing to do with stretch marks. Or wrinkles. You could still be seventeen.'

'Don't. I'm not a child.'

Irishwomen never believe compliments. He twisted towards her and John Donne fell out on the floor. 'Listen to me, Alice. I mean it. You haven't changed a bit and you'll still be beautiful when I'm pushing up nettles. You'll live forever. Look at your grandmother – eighty-three and still getting her hair done to go to bingo every week. Now come on and don't be acting like a' – it came out before he could stop himself – 'like a child.'

She opened her swollen eyes and looked up at him in utter hatred. 'You and your bloody poetry.'

'What!'

'It's only all talk with you. You don't live any of it. You're in a rut and you don't even know it.'

'For God's sake what has poetry got to do with it? What are you talking about?'

'All the romance is gone out of you, that's what. If I'm not changed, then you must be. Something is missing anyway.'

'Romance!'

'Call it what you like. You think you have everything worked out, everything finished and in its place. No more adventure or taking a chance or doing something unusual. And then when you're drunk enough you go on about poetry and stuff . . . ' She glared. 'You're only a big fake.'

'Alice, listen. You're upset. Can't you try to relax and go to sleep? In the morning things always look different. You can't expect life to be like a fairytale.'

'What do you know about it? You think it's all fixed and done now. The only place you want to live is between the covers of a bloody book. Because it's nice and safe.'

"What the hell am I supposed to do – ride up on a white horse and serenade under your window? A semi-detached knight in shining armour? You were always the same. Life must be magic all the time. Rabbits out of hats and leaps through flaming hoops. You notice, ladies and gentlemen, that while I perform this trick the fingers never leave the hand. Watch carefully while I turn the mortgage and the nappies into a magical – '

She reached over suddenly and gave him a vicious pinch in his unprotected paunch. He gasped. She was always a girl who could pinch. With the nails, and leave a mark.

'Holy God!' He jumped out on to the floor. 'You little bitch!' He dragged the coverlet from the bed and draped it around himself. He was angry, but he felt a mad urge to laugh, which made him angrier still. 'Assaulted in my own bloody bed, after I spend the night at home to leave you out with your women friends. I'm going downstairs. For a drink.' He stumbled over the book on the floor, reached down and tossed it at her from the doorway. 'Romance! Try the Dean. Still standing up and saluting after four hundred years.'

Passing the mirror in the hallway he saw himself, flushed in his toga, questing wine, making a wild face at his own reflection. Mr John O'Brien MA, HDipEd, looking like a goat dragged through a bush. The unsuspected dramas that go on inside the mortgaged privacies. As sure as God the cupboard would be bare. Give them romance and they want security. Give them security and they want romance. Search. Empty whiskey bottle and one stale beer since Christmas. Drawer of cabinet. Insurance policies; bulwarks against adventure. Life insurance, fire insurance, car insurance, mortgage insurance. Insurance insurance? All risks and personal liability. Keep at bay the lizard in the grass, arm against the tiger in the dark. The unexpected foreseen, forestalled.

Take life and multiply by age, profession, number of dependants, congenital defects, original sin. Express in terms of possibility divided by probability, allow for earthquakes, floods, wars, racial characteristics, climatic variation, longitude and latitude. Relate to profit-curve for company. Press button. Say sixty pounds a week. Sleep safe. With benefits. Family provided for in the event of. Go gentle and dead safe into that good night, easy in your mind. Large and representative attendance present at the final obsequies. Quiet and unassuming disposition. Exemplary family man and dedicated in his profession. Generations of past pupils attest. Love of books and cultivation of the highest ideals as embodied in the enduring outpourings of the great poets.

No drop to be had but this flat beer. Wait a minute. Yesterday in the garage. Beside the driftwood and the back numbers of

The Times Lit. Supp. A gallon of the stuff. Dark red in a big dusty jar. Elderberry? From the château of Brother O'Rourke, science master. Swinging chalk-stained soutane and bare ankles. 'Socks, Mr O'Brien. Unhealthy. The enemy of clear thinking. The unimpeded circulation of the blood from the brain to the extremities. *Mens sana* yes? Essential. A few moments of your time in the science room after school. I'd like you to taste some dandelion for acidity.' Two dozen bottles exploding in his room one night. Community sleep disturbed. Wine flowing out under the door and down the monastic stairs. Resignation of housekeeper.

Kitchen door to garage locked. Security. Key God knows where. Lateral thinking into play. Slip out front door and across patch of grass, toga flapping over his night-nakedness. Old Vermin's light still on next door. Worrying about his repayments. Up-and-over lock broken. Thank God for small mercies. Grope in the dark. There it is. Lug out, pull down door behind. Twitch of Vermin's curtain above. Vocal member of Laurel Grove Residents' Association. 'Through the chair, Mr Chairman. Tree-planting would be a visual amenity but there's the problem of leaves in the autumn, and the danger of encouraging vermin in the estate.' Poor bastard. Nightmaring about birds, snails, caterpillars and primeval forest advancing on his tenth of a territorial acre while he sleeps.

Prise bung out with screwdriver and pour gurgling dark-red glass. O'Rourke, eccentric celibate, from your grave you come to my aid. Temperature, acidity, fermentation. 'Any port in a storm of course, but a good body, Mr O'Brien, is everything, while I prefer my bouquet to be modest and unobtrusive.'

Dark juice of the elderberry, work of monkish hands, bring me the true, the blushful visions. The king sits in Dunfermline town, drinking the blude-red wine. Fill again and bedamned.

Safe between the covers of a book she said. Do something unusual. Warm glow kindling in the innards. Romance and adventure. First they fix the balls and chains and then they wait for you to perform triple somersaults and other astounding tricks. Woo them constantly with wonders, keep the canker from the rose. See how the fermentings of yesteryear release in the fullness of time and chance their glow, their sun and solace. O'Rourke, mad cleric, you weren't the worst of them. 'The Tuatha de Danaan type, Mr O'Brien. Easily distinguishable in the physiognomy of the midlander. Don't you think? Try another drop, though it won't be at its best for another couple of months. A second opinion is always interesting and the community are all abstainers. Except Sullivan who has no time for anything except big black bottles of stout. A Kerryman of course.'

O'Rourke, sad celibate, I drink to your memory. Rotting now in the clay while I taste the water you reddened. 'Married life must have its consolations, Mr O'Brien, though we choose otherwise. Who can know the greater wisdom? *The tragedy of sexual intercourse is the perpetual virginity of the soul.* Mr Yeats was it? I am unlettered in these matters; a celibate scientist standing aside from the hurly-burly of human relations.'

And she above now, mourning the loss of wonder, of magic and surprise. Crying for golden lads and lasses, still sad music. Link by cosy link the chains are forged; the horizons narrow down to a small town with a hill over it, a river, a bridge, tight streets. Thirty pairs of young eyes in a classroom. What is the poet trying to say in these lines? Can you find a parallel in your own experience? Revise Wordsworth, look up 'Lycidas', brush up on the sonnets and watch out for *Paradise Lost*. Sir, what use is poetry? Chalk, duster, syllabus; another thirty pairs of eyes next September. Brilliant lad; choice of Electricity Supply Board, civil service, teaching profession. Grateful past pupils owe their success. Weep no more ye shepherds.

Toes and knees turning chilly. Go up to her. Bring jug of wine and extra glass. Capitulate. Human comfort. No man is an. Paddy Cleary in the pub. Folk wisdom. 'Listen, you're an educated man and tell me if I'm wrong. In the long run what have we in this life only the few bottles every night and the wife's arse warm beside us in the bed? Listen, there's a lot of people over in the cemetery would like to be like us. Am I right or am I wrong?'

Gather thy shroud about thee, bear gifts to the nuptial chamber. I come with wine for wooing, unsteady but ardent; fain would I gather rosebuds.

Her forehead frowning over John Donne.

'Alice, I'm cold.'

She closed the book and looked. 'Mother of God, would you look at the cut of him! Where did you get that stuff?'

He put down the two glasses on the bedside table and poured. 'O'Rourke, the late brother. Master of Science, maker of wine; the cracked cleric who refused to wear socks. Elderberry and two years old. I found it in the garage.'

'I heard the front door. It's a pity I didn't think of locking it after you and leave you out there in your shift.'

He sat down on the bed and drank. 'It's not bad stuff at all. When you get used to it. Try some.'

'Wouldn't it be great! Locked out on the road and nothing on him but a bed spread. I'd wet myself laughing. Imagine the boys in school hearing about it, not to mention Vermin.'

He handed her a glass and she gulped it back, making a face.

'The trouble with old Vermin is he has no sense of irresponsibility. You wouldn't do that to me anyway. Leave me naked and alone, at the mercy of middle-class outrage?'

'That's what amuses me about you. That really kills me. Which class do you think *you* are?'

'I don't dream about double-glazing and holidays in Tenerife anyway. Or worry about the golf handicap or whether to order red or white. Let us be thinking about life and love and death, not about mowing lawns and washing cars. I have immortal longings in me.'

'That's only your excuse to get out of doing things. You're no different from any of the rest of them. Except that you can't hammer a nail or paint a door.'

'Alice, I'm famished with the cold. Would you think of shoving over in the bed before I get my death? When I have thoughts that I might cease to – '

'Give me some more of that stuff. I might as well be drinking, seeing as you are.'

He topped up two glasses. She moved to make room for him as he turned the clothes back. Flash of white thighs by God. Home is where the heat is. The dead O'Rourke's elderberry setteth us on. He was wont to lace, to fortify. 'Rather potent, Mr O'Brien. Needs more time to mellow. The Roman civilisation. A pity we missed it. You remember Horace? The cask of Falernian. Loved his wine. *Falernum*, neuter noun. Ah yes, the Mediterranean, a pity. The white light, the terraced vine; *O fons Bandusiae*. Our own ancestral experience distilled a dark fatalism Mr O'Brien. Caught in a pincer movement between endless troughs of low pressure from the west and Anglo-Saxon injections of puritanism from the east. A people shaped by constant rain and colonial humiliations. We have something of the Mediterranean instinct but without the climate to match. So we drink whiskey for oblivion rather than joy. Are we a lost tribe in the wrong place? Try the dandelion. A little dry? Sullivan refuses to taste, even on feast-days. A Kerryman. Black porter. Extraordinary.'

Love and wine. Illusions to distract us from the dark? Still, the best illusions we've got. Leaning on elbows, the warmth of her soft beside him. And dead O'Rourke – my God, yes – O'Rourke is here, a part of this communion. He reached and put a hand on her stomach. 'Alice, you're lovely.' Yeast of life, his, hers, swelling within.

She jumped at his cold touch and the elderberry splashed over her neck, trickled down towards her breasts.

'You chancer. An hour ago you wouldn't look at me. Stuck in your bloody book. Now you're three sheets in the wind and getting worked up. The eyes are dancing in your head you eejit.'

'Alice, I meant it, honest to God.' He stroked the soft, blue-veined skin of her shoulder, sitting upright and speaking with a sudden passionate clarity. 'This is the terrible, Godawful truth, Alice. We lie all these average nights together, never knowing how many nights there will be for us, except that in the end, in the final wind-up the two of us will be stretched together in a bloody grave. A hole in the ground for Christsake. A black hole in the bloody ground. Jesus think of it. Just think of it!'

'Thinking is poisonous. You're giving me the creeps. We won't know anything anyway. It's while we're here that matters. And you ignore me half the time.'

'Sometimes I'm blind. It's hard to see the important things clearly all the time. Alice – ' he reached ' – give us a feel . . . '

Her face turned scarlet. She could still blush, after eight years. Blushed, but did not draw away.

'Oh God John it's not fair. You take me for granted. You expect me to be there waiting for you when you want me. It wasn't always like this. You used to give time to me. You used even sing to me. It's a long time since that happened.'

First on the roadside outside a country pub one night in summer. Still half strangers to each other, but something was sealed in the singing of that song of Burns which came unbidden into his head on a summer night. Unspoken then but sealed. In a song by the roadside.

'I remember, Alice. I remember. Bobby Burns had a hand in it.' And knew all about it. The silver tassie and the pint of wine, ploughland and red lips and candlelight, winds and tides of meetings and partings, the boat rocking at the pier of Leith, the need to sing.

'Drink, Alice. The last of O'Rourke's wine. I'll sing for you now.'

'You'll wake the child. And the neighbours. It's all hours.'
But smiling.

'To hell with all the neighbours. I'll sing for you now and let the dead rise if they're able.' Clearing his throat to let out the song, he leaned warm and tipsy over her, singing as he did first in a moment of recognition shared on a country road one summer night.

O my love is like a red, red rose
That's newly sprung in June;
O my love is like a melody
That's sweetly played in tune.

His voice lifted, affirming love till all the seas gang dry and rocks melt with the sun. Suddenly her hand reached up to stop his mouth.

'Whisht! Listen!'

Whimper. Next room. My child, my son.

'Mammy! Mammy!'

She stiffened, alert on an elbow. Girl. Mother.

'Easy, Alice. He'll go to sleep again; he's only dreaming.'

'Mammy! Mammy!'

'All right love. I'm coming.'

Gone to comfort him. Fare thee well my bonnie lass. Head throbbing. Grey light creeping cold under curtains. Thirty pairs of eyes. Sir, what use is poetry?

STILL LIFE

BARBARA McKEON

There are times when you know right from the start that someone is wrong for you. But you go ahead anyway. You haven't got a man and you wait for either divine intervention or plain sexual attraction to intercede and have one turn up . Sometimes you resort to fantasies that leave you sleepless at four in the morning, giving your life another reappraisal. A line of a song goes: 'It feels so right, how can it be wrong.' And that's the truth. At four in the morning alone in bed you don't think of poetry, you remember lines from gutsy rock 'n' roll numbers. Poetry's romantic, and it's not romance you want, it's something more honest, more basic, more human. Romance is for poets, life is for people.

Walking into the library I saw him ahead of me at the counter. He was propped on one leg, tapping his loose foot monotonously off the tiled floor, his head jigging up and down rhythmically, while the librarian fiddled about with his returned books. Turning around he saw me, and threw me a careless smile. I shrugged it off and put Shakespeare down on the counter, and then set off on my hunt for similar sized reading matter, acutely conscious of being watched all the time. After a few minutes I came on a perfect two inches in the shape of a hardbacked volume of the shorter works of Franz Kafka.

He was following me, his eyes peeping over the spines of books. He wasn't particularly good-looking, but I'd learned long ago not to expect too much. It was enough that he paid attention. He shuffled self-consciously, averting his eyes when I glanced over, waiting for the courage to come that would ordain his actions. He banged his book shut with excessive bravado and clumsily replaced it in the wrong section. Slowly he trailed along the shelves towards where I stood flicking through the pages of Kafka. He blew his cheeks in and out, nodding his head as if thoroughly satisfied with the selection offered him. He reminded me of a farmyard rooster scratching his way across the dirt. That irritated me.

'Ah, Camus,' he would cluck, his head jerking forward to peer closer. Or, 'Oh, Canetti.' His Adam's apple strained in his throat as he made silly noises indicating his intimate knowledge of literature.

From the corner of my eye I followed the dance of the male urban peacock, and was torn between ruffling his feathers by turning and walking out, or staying where I was while the great divide narrowed and he eventually staked his claim to my attentions. Even as I deliberated, I knew I would stay. Though I also knew at the back of it all that I really didn't want this man to talk to me. Indecision, or paralysis, transfixed me to the spot, had me perusing a book I wasn't going to read, awaiting the crucifixion of my pride on the off chance that a tarnished ego might for a little while pretend it was glittering.

I wondered what he was. A bank clerk, or a civil servant. Could be a teacher, or a renegade on the loose from a seminary.

He had the look of a priest about him, trying to put life in terms of a redundant catechism. Searching for truth among the Existentialists, patently misunderstanding them so he could be sure that what he was brought up to believe in was right all along. But he wasn't a priest, as it turned out. Customs and Excise. Or was it Weights and Measures?

Almost imperceptibly he was edging closer chronologically. He was at 'G' by now and André Gide was suffering unmercifully at the hands of a psychotic philistine. A library on a Saturday afternoon is comparable to the dark side of the moon. The gravitational pull attracts all manner of lunatics, devouring the mysticism of art and literature to regurgitate it on the mundanity of their lives.

'Excuse me,' he smiled and proceeded to scan the row in front of me.

I stepped back to allow him room, watching his pale and slightly freckled hand roam over the titles. I was pleasantly surprised by his smile. It seemed to tie up his awkward features into some kind of order. He had a pimple on the back of his neck that his collar rubbed against, making it appear angrier.

'Oh,' he said, his gaze finally alighting on the book in my hands, 'You've got it.'

'Got what?' I asked innocently.

'Kafka.'

'There are plenty of Kafkas on the shelf.'

'But you've got the one I want.'

'Oh really?'

'But I can read it after you.'

'No, you take it. If you want. I can get something else.'

'No, no,' he protested, shielding himself with his large hands. 'Be my guest, I've already read it. I just wanted to read it again. I can recommend it. Marvellous writer, don't you think?'

'Mmmm,' I replied.

In the pause that followed, he blew his cheeks in and out once or twice, protracted and retracted his head in his rooster-like fashion and exchanged the weight of his body from his left to his right leg. He never seemed at ease with his body, he continually shifted it to the left or to the right. I eventually figured out he had a chip on each shoulder and couldn't decide which was weighing him down the more.

A stroke of inspiration blundered to the fore.

'You bear a striking resemblance to Rossetti's "Dying Beatrice". Has anyone ever told you that?'

'Not lately.'

He studied me closer, pointing the line of his gaze with his chin. Seeing I was flattered by his comparison (though I don't know why I was as I had no notion of what Beatrice looked like on her demise, but assumed it must have been poetic), he decided he could best allay his hesitancy by this line of approach.

'Yes, definitely. I think it's your hair, or your eyes. Is that your natural colour?'

'Yes, they've always been green.'

'No, I mean your hair,' he said with an embarrassed laugh. 'My name is Colin.'

'I'm Angie.'

'Short for Angela?'

'Well, Angelina actually.'

'Angelina, Angelina,' he repeated, rolling his hand in the air as if to encourage the name out of his mouth. 'Yes, Angelina is perfect.'

'So glad you approve.'

'Well, you take the book. I'll get this one, Angelina,' he said, grabbing the nearest one and starting towards the counter, still mumbling my name and rolling his hand about.

We stepped out into the afternoon and, having elicited which direction I was going in, he volunteered, uninvited, to accompany me.

A cumbersome silence replaced conversation. A passing bus fortuitously gave him the topic of an impending bus strike. He was unable to talk without his arms threshing geometric designs in the air.

'Cigarette?' I said, holding the packet out to him.

'Given them up,' he replied. 'Took ages but I finally won. The thing is will power...'

'God, is there anything worse than a reformed smoker!'

He grinned in submission. He was trying so hard to be liked that I felt a pang of sadness for him. He was constantly on the defensive, and I defended by attack. The pang I felt ricocheted.

We were crossing the park and he suggested we sit down on the grass and discuss our mutual interest in Art. That really amused me, nowhere had I professed the remotest interest in Art. I was more at home with the bus strike issue. The tortured soul of the artist, I chuckled to myself and sat down.

While he launched into a one-sided discussion as to how a 16th century playwright (Shakespeare) compared with a

20th century Jewish Czech psycho (Kafka), I wondered where Robert was and what he was doing. I supposed he must have married her by now, it was ages since I saw the engagement in the paper. I remember cutting it out, though I can't remember why, or what happened to it. It's funny the things you do sometimes, for no reason at all. There must have been a reason or I wouldn't have done it. Or would I? Could have been my name on that item in the Personal Column... Mr and Mrs Mulvanney are pleased to announce the engagement of their daughter Angelina to Robert Morrisey... But it wasn't.

Colin sat opposite me in what more or less resembled the lotus position, his arms flailing about descriptively. I didn't know what the hell he was rambling on about. To tell the truth, he would have bored me stiff if he hadn't taken the precaution of holding my hand and squeezing it every so often to make sure I wasn't an aesthetic illusion.

'Why did you choose Kafka? Was it the subterranean depths he visualises so brilliantly, or the despondency of man which he evokes with such disillusioning realism?'

'Neither,' I said. 'The book was exactly two inches thick.'

Colin looked at me puzzled, then burst out laughing.

'The wit and charm of Beatrice,' he said.

Perhaps I'd better explain about this two inches business and the size of my reading matter. As far as I was concerned Shakespeare and Kafka compare beautifully. One leg of the kitchen table is two inches shorter than the other three and we were waiting for the landlord to get around to repairing it. Anyhow, my sister's library book fitted perfectly, being an exact two inches. After one or two reminders I returned

Shakespeare and got out Kafka, having compared spines and found them equal.

'Would you like to come back to my place for coffee?' I asked. 'I live over there.'

He smiled at me. 'Okay.'

I tried to remember what state the flat was in. It's not the tidiest place on earth, but nobody really sees it except my sister and myself. And occasionally the landlord when he's trying to pick up the rent and Shirley simultaneously.

He was waiting for me to move, but I didn't, so finally he asked me where I worked.

'I'm a typist in an Insurance office. Been there seven years,' I added.

'You must like it.'

'It's a job.'

'Look at that,' he said suddenly, pointing to a beetle crawling through the grass.

'What's the matter, don't you like beetles?'

'Metamorphosis,' said Colin.

'Meta-what-osis?'

He picked up my library book, looked down the index and turned to a page.

'Read the first sentence,' he said, handing me the book.

'"As Gregor Samsa awoke one morning from uneasy dreams he found himself transformed in his bed into a gigantic insect". I didn't know it was science fiction.'

'It's symbolic,' said Colin, drawing out the word with a sweep of his hand.

'Oh.'

'I had a girlfriend once,' said Colin to the expanse of sky overhead, as if it gave a damn anyway, 'who had a pet beetle.'

'A what?'

'A pet beetle. She found it in the bath one night and caught it in a matchbox. Then she took her bath and forgot about it. Next morning she opened the matches to light a cigarette and the beetle was in it looking up adoringly at her. I loved that girl.'

At this point he redirected his remarks from the sky to the insect scrambling around a pebble.

'She sounds pretty weird to have a pet beetle.'

'Ah, she wasn't weird. Not a bit. The nicest girl you could meet, kind and gentle and loving. She worked in a theatre booking-office and got tickets to all the shows and we'd go. A great cultural experience was Alison.'

'What happened to her?' I asked, chewing thoughtfully on a blade of grass.

'She . . . I don't know. But I loved her anyway.'

'Did she love you?'

'Yes, but . . . She put the beetle in a bigger box and fed it on whatever it is beetles eat. She called it Attila. Then one day, for no reason at all, she let it go.'

'Where?'

'In the garden, I think.'

'Is that where she let you go, too?'

'What?'

'When she let you out of the box she'd been keeping you in, was it in the garden?'

'Yes. I believe it was. She said . . . She said . . . Oh, what does it matter what she said. I loved her, I really did, but she let me go.'

'And like the beetle, you've been scrambling around trying to get back into the matchbox so you could gaze adoringly at her while she fed you whatever it is you eat and took you to the theatre for nothing.'

'You're very understanding. Have you been in love?'

'Yes.'

'Were you let down?'

'Like an inflatable tyre.'

'Would you like to be in love again?'

'I don't know. I don't know much about anything.'

'Don't be so negative,' said Colin. 'Everyone is afraid to commit themselves to a positive action because of the repercussions.'

'You want something positive,' I said to him. 'I'll give you something positive.'

I picked up the stone the beetle was still scrambling around and, placing it directly over the insect, pressed down. There was a crunching sound as its back was crushed.

'That was destructive, therefore negative!' exclaimed Colin.

'It was an action, therefore positive,' I insisted.

'Poor beetle,' he said. 'Do you realise, Angelina, you've just killed me.'

'It's going to rain. Come on, let's go back to my place.'

Funny how people's moods change. The heavens opened and it lashed rain, so by the time we got to my flat, we were drenched. As we ran through the downpour we couldn't decide whether to use our library books to cover our heads or to shelter them under our clothes and that made us laugh.

We got to the flat and I gave Colin a blanket to wrap up in while his clothes hung on the clotheshorse to dry. While I made coffee he sat in front of the electric fire, poking the bar with a match stick, blowing out the flame and lighting it again. Sometimes he would see how close to the bar he could keep the match before it set alight. Eventually, I had to take the matches off him as I was running short as it was.

I put two cups of coffee on the floor and squatted on the sheepskin beside him to dry my hair.

'You're very pretty,' he said, not looking at me, but gazing absently at the red light that glowed under the artificial coal. Charred matches littered the impotent embers.

'Thank you.'

Rain pummelled on the window, the glass shaking in its frame. Steam from the coffee mingled with cigarette smoke. His arms were practically hairless and where the blanket fell from his shoulders the pale white flesh of his chest reflected the red glow of the fire.

He caught my fingers in his and we sat in silence, facing the fire like two meditating Buddhas glorifying the mysteries of electricity. He turned his head and openly looked where the folds of my dressing-gown parted to reveal the curve of my breasts. With the same gentleness he had run his hands over the books in the library, he reached out and touched them. He never went farther than the delta of flesh exposed by the dressing-gown. Just tracing circular movements that dulled my senses of all awareness other than the slow, sensuous flow of his fingers.

'You've got a lovely body.'

In my fantasies I would be working late at the office. I am alone and it is dark outside. I am wearing a black low-cut dress and one of those push-up bras that I would never dare wear. The door of the District Manager's office is shut, but I know he is inside working late too. He does not know I am here. I am surrounded by covered typewriters and neatly filed insurance policies. The District Manager's door opens and Mr Conroy appears. He sees me and smiles. He bends over me pretending to see what I am typing, but he is really looking down my bosom. Slowly, he slips one hand over my shoulder and begins to caress my breasts. I lean back and offer my mouth to him. He kisses me, our tongues touching. He pulls me to the floor and seduces me. Suddenly we hear the cleaner out in the corridor. She will begin with the office at the end and work up to where we are. As she moves nearer, room by room, our passion heightens at the prospect of being caught. We make love as the sound of banging and sweeping and water flooding the office floors crowds into my head. Mr Conroy can no longer contain himself and a bucket crashes to the floor and the passion reaches its pinnacle. We lie quivering and sighing as the cleaner opens the door and sees us lying in dishevelled clothes. She gasps in horror and we laugh.

Colin was gently pushing me back to lie on the floor. His breathing was uneven and his kisses hard and coaxing. But my sister could be back any minute. Still I think I would have. I know I wanted to. Besides, it wouldn't have been for real. He kept calling me Beatrice.

That night I was to go to a party at Sarah O'Brien's, so I

thought I'd take Colin as I was dying for him to use meta-what's-it on her. Any word with five syllables was a sure-fire entry into her circle.

The party was all right. There was a good crowd and plenty of food and booze. Colin launched into the alcohol with a vengeance and was drunk in no time at all. To complete whatever image it was he was trying to create, he kept saying odd things like – 'I witnessed a murder today.' Or – 'I saw the nothingness of reality seduce a myth and produce an illusion.'

The room was dimly lit, candles threw strange shapes on the walls and snatched them away again, music pumped relentlessly, people drifted or darted about, painted faces and fantastic clothes loomed out of nowhere. With alcohol to fortify him, Colin was a different person. Every inch of the floor was occupied to demonstrate his ungainly dancing. At one stage he leapt onto the table and did a striptease. The whole effect was ruined when he unbuttoned his shirt to display an interlock vest. Sarah O'Brien asked me where I found him; I said I had him out on loan from the library.

In a way I was enjoying myself. I was with a man who liked me and I had just enough drink taken to almost believe I liked him back.

Colin uncorked another bottle of wine.

'If music be the food of love, play on!' he roared, slopping wine on the carpet. It splashed into his face and tiny rivulets trickled down his neck. Impulsively I moved towards him to lick the wine away, but he was already wiping it off with his shirt tail.

Shirley was standing beside me, looking my man up and

down. She was dressed beautifully and perfectly made-up. She could afford it, sleeping with her boss and screwing him for every penny she could get. Shirley's very attractive in a no nonsense sort of way.

'Yes,' I said. 'This is Colin.'

'Hi,' she said with a grin and then ignored him. He wasn't her type. She didn't waste her time on anyone who wasn't her type.

'Have some wine?' asked Colin.

'Don't mind if I do.'

'Wait till I get you a glass.'

He elbowed his way off into the crowd to fetch a glass. Something he hadn't found necessary to do for me—I was obliged to search for my own.

'You weren't home for tea,' I said.

'No, I was meeting Philip.'

'You might have phoned.'

'Why,' she said smugly, 'was there something hot for tea?'

'There might have been, if you'd phoned to say you weren't coming.'

'With him?' She jerked her thumb in the direction Colin had gone.

I didn't answer, but she let out a snort of laughter anyhow.

'Fancy him, do you?'

'He compared me to Rosetti's Dying Beatrice.'

'Seems to go in for poetry rather than accuracy! Still, it's a nice compliment.'

There was sarcasm in her voice. It didn't bother me. Why should it, you should see Philip.

'Here.'

Colin thrust a glass into her hand and poured the wine.

'Salut,' she said and took a sip.

'So,' she said after a moment. 'You think Angie looks like Rossetti's Beatrice. Who do I remind you of?'

Colin's body weight alternated from the right to the left, and he held the bottle to his chin thoughtfully.

She waited, one hand resting provocatively on her hip, the other holding the glass, with her index finger stroking the black velvet band around her throat. Her dark hair was pulled back, showing the perfect outline of her face. I rolled my eyes to heaven.

'Got it!' he said. 'Wait.'

From a vase on the table he plucked a pink carnation and slipped it behind her ear.

'Olympia,' he announced.

'Olympia?'

'Manet's Olympia. A beautiful woman lying naked on a couch, with a flower in her hair. And there's a negress holding a bouquet from an admirer.'

'Well,' she simpered. 'Aren't you the flatterer. Only one thing, I'm not naked.'

'Ah, but her real nakedness lay in her eyes. The same dark pools that are your eyes.'

'You're quite the boyo when it comes to impressing the ladies, aren't you? Why don't you ask me to dance?'

'Is it all right, Angelina?' he said, pushing the bottle of wine into my hands and taking Shirley's arm.

'Sure.'

I watched him lead her away. Only he wasn't leading, he was dangling. And if he was too stupid to see it, I wasn't going to tell him. I took a slug from the bottle and told myself I never wanted him in the first place anyway. After a few dances Shirley would let him go, send him packing and he'd come looking for me. But I wouldn't have him back. My dignity couldn't take it. Shirley doesn't mean to be the way she is, she can't help it. She squandered her pride when she gave up dreaming of tomorrow and settled for a down payment on today. She's a real 'one-up-man', that girl. Right back to when we were kids and we both won Bibles, only hers had colour illustrations and mine had black and white. She has the edge, all right, and she's learned how to exploit it. If I remember rightly, I tore all the colour pictures out of her Bible. But I don't do that anymore. You settle for what you've got and try to pretend that's what you've always wanted.

'He came with you, didn't he?' said a voice behind me.

Tucked in a corner was someone I could hardly see, it was so dark. He was sprawled on a chair with his feet up on the table.

'Yes, I was his Beatrice. He fancied himself as Rossetti.'

'And now he's making his play as Manet and Olympia. What a smooth artist he is, from the pre-Raphaelites to the Impressionists in one clean sweep.'

'You seem to know about Art,' I said indifferently.

'Yes, I paint a little myself.'

'Really.'

'I do flowers and fruit and vegetables, that sort. Still Life. They don't move about.'

'Why don't you paint me?'

'I can only do Still Life.'

'It's the same thing.'

An attractive blonde passing by smiled at him. He waited till she was gone a respectable distance and then said, 'Excuse me. Must go to the john.'

Something must have fouled up his intestines because he never came back.

I slipped away to get my coat. I opened the door and stepped out into the street. The darkness made it seem terribly unreal. A few cars stood motionless, the street lamps casting immobile shadows. The houses, some lit, some not, showed no trace of life. Overhead, the night was a dark shroud draping the corpse of a city. The nocturnal remains of Dublin, its soul having departed to its reward. Suburban somnambulance. Its deathly appearance seemed so peaceful and beautiful. The stillness was perfect, as long rigid shadows lay in serene blackness. Not a sound touched the canvas. The party taking place in a back room was inaudible out here.

I clapped my hands together once and broke the image. Then marching down the street with clattering footsteps, I shattered the stillness with the cruel intrusion of life.

1978

THE SMELL OF THE SEA

ANNIE ARNOLD

'Early July is the loveliest time of the year here,' said Fr Donellan, the elderly parish priest, as he seated himself at the head of his table. 'But it can be very stormy and dreary here in winter, and our winter lasts six months! Sit in here, John, and have your breakfast, a rural backwater like this is a great change for a man fresh from Maynooth.'

Fr Friel, on the very first morning of his very first curacy, had liked all he had seen so far. He moved gracefully to the seat indicated, listening with one ear to his parish priest's bantering conversation, and with the other to the myriad sounds that make up a summer morning. The sky, a clear, cloudless blue, was reflected in the glass-fronted cabinet which was placed opposite to the dining room window, and the air was already beginning to warm up in a prelude to what would be a swelteringly hot day. He applied himself to the task in hand, and did justice to the ample breakfast placed before him.

'I consider myself very lucky,' he said. 'I think this is a lovely place and this morning is just like something conjured up by the music of Greig. Are you familiar with the work of the northern composer, Father?'

'I never was much of a man for music,' replied the other

with a twinkle in his eye, 'and God knows it was just as well, for I had to endure some very queer sounds for benediction in my time. But I do like a good reel, well played on a violin, although to tell you the honest truth, John, I never could distinguish between a jig and a hornpipe.'

The young man smiled dutifully, but in some dismay, for he was a musician. But he rallied and took another piece of toast and put on a layer of home made marmalade on the top of it. 'I repeat that this is a lovely place to live. See the amount of light in the sky, and the fresh smell of the beautiful blue sea.'

'Wait until you see it a grey sea full of foam and fury,' said the parish priest. 'Wait till you go to console a family who has lost a son to the sea. So many times I've had group drownings, searches for bodies, sea-widows and sea-orphans. I hate the sight of the sea.'

'Disasters are not confined to the seaboard,' began the young man in his best school-debating manner. 'We had more people killed in car crashes last year than you had drownings in a decade.'

The priest's attention was diverted. 'Excuse me, Fr Friel,' he said, 'did you hear a knock? One thing a priest must always listen for is a knock.'

'I didn't hear anything, and I can see out to the front door from where I'm sitting. There is no one there.'

'All right, it is broad day and I need not worry. But at night a priest must always pay attention to a knock. Hold on to your youthful beliefs and enthusiasms by all means, you'll need them. Thirty-five years I've been here, spell as curate and the rest as parish priest, and I was a curate on an island for nine years before that and I've seen my share of the havoc wrought by the sea.'

They were interrupted by a light knock on the dining room door. 'Come in,' said Fr Donellan, turning to face the door.

His housekeeper put her head round the door and said, 'Excuse me, Fathers, but John Roarty is here from Slatamara. He wants a priest to go out on a sick call to Murphys of the headland.'

'Which of the Murphys is ill?' asked Fr Donellan.

'The brother James. The sister Ellen called to John when he was walking their strand this morning. She asked him to cycle in for the priest. She wants a priest to go out as soon as it is convenient.'

'Make Roarty a cup of tea, Mary, and seat him down in comfort till a priest is ready to go with him. Keep him talking for a while.'

'All right,' said Mary, withdrawing her head, and closing the door behind her.

'You did hear a knock,' exclaimed the young man.

'I listen for them all the time, but enough of that. I'm going to send you out on that sick call, and you'll learn a lot about the sea before you're a day older. The very first year I came to this place, the Murphys were a fine young foursome, two men and two lovely girls. On a day like this the girls went out for a dip in the quiet sea and were nearly drowned. They were rescued by their brother Mick, as fine looking a young fellow as I have ever seen. Mick had his passage to America, and was getting married to a neighbour and taking her out with him. They were within a month of the wedding. But the belief here is that if you take anyone from the sea, the sea will get its own back, and everyone started to tell Mick not to sail. He didn't sail, but as he was also leaving the girl, he ran away, disappeared, was never seen afterwards. His two sisters got afraid even to look at the sea, and his brother wouldn't go down to high water mark to pick up timber. They grew odder and odder, stopped going anywhere except the odd trip to chapel, and now they are three ageing persons who associate with nobody.'

'How old would they be?'

'The three of them must be over fifty now. I see the younger woman pretty often in chapel, but the other comes seldom and the man – never. Treat him gently, the poor fellow must have had some hard experience.'

'Is he – are they simple – or mad?'

'Neither, I'd go out myself and welcome, but knowing the Murphys I think they'd be happier to have everything settled up by a stranger. Remember, this is your first sick call, the simple faith of country people will put you to shame. Anything they ask you to pray for, do it. Remember Him Whom you represent and treat the penitent as He would. Hurry up now, come out to the kitchen and I'll introduce you to Mr Roarty, a clever enough boy in his own way, and without him the Murphys would be lost entirely.'

In the kitchen the messenger was seated at the head of the table twisting his cap in his hands. The empty tea cup was on its saucer, and he looked a little frightened. But the old priest soon put him at his ease, brought him outside, and helped him to put his bike in the boot of the curate's car, while the curate was in the church getting what he needed for a sick call.

The two set out together, the road shimmering in the sun, the countryside looked like heaven. Fr Friel took stock of his companion sitting uneasily in the seat beside him, his cap still being revolved in his nervous fingers.

'Put on your cap, John, and pay no heed to whatever the parish priest told you about me – he is a great man for a joke.'

'A great man for a joke indeed, but a true friend in trouble. No offence to you, Father, but I wonder why he didn't come himself. He is so long here he is one of ourselves.'

'I don't see much sense in the bishop sending you all a curate if you are going to consider him a stranger. Fr Donellan was a stranger once too, you know. Tell me about this family, the Murphys. What age is the sick man?'

'About sixty-two, but he has been in poor health this long time, part of it maybe due to all the fresh air the sisters need going through the house. The Murphys were a grand family, but some kind of a curse fell on them.'

'Nobody believes in curses, John, you should know that. What would make people think of such a thing?'

'Nobody knows. There were four of them, the youngest boy Mick was to marry my sister Katie. He disappeared in the month before the wedding and was never seen again. He wrote to Katie one letter telling her he couldn't come back to marry her, that if she could see him the way he was she wouldn't want to marry him.'

'Was the letter posted locally?'

'No then, it was not, it came from away down in County Derry. Mick was working down there when he was a growing boy. He put it in the letter for her to go to America and get herself another man, not to think anymore about him.'

'Did she go?'

'Aye, after some forcing she went. She told a girl pal of hers what was in the letter and the rumour went round the neighbourhood that some sort of a beast or a fish came up out of the sea and bit the nose off him, maybe it was true, maybe it wasn't. The Murphys never came to visit us, they never went down to the beach on their own land anymore, not if there was heaps of firewood lying on it – and many's a time they needed firewood – that's for sure.'

'Did your sister marry in the States?'

'No, she never took a trip home either. She died last year. Every letter ever she sent home she asked did Mick come back. She used to write to the Murphy girls – they were all girls that time, after a while they quit answering her – they got very peculiar. They started washing everything in the house every day and they used to hang their Sunday clothes out in an open fronted shed they had for carts. Even in the depths of winter I saw Ellen take off her coat when she came from Mass and hang it in the cartshed. They had washing out the coldest day in winter, and the day a storm would be blowing up would be the day they would hang out their bedclothes. They were always clean, but they went crazy washing.'

'Are they in good circumstances?'

'They were very well off once. Their father was a great man for picking up stuff washed up by the sea. He got valuables during the First World War. He had a lookout place near his own front door – the house is built on the headland there in front of you. But there is no luck with drowned stuff. Anyway the Murphys are not so well off now, they sold the farm and they are living on the price of it. The older sister, Ellen, will be fifty-eight this year and will get some sort of a wee pension as a spinster – the other sister will get the same in two years time. They'll make out after that.'

'Who bought the farm?' enquired the priest.

'I did,' replied his companion, 'but only because James came to me and asked me to do it as a favour. I just give them the money as they need it, they'll have the house for their lifetime.'

An unfortunate family, thought the priest, but he said nothing aloud. 'Stop here,' said his companion as they approached the end of a steep second class road. 'You turn up that lane to the right now. They wouldn't welcome my coming up, they'll be looking out for you. You needn't bother about my bicycle until you come down again. I'll be waiting here for you. They'll maybe be needing messages and some of their money.'

The priest stopped, let his guide out, and turned up the steep lane. In a minute or so he arrived at a small, compact, well-kept country cottage. A woman was awaiting in the doorway with a lighted candle in her hand. Her face was lined and seared, and tears were running down her cheeks.

'You are both welcome,' she said in a soft voice. 'I'm Ellen Murphy, I expect you are the new curate.'

'Yes, I'm John – Fr John Friel.'

'You are welcome, Father and Your Master with you. Down here my brother is in bed in our lower room.' She preceded the priest to a door in the gable, opened it, and walked with her lighted candle to the bedside, where she placed it on a small prepared table. In changing from the bright sunlight outside the priest had some difficulty in adjusting his eyes to the gloom of the room which had the blind drawn on its one small window. But in a few seconds he saw in a spotlessly clean bed the worn face of a man with the death shine already in his eyes. Another figure rose from the bedside and he found himself looking at a face which must have once been very beautiful, though drawn and worn now. The elder sister said, 'This is my sister, Margaret, and this is our brother James who is ill and wants to see you. James, here is your priest at long last. It is the new curate, Fr Friel.'

The man in the bed made an effort to rise from his pillows and extended a hand in welcome to the priest. The women went quietly out of the room, closing the door behind them. The priest turned to his penitent.

Later the priest opened the door and called softly to the two women who were kneeling in prayer on the kitchen floor. They rose and came down to the sickroom. Their brother was semi-seated now, his eyes even more glazed, but he had a smile on his lips.

He tried to speak, but couldn't. His sister gave him a sip of water and he managed to croak, 'The priest will read a burial service over Mick's remains, and he says Mick can have a Christian burial.'

'You instruct them,' the priest said. 'They are not to mention anything to me. You instruct them.'

'Go up, Ellen,' said the dying man, 'and bring down the box.'

Both sisters left and in short time returned with the sawndown bottom of an old tea chest with a lid on it. Ellen left it down beside the priest. The priest looked at it in wonder.

'Could you bring me a basin with some earth in it?' he requested.

The sisters left the room together and the priest turned to the man and said, 'This is very small looking. Is the whole body here?'

'That is all that was left of him when we lifted him – a man gets small in thirty years beneath the soil.'

The sisters returned with the earth, and the priest read a normal burial service over the remains, as he might over any coffin. Then he turned to the man in the bed again. 'You could get it buried now in your family grave,' he said. The dying man, whose face now wore a look of such happiness that the priest saw him as he must have looked before the tragedy, said weakly, 'Mick is going in the coffin with me and that will be before this week is out. We are thankful to you, Father, and maybe now you'd say a prayer for Mick, it's his wake at long last.'

The priest did as requested, mindful of his instructions from his parish priest. The sisters joined in the responses, the man whose lips were moving though no sound could be heard from him, fell back on his pillows. In a minute or so he went into a sort of coma. The priest felt that he couldn't very well leave the two sisters alone; he asked them if they wanted to send for anyone and they shook their heads. He began the prayers for the dying. Before he was finished James Murphy ceased to breathe. His sisters opened the windows, took down the blind, put a prayer book under the dead man's chin to keep his mouth from hanging open, and beckoned to the priest to follow them to the kitchen. Ellen carefully put the old box in beneath the bed on which the dead man lay. To the priest's surprise the sisters were not crying. They appeared to be bracing themselves for a bigger test even than the one they had just undergone.

Ellen placed a chair for the priest, who was far more shaken than he cared to admit: his first sick-call, his first death-bed and an encounter with events his text-books had not anticipated.

'We think James was too far through to give you the whole story this morning,' began Ellen.

The priest put up his hand to stop her.

'If either of you say anything about Mick's death to me, it will be my duty to go straight to the police.'

'But you must listen to us,' said Ellen, 'and if it is your duty to go to the police, then do it. We are prepared.'

'If you understand that, then I suppose I must listen to you,' he said uncertainly.

'It was the sea that caused it all. Mick saved Margaret and me from the sea. It was a nice day like today, and a wave followed Mick right up to dry land. Mick pulled us all safely through it and we came up together here and we were so happy to be alive. But when James came back and heard the story he said that the sea would have to be watched from then on, for it hates to let go anything it gets a grip on, so we all promised him that we'd go near the sea no more.'

Margaret took up the story. 'There was a young Irish

wrestler at that time, his name used to be in the papers every week. James and Mick used to be reading about him, and trying to do throws and things would be mentioned in the paper. They used to try it in the hay barn where they wouldn't hurt themselves. One evening James threw Mick and broke his neck. He was dead before James could believe that he wasn't codding him and he was stiff before he came in for us. Then James got afraid that people would think it was a fight and that he killed Mick, because James and Mick were both fond of Katie Roarty and she was promised to Mick. James didn't go for priest or doctor until it was too late and we couldn't do anything that would harm James, so we agreed to let him bury the body, in secret, down under the floor in our upper room.'

Ellen broke into the conversation. 'We were very fond of Katie Roarty, and we didn't want her life to be affected. So we made a plan. James went away one night and walked all through the darkness and in the morning he was far enough away for no one to know him, and he took a bus down to county Derry where he posted a letter to Katie telling her to go to America and forget him. He signed it with a nickname Katie had on Mick, she thought no one else knew it. So we got her to go away and make a life for herself – we even stopped writing to her, hoping she'd take a spite at us and forget about us.

'And this is why you must help us, for a terrible thing happened to all of us when Mick was a year dead. Everything in the house took a musty smell, our clothes and shoes and bedclothes and even the baked bread. You must smell it now yourself, Father, you're here in this house at least an hour.'

The priest paused. Since he had come into the house he had smelt nothing but the clean fresh smell of the sea, and the smell of sun-warmed earth. As late as this morning he would have rushed in and said it was just imagination, but he had learnt a lot in this one day. 'We will pray together and ask the Lord to remove it,' he said humbly, and all three of them went on their knees to pray. He finished by reading an account of the resurrection and they got to their feet. The younger sister cried out of joy, 'It's gone, Ellen, I can smell nothing but the turn of the tide.'

'Thanks be to God,' said Ellen. 'Now we can have a wake on our brothers. It won't matter what happens to us afterwards, even if we have to go to court.'

The priest found that he had taken a big decision.

'I'll never mention anything I heard in this house today,' he said. 'But you two must never mention any of these things again, either to me or to anyone else. I see no point in adding publicity to your other troubles. You have all suffered enough keeping a little secret about a simple accident. Do as your brother said, put the two bodies in the one coffin, and leave the rest to God.'

'You do understand that we couldn't inform about Mick,' said Margaret. 'We couldn't give James away, could we?'

'You were a very loyal family, and you all did your best. I pray God makes it up to you all, for all the suffering you endured. Now you have a funeral to prepare for and if there are any messages I can do, or any help I can give . . .'

Ellen wrote it all out for John Roarty: a big coffin, enough provisions for a wake, the arranged funeral time, and gravediggers to be employed. The priest drove away and found John Roarty where he had left him, and everything then passed as normally as any such event in rural Ireland.

On the morning after the funeral, another lovely summer day, the two survivors of the Murphy family went to the lookout post built by their father, and stood gazing down on the little cove that used to be their very own. The sun was shining and the sea stretched itself along the sand as calmly and as lazily as a kitten.

'I was dreaming last night,' said Margaret. 'I thought we were both dead, that we died the day we were in the sea.'

'I didn't dream it,' said Ellen, 'but I'm beginning to believe it – all four of us were lost on that day supposed to be thirty-five years ago.'

EXILE

EDWARD O'RIORDAN

'I never saw such a crowd. Where did they come from at all?' said Mary Conroy as she followed her two brothers into the house.

'There were a lot of representatives from the GAA,' said the elder brother, Sam, 'they came because of me.'

In the sittingroom Mary went immediately on her knees and tried to blow life into the dying fire; her brothers settled themselves into comfortable chairs on either side of her.

'It's hard to realise he's gone,' said Sam piously.

'He was a good age,' said John, 'not like Mammy. I can't think of him at all, I keep thinking of Mammy. Even at the graveside – when I saw her name on the headstone.'

'And why wouldn't you think of Mammy,' said Sam, smiling. 'Weren't you her favourite? Didn't she put you where you are today?'

'She was very hard on me,' said John defensively.

'That's because you had the brains. She wanted you to get on. She kept you at the books.'

Mary had got the fire going. After surrounding the glowing centre with lumps of fresh coal, she pulled a chair forward and sat down between her brothers.

'I'd have liked to have helped on the farm,' said John, 'but she wouldn't let me.'

Sam crossed his legs comfortably and looked at his brother with an amused smile.

''Tis easy known you don't know what you're talking about,' he said. 'You should be thankful she kept your feet out of the muck.'

He stood up. 'How about a drop of whiskey to get the cold of the graveyard out of us.'

John nodded. Sam went to the sideboard, the top of which was covered with trophies he had won on the hurling field. He picked up a few of them, turning them around to see the dates.

'Everything but the bloody county medal,' he said bitterly. 'To think that we won it the year after I went to America.'

John glanced cautiously at his sister. She sat forward in her chair, her chin resting on her hand, staring into the fire.

'Would you like some?' he asked her as he took the glass of whiskey from Sam. She shook her head.

'About the same county medal,' continued Sam, sitting heavily back in his chair, 'Tom Corbett tells me that Daddy went down to the County Board and demanded a medal for me even though I was three thousand miles away when the match was won. He created a holy show.'

He took a long slow drink, choking slightly as the whiskey hit his throat.

'He was a tough man, and no mistake,' he said feelingly.

'He struck the Chairman,' said Mary suddenly. 'He accused him of putting his own son on the team to get a medal even though the whole parish knew he was a coward. There was bad blood about it afterwards.'

'Ah, that was going a bit far,' said Sam. 'Jim Flynn right enough wasn't one to mix it. But he had some nice touches. And by the same token, that reminds me of the Ferret Farrell who, unlike Flynn, would put his head where another man wouldn't put a crowbar. Tom Corbett tells me he has gone and got himself married.'

'Who is he?' asked John.

Sam looked at him in mock exasperation. 'Do you know anybody around here? For God's sake, you must know the Ferret. Do you remember his brother, Spider, the fellow who took the fiver from the jug on the mantelpiece and headed for England.'

'That's years ago.'

'Yeh. But Tom Corbett was telling me – only for my father-in-law I'd have no news at all – that the Spider is back, and back with more than he went, a wife and five children. The Ferret got the wind up and made a dash for the altar to secure the mother's cottage. Who'd have thought,' he continued, slapping his thigh delightedly, 'he'd have sobered up long enough to do it?'

'I think I remember him,' said John politely.

'A cranky devil,' Sam chuckled reminiscently. 'You couldn't tread on the tail of his coat, he'd take the head off you. But he got the scores, that's what mattered.'

John moved uncomfortably in his chair. Mary's air of remoteness and inaccessibility disturbed him.

'It will be lonely for you now,' he said to her solicitously.

She turned her head and looked at him.

'What makes you think it hasn't been lonely up to now? I've been on my own since you two left home.'

'I hope he is in heaven tonight,' she went on, 'but I had the hard life with him, especially the last few years.'

'He wasn't an easy man to get on with at the best of times,' Sam conceded, 'but then again, I suppose we all have our faults.'

'He got very peculiar in the latter end,' Mary continued in a low voice.

Sam looked at her sharply.

'How so?'

'He took to getting up in the middle of the night, shouting for his breakfast. And then going out wandering the roads. The Guards brought him home several times and didn't get thanked for it either.'

'I suppose 'twas to be expected at his age,' said Sam, shrugging his shoulders, 'the oul' brain was softening.'

'Then there was the matter of the Friesians,' said Mary. 'He could have got jail for that but no one reported him.'

'What's this about the Friesians?' said Sam, turning to John. His brother shook his head. They both looked uneasily at Mary.

'He had trouble getting them in from the fields and he got it into his head that they were conspiring deliberately to thwart him. One morning he blinded them in their stalls with a red-hot poker.'

'My God,' said Sam, horror-stricken, 'was he gone that bad!'

Mary persisted quietly. 'He used to sit at the fire glaring at me. I felt his eye on me every move I'd make. I think he thought I was trying to put him out of the house. As if I could.'

She began to cry, making no effort to hide the tears streaming down her cheeks.

'It's a hard thing to say, but I hadn't a minute's peace until he passed on.'

She got up and went quickly out of the room.

'What were you doing when all this was going on?' said Sam, turning angrily to his brother.

'I didn't know anything about it. I'm in Dublin all the time.'

'In Dublin, in Dublin,' said Sam contemptuously. 'You'd imagine it was the backside of the moon. Surely to God you could have kept an eye on Daddy!'

John stood up.

'I'll see how Mary is,' he said.

In the kitchen Mary was standing in front of the mirror dabbing her eyes with a handkerchief. He stood looking at her impotently.

'I wish I could have done something,' he said, 'but I didn't know.'

'What could you have done?' she said. 'He'd neither be led nor said by anyone.'

She came up close to him and gripped him by the arm.

'There's something I want to ask you,' she said urgently. 'It's about the farm. I know it's Sam's and if he is coming back for good, well, that's that. But if he decides to stay in America! You've a good job, and anyway you're in Dublin. I have nothing.'

'Yes, of course,' said John. 'If Sam doesn't want the farm,

you're the obvious person to have it. I'm sure he'll see it that way.'

'What I want to know,' said Mary, 'is, will you back me if I look for the land?'

John looked at her doubtfully.

'I'll do my best,' he said, 'but, as you know, I've little say.'

Sam refused the tea that Mary brought back from the kitchen. Glass in hand, sprawled in the chair with his legs stretched out, he was in a mellow mood.

'Nineteen years in America, and this only my second trip home. The first time to marry Patricia Corbett, the second to bury my father. A wedding and a funeral.'

'But we'll be seeing more of you now,' said Mary. 'Maybe you'll be coming home to us for good.'

'If only I could,' he said sorrowfully. 'Everything I want is here. But it's not to be. What can I do?' he went on, looking at them appealingly. 'Patricia likes it, over. She doesn't want to come home. And the children! They know nothing but America – they are Americans. I can't uproot them all and bring them back here.'

'I'll be on my own so,' said Mary, 'but sure I'm used to that.'

Sam leaned towards her smilingly and put his arm about her shoulders.

'No,' he said, 'the days of your loneliness are over. I'm going to bring you out to America.'

'I don't want to go to America,' said Mary quietly.

'Ah, for God's sake, you always wanted to go to America.'

'That's when I was young. What would a woman near forty be doing going to America?'

'But you can't stay here.'

'Why not? This is my home. I've seen the worst of it when you two were away. Things will be easier from now on.'

'John,' Sam appealed in exasperated tones, 'will you talk some sense into her!'

The younger brother looked uneasily from one to the other.

'I suppose she knows what's best for herself,' he said.

'She can't stay here,' said Sam abruptly.

'*You're* not coming back,' cried Mary, 'you don't have to sell the place – you're a wealthy man. Do you want to put me out on the side of the road?'

'Look, Mary,' said Sam in a more conciliatory manner, 'there is no question of putting you out of the house. You can stay here as long as you like. As a matter of fact, I've let the land to Tom Corbett and arranged that the rent be paid to you. Of course, I'm hoping that you'll eventually come out to me in America. You'll be happy there. I'll look after you.'

'Well, if she doesn't want to leave, she might as well have the place,' said John nervously.

Sam rounded on him. 'Listen here,' he said, trying to control his temper. 'I hate to say this, but all this is none of your business. You keep out of it.'

Mary stood up.

'So that's that,' she said, 'that's the end of the story. I suspected as much.'

She went out. They heard her going up the stairs. Her bedroom door opened and closed.

Sam breathed a sigh of relief.

'Thank God that's over,' he said.

'Why can't you give her the farm?' John asked.

'Do you know Micky Moriarty?' said Sam slyly.

'He used to work here when I was a kid.'

'He got great with Mary so Daddy threw him out. She kept seeing him. I can tell you, there was hell to pay.'

'She used to stay out late sometimes,' said John. 'I remember lying awake hearing her come up the stairs. She could never avoid the creaking board. Daddy gave her some terrible beatings.'

'Tom Corbett tells me Moriarty is still around and he's not married. More than that, he and Mary are still very friendly.'

'Well?'

'Don't you see the dodge. Mary wants the farm so she can bring Moriarty into it.'

'Would that be bad?'

Sam looked at him in amazement.

'Have a penniless farm labourer in my father's place? Are you out of your mind?'

"What matter if Mary is happy. Why should it worry us. We won't be here anyway to see it.'

'I envy you, John, I really do,' said Sam viciously. 'You had it soft all your life. Never did a stroke of work at home, thanks to Mammy. And now a nice cushy job in Dublin. You don't know what hardship is.'

'I don't see what this has got to do with it.'

'You have no feeling for the land. Your sweat never watered those fields out there.'

'Mary gave more years to it than you did,' said John sullenly.

'This farm is not going to a landgrabber, a member of the Ferret Farrell clan. We'd be the laugh of the countryside. I am letting Tom Corbett have it. It's more or less the same as keeping it in the family. After all, he's my father-in-law, and the grandfather of my children. And if you must know, I owe him a lot. Who do you think financed the buying of my first bar in New York?'

'Where does this leave Mary?'

'As I said, she can stay here in the house for as long as she wishes. No one will disturb her. But eventually she'll come out to America. I have no doubts about that.'

'Maybe she'll marry Moriarty after all, land or no land.'

'Not a chance. She's too proud. They'd have nothing. She wants the land at her back.'

John woke about seven. He heard sounds below in the kitchen. Dressing hurriedly he went down. Mary had her overcoat on and a suitcase stood on the floor beside her. She was drinking tea. She filled out a cup for him without speaking.

'I'm sorry,' he said, 'I wasn't much use.'

'You did all you could.'

'I seem to lack something,' he went on. 'Even in the job. I've done very badly. I haven't got on as well as I should. I'm sometimes glad Mammy isn't alive to see it. I'm sort of . . . ineffectual.'

She stood up, drawing her coat about her.

'I suppose we all have our crosses to bear,' she said.

'What are you going to do?' he said.

'I don't know. I'm not fit for much. I'll ask Fr Cullen. He might get me a job as a priest's housekeeper.'

'You wouldn't change your mind about America, then?'

'God help your head,' she said pityingly, 'you'll never understand. Is it me, a servant to Patricia Corbett. A skivvy to a publican's daughter!'

She went out. The front door opened and closed. Quick footsteps and the creak of the wicket gate, and then footsteps again on the roadway, gradually dying away. Through the window he could see the dark glimmer of lakewater and the vague bulk of the mountains emerging out of the fading darkness. He felt an indescribable weariness. Closing his eyes, he rested his head on the table and waited.

Sometime later a door above banged shut and then a heavy tread on the stairs.

'Are you there, Mary?' came Sam's voice. 'Any chance of a bit to eat. I have a long journey ahead of me.'

DISPLACED PERSONS

MARY LELAND

She was taking alone a journey she had hoped to share. She hadn't actually asked him to come. Instead she had just said where she had to go, how pleasant it might be, the people they could call on, Skibbereen, Kealkil, Ballydehob, Schull and Goleen, the lure of Roaringwater Bay. On his dismissal the day fell apart.

All it meant was that she would miss the pleasure places, the places she would have gone just to show him, the spilling lakes seen from the hillside, the forgotten slate quarries hidden by forest, the roads she knew, unseen from the main road, but they were there and she knew them, leading to a cottage, a castle, a dark pool set in secret heather. That was all his refusal meant. No, it also meant that he could do very well without her, even though their days were numbered now. Oh, well. Perhaps he didn't count the days the way she did; it was like going to Dublin sometimes. 'Are you up for the day?' everyone said. 'When are you going back?' Her own instinct, meeting him and recognising him, had been the same as that: to fix the day, the time, in which she would have to be ready to let him go again. So from the beginning she had known; that was supposed to make it easier, but not easy.

Changing gear for the corner looming among great boulders she shifted in the driving seat, feeling sticky with dazzle from the windscreen. The landscape danced around her passage through it, she felt the ripples of air, the accelerator beneath her sandalled foot plunging her through the light, the heat, the day that she had longed for. The smell of leather came back to her, the hot smell of the sunny car, the slightly worrying smell of the hot engine.

'What did you say your name was?' he had said, struggling to accommodate this woman who had thrust herself – yes, she was only slightly ashamed of that, but it did come back at her sometimes, at times like this – who had thrust herself positively at him saying, 'I remember you: remember me?'

It was not possible for him to remember her. The glow began when he did not pretend; that made it easy for her to laugh, to apologise with some grace, to smooth a hollow in their encounter into which he could pour a little of his own charm. She made it plain that nothing was his fault, she had been so delighted to see him again, in Cork of all places, he need not blame himself for a second. He didn't; relieved, he had laughed too. They had formalised it, pleased with themselves. He was Kevin Murray, she was Orla Bracken, I've read so much of your . . . I've seen so much of your . . . Very pleased to meet you.

It was only the heat, and the long steady driving pressure on her arms and her right foot, only these made her feel uncomfortable now. It had not been a bad start, after all. The things she had been able to tell him about himself had pleased him. He had enjoyed being reminded, what she remembered he had forgotten, her recall amused and disarmed him, she had made sure of that. Right then, right then and there she had established that he was going back to Edinburgh within a few days, three, she had been exact. It was important, she had found long ago, to know these things. But that evening she had felt, not loose, but, well, loosed; let off, let out. It was early summer. The light was gay, the splashed poppies on her cotton frock reinforced a feeling of safe abandon, she was going among cheerful friends who expected nothing from her except her company.

She hadn't even been bored when she saw him. She had not reached that stage of feeling she had remained too long in the same conversation. There had been easy passages among both friends and strangers, and there was no doubt about it, she had been buoyed up by some new sense of herself, an almost physical lightness. Oh, all right, and she wrenched the handbrake up to hold her against the hill while she changed into first, stupid mistake on this incline, she knew it was coming, stupid! But all right, it was true, that evening she had been happy. It was as simple as that.

The windscreen misted with tears. It had been as simple as that. She slowed, pulled in and stopped, the low hills spreading out like a badly-made bed. Not seeing them she leaned her head against the hot steering-wheel, its corrugations pressing into her forehead. With wet eyes she saw that the horn-button in the steering column had loosened with the heat; she hit it, disgustedly, and there was no sound. Still, the action and the care with which she had to replace the button revived her. The fact was this: that evening it had been quite logical to be happy.

There was no point in being wistful and sentimental now about it, and if she could be tough with herself, even for a second, she would have to admit, as she wrestled with sweating hands on the steering column, she had to admit that just as she would once again have all those reasons for being legitimately and unquestionably happy, so she would once again be so. The reasons, at least, could not change for a long time.

The children and the dog had been playing all afternoon in the field behind the house. A long, intricate game, which yet made room for the assorted ages of the children of at least three families. The older boys had posted themselves on walls, with hurleys as weaponry, or hunted for stones and old branches with which to mark out boundaries. Within the boundaries the girls had played with the smaller ones, sending them on mock messages, or to bed, or to hospital where they were visited with a great deal of ceremony and some drama.

In the garden she had heard how the throb of a ship on the river had brought them all rushing to the wall near the road, and the girls had used this break as an opportunity to beg for orange juice or milk or even water, and whatever broken biscuits and unimportant fruit was available. All these they took back to the field, where they ate, among the grasses, within their careful walls. She had worked away in the garden, swearing sometimes of course; some things had gone wrong, a branch had been broken from the pear tree, a football had damaged the seedling sweet pea, there would be no way at all of dealing with some of those weeds except by getting down on her hands and knees and digging them out one by one. But the new aubrietia had come on wonderfully and had delighted her by encouraging the older plants, which now hung in cascades of purple along the wall.

The smallest boy had found a ladybird, and brought it, almost stumbling with care, in to her so that they could put it on a rose bush. They sat together on the hot lawn for a little while.

Ladybird, Ladybird,

Fly away home

Your house is on fire,

Your children are gone!

Several times she had to say it; he loved it, he loved being reassured that it was not really so, that the ladybird's children were safe and well and that the ladybird knew where to find them.

Teatime had been early, distinguished by a strawberry shortcake made, she understood from the recipe, the American way. The children had enthused about it. There was enough left for the babysitter. She had been able to bathe in the comparative peace of a television programme they all liked. The sitter was one they all liked too, and when Orla came back downstairs, 'dressed up' as they loved to say, they had teased and played the game from *Young Frankenstein* – they had to beg to kiss her, to kiss her goodbye, and she had to shriek: 'Not the lips!' and 'Not the face!' and 'Not the hair!'

She left on a litany: the story to be read for the youngest, already in pyjamas; the time at which the others were a) to go to bed, and b) to stop reading. Sometime, she thought, scattering telephone numbers and the likely time of her return into whichever ear would receive the information, sometime I'll have all this written down, it will be fixed and unchangeable, sometime.

Jaunty in high heels and buoyant with petticoats she had sat into the car and the machine, catching the mood of the day, had started immediately and sweetly. Sunglasses softened the road into town, across the two rivers, up the hills to the north side, to the house, to the party, to him. It had been such a happy day.

It was too hot to sit any longer in the car. She had better keep moving. There was work to be done, people to see, arrangements to be made. When she had had to make this journey before she had thought that driving into West Cork was like driving into a hive of particularly industrious bees; they would buzz and whir round her, offering the handwoven blankets, the hand-thrown pots, the glass, ceramics, the quilts, as though they were superior types of honey. And then, within the hive, she found cells of uncompetitive warmth, of enlightenment and kindness. She had looked forward to going back there.

Moving off, she took the usual small comforts to heart: the seatbelt strapping her to safety, the red jacket on the back seat ready against the chill of the evening, the book, and Skibbereen ahead. She would stop there and buy good things at the cake shop; something creamy for herself which she persuaded herself was enough for lunch, a currant loaf to take home, sparkling with sugar, buns and a brack for Una and the children. Una and *Dáithí* and the children. Where there was resident husband, what was she doing disposing of him even mentally? She hadn't intended to visit there, at first, they weren't on her list. But she felt a need growing in her for their self – absorption; they would never assume she would not be interested in their concerns, she couldn't be bored or idle or lonely there.

Just how true this was she realised only a few hours later. She took the turn into the rutted track that led to their house above the sea before she had meant to. Losing heart in the honey of macrobiotic contentment, shaken by the thin and silent children who snatched the wheaten crumbs from her plate – she had never been able to convince herself that hunger was a healthy state – she had abandoned her main reason for making the journey at all and had turned back to the town from which the path to Una's house could be most easily reached. As she drove noisily and fearfully up, sounding the horn at each omnivorous bend, she met Dáithi coming down, his car full of people and children. Of men and children, she realised, when they stopped and smiled at each other and explained themselves through the open windows. Brendan was on holidays, so was Peter, both with their children, both staying with Dáithi and Una, they would all be back at the house before she left. They went on down to the village for lemonade, ice-cream and Guinness, she went on upwards.

At the house she realised they had been evicted. Una met her with wails; God was to be thanked that she hadn't brought any of her own children. There were notices up on walls, leaden with the irony that children love and that adults use as a pretence that they're not asking for anything unreasonable. Una didn't mind, she said now, being a house-mother. But surely she was entitled to the privacy of her bedroom? She laughed, but spoke as if she were trying to recognise the shape of her own life under this rubble of visitants.

To Orla she explained that Brendan was finding out whether or not he could live without his wife, who anyway, in anticipation of his conclusion, had left him. Briefly the two children had been taken to another farm further up another mountain, but this, Una said, was only temporary, and Dublin was the eventual destination. In the meantime the children had been sent back down to spend some time with their father, who was not at all sure what to do with them, or with himself. Except to lodge them all with Una for a while, using the summer as an excuse.

'I feel as if this house is a clearing centre, a camp for displaced persons,' Una said, pushing Orla in front of her into the garden, where they drank tea and ate the sugared bread in a precise, deliberate ceremony, using china cups, a delicate old teapot, lemons cut with frilled edges. The sun was sinking on the hills that curled towards Mount Gabriel; immediately beneath the low wall edging the grass the rocks tumbled down to where their bits and pieces made walls for fields, small rocky fields that clung to the hillside until they became vegetable gardens, backyards, and a street that led to the glittering sea.

Listening to Una, watching her careful movements with cups and spoons, Orla thought that West Cork had its own sense of order. Wild though the landscape was, yet it fell into place; the lack of discipline in the lives of its newer inhabitants was only apparent. They lived by their own rules. And when disaster disturbed those rules they knew where to rest until new structures could be designed.

'Yes!' said Una. 'Yes. With me, with Dáithi. Because we've

held on to things that they abandoned when they left the cities. Not everything, obviously, but we're not so dedicated to the idea that our own rhythms are the only timekeeping we need to observe, and we do think constantly about our kids, what they're doing, what they should be doing, and we still respond to the notion of comfort in our lives – we have worked to achieve it.'

'Oh,' she sighed and moved to the garden chair, 'it's not that I mind all this. They are our friends, really, and of course I want to help. But they won't admit that their lack of order matters. Here they are now, shipwrecked to all intents and purposes, and they don't even know which lifeboats are sea-worthy. With such a precious cargo! The whole thing exhausts me. I'm exhausted.'

She was glad Orla had come, she was viciously glad she had pushed everyone out of the house. She wanted one small piece of this day to herself, the uncomplicating company of another female, the opportunity to grouse and grumble to someone who wouldn't be around to remind her of it. Orla knew, smiling as she thought of it, that only Una would feel the need to apologise for kicking against this situation. She knew too that the instinct of the men had been absolutely right; they had homed in to Una because in her atmosphere, in the calmness which she and Dáithi maintained around their days, the various children could live without any extra anxieties.

They lazed in the garden, talking or not. They never used the word 'sad'; they knew it, that was enough. The sound of a toiling car brought Peter back; he had left the others below, he had been anxious to be there when small Petey woke up from his afternoon sleep. 'Petey', wondered Orla. That must mean that Peter and his vanished, faraway, unforgotten wife had loved one another enough, such a short time ago, to name the baby boy for his father. It was something that spoke of such expectation, 'Petey'. Now Petey had to live with their disappointment.

When he came into the garden in his father's arms the small boy did not like another new face. He turned from Orla, moping into Peter's shoulder. Peter was rallying, asking for a big-boy display of manners. Watching him doing exactly the wrong thing for the child, a child apart from his mother for a brutal month and for the first time in his life, Orla wondered at what stage Petey would realise that these months were to be the pattern of his future existence, and whether Peter, or the child's mother, would understand before then how ill-equipped they had left him, and try to change things. It was most unlikely, she thought, hearing Peter now encouraging the three-year-old to be a man. Peter spoke of him with love, but the love of a deprived person for something that he sees as unattainable. He could not have Petey for himself; for this month he tried to get everything from his son that he would long for, miss, extol, boast about in the coming year.

When Petey, contented for a while, whispered against the sea-tanned skin of his father's neck, Peter smiled and moved his hand smackingly against the seat of the small boy's jeans. Smiling too, the child slipped onto the grass and ran across the garden, his plimsolls skipping over the flower border, his bright blue T-shirt shrining the small body, the garden itself containing his bright brief image for a second after he had vanished into the shadows of the house, where he was to demonstrate his manhood to himself in the bathroom.

When Peter asked Orla how things were with her she responded with questions about what was happening to him. Things were all right, really, considering. They both knew what he had to consider, and considering it were silent. When he spoke then about his wife, Orla was dismayed to hear the venom in his voice. She had seen them together once, linked, she had thought, by a glowing, delighted love. Now Peter spoke in pounds and pence, weighting maintenance like a payment on the child's body. It was unbearable; gasping at him, laughing to hide her anguish, Orla said, 'Stop it, stop! You're talking about me, you know!' He laughed too. Perhaps for the same reason. But it was true. To someone else, to her own children's father, Orla was the paid-off wife, bartering her children's bodies like goods for money.

Getting ready to go she groped for sunglasses, handbag, the tea-tray for Una. Stepping from the sun into the flagged kitchen her foot rustled on a piece of paper, and when her hands were free she picked it up. It was a child's drawing. One of Brendan's girls, Una said, was always drawing. Quite a talented child, she said.

The picture, drawn in crayons on lined paper from a school copybook, showed a large ladybird with a headscarf and an apron, mother ladybird. Another ladybird wore only a headscarf, but carried a parcel, or perhaps a satchel, or a suitcase; something almost square, marked into quarters. Careful letters along the lines told the story:

'The Ladybird. One day the mother ladybird said to her

daughter, you are big enough now to live by yourself. Pack your bag and fly away. The little ladybird packed her bag and watched her mother fly away from her, far far away, and then she flew away herself, carrying her bag. That's why when you tell a ladybird to fly away home, she doesn't know where to go. The End.'

Orla left the sheet of paper on the kitchen table. She felt like marking it 'to whom it may concern'. All her goodbyes were said, she kissed Una, laughing at her, seeing her laugh back, life would go on, they would manage. But as she buckled herself once more into the car, chasing a bewildered bee out the window, she felt as if she were dragging something from the house with her. She rejected the image of a ball and chain, of course, but it was something weighty, something that would not leave her mind alone. She had happened like an accident in that house – why did she feel its several groupings coming together to present her with a single message?

For a while she did not think at all but drove. By the time she reached Leap the sun had not yet begun to set, there was still no chill in the evening, there was no hurry on her. She turned left before Rosscarbery, a long way before, and took a thin road across a broad mountain, not knowing where it went. Where the hill crested and the road sloped again towards a dim valley she pulled in against a gateway. Up here there was a light wind, smelling of the hay in the small yellow fields. She took out her book, the buns, the apple, and began to read and to eat. But the thrill of guilty surprise which disturbed the amateur theatricals at Mansfield Park on the famously inopportune return of Sir Thomas failed her for once. She could not eat without words before her eyes, and putting both book and cake aside she got out of the car and walked a little way along the path.

How sweet the fields could smell, how gentle the colours on the evening hills above them; a bird sang his last song of the day, and she knelt into the clovered grasses of the meadow beyond the ditch, digging her knees into the yielding pasture and then lying her body into it, nothing around her at all but the grass stirred by her own pressure on it. And how she longed for him. Forget, she told herself, forget that he might not feel like this, forget that life is not earth for him, nor growth goodness. The heat of the land she lay on swelled back to her, and thinking of him, of his white body when they were last together, a surge of liquid warmth filled her with such grief that she turned her head into the pillowing grass and wept.

At their second meeting she had meant it to happen, she had brought her diaphragm with her, the pessaries. She had meant it, she must have meant it. But it had been he who asked. She had been delighted to agree. It was good, after all, to wait until opportunities like this came. She had not hungered for sex before this; a long abstinence had whittled her desire to something thin and frail. Now, oh now as their bodies parted at last on that flower-spread bed, now she knew that she was condemned to appetite, to hunger.

It had happened, for all that, so quickly. The question asked, the answer given, they had returned to the hotel room and stood looking at each other inside the door. They had both laughed at the same instant, at the realisation that all the necessary preliminaries had already been observed, that all that was waiting for them was to love one another. Weaving between the sheets in grateful exploration she had recognised the delicacy of his approach, the advent of his body on hers was not aggressive or demanding. Her body was grateful, grateful and amazed. His was more subtle, almost shy, and seeing this her hunger was held back. Held back, but it filled her so that her mind was a dam against its insistent tide. It blocked her ears to what he said, to what he meant beyond the words.

'I hope you won't fall in love with me,' he said, and she had smiled. First at this gentle arrogance, the assumption itself seemed funny to her. Then at the fact that she did not, after all, feel what she could call love. Was it possible, she wondered, to fall in lust with somebody? What she had not done was question him. And weeks later, when he had returned to the city and called her, she had not questioned him then, either. She had been insatiable, there was no time. She poured over his body, her own by now – the weeks of absence and distance had made sure of this – was now too full, too blown, too old, to be important.

She had gone to him then feeling blessed. Something she had been dreading had taken place. Not this absence. She had not feared that then, although now she did. No, it had been the threat of another absence, the children were to go to stay for a week with their father. The week selected, the arrangements made, they had gone. She was blank with surprise at its painlessness.

Before inviting him to it, she had looked at her house, wondering how it would hold him, what he would think. But when she did ask him he had asked instead, 'Will your children like me?' What an odd question, she had thought. Relieved, licensed, she had said that they wouldn't be there, and thought no more of that. What had stopped her then, why had she not explained, let him into her own life, instead of just saying that they were away, on holidays? And oh, how she had wrung the muscles of her heart since then, searching for the reason why she had not listened to him, had not noticed that he too was seeking the sound of children's voices.

Ah, she thought as she moved in the grass, turning so that once again she looked up at the sky that was now growing dull, she had not asked these questions because she did not want him to know about her, about her children gone for a court-certified week with their banished father, about her children for whom some other woman was now caring, complaining in a mild undemanding way.

It was dusk. Something swift, long and brown leaped away from her feet as she climbed over the ditch; startled for a second, her next thought was that Betsy would know what it was, that she would tell Betsy about the small animal in the slumbering hay. Betsy, whose grave little face had shone at her over the back seat of their father's car, eager for the journey but sorry to leave, whose look then and so often these days reminded her of the line from Patrick Kavanagh, 'smiling at me with violets'. When it was spring again they would search for violets together, and primroses, and note those which they might later transplant to Betsy's own little patch in the back garden. Those days were not so far away, now, after all.

She thought, on that thought relying on next spring. One

day I will be surprised to realise that this all happened a year ago. It was a little bit like having a baby; you had to get through this contraction, because the next one might be worse. She had to get through this day, tomorrow would be worse.

It had happened already that it had turned out worse. All that time he had been away, the time after their first few meetings, she had wished with shame for solitariness. The children had hummed like flies among the heat of her obsession. When they were gone, and she was free, and he had come back, within a day or two it had faded into this emptiness.

She heard his voice above her hair. 'Use your muscles,' he had whispered fiercely at her. Those were the muscles which had ripped apart on the exploding birth of one of her children. She had used them once and after that there was nothing left to use. She could not tell him that. She had wanted briefly to try, but then knew better. She shrank, folding herself limp and still, grief creeping into every crevice of her closing body.

Well, in time, she told herself, putting the car in gear, moving into and down the rutted track, driving into the looming dark, in time I will forget those words too. I will forget that last meeting, the dinner-table, candles and wine, the official 'thank you' meal. He was so polite, so courteous, and so distant, while there seemed to be no language left for her but touch. But if she had reached for him he would know everything. She did not move towards him, he did not ask her to. She left. It was over.

Driving home, across the luminous causeway at Rosscarbery, she was travelling towards a still empty house. She thought of the children, away in someone else's home, learning what it was to be displaced persons. When you peel an apple, she thought, the flesh comes as no surprise; although so different from the skin it is only what we are accustomed to find. If she peeled the skin of love from the children's lives, what would she find, now that she no longer knew what to expect?

ASHES

NESTA TUOMEY

Higney stepped lightly into the hallway of Connolly Mansions and stood for a moment listening to the early morning sounds filtering through closed doors. His small bright eyes missed nothing as they darted from the pile of empties outside number three to the big shabby pram blocking half the passage, with its bag of refuse already punctured by the claws of some early cat.

He mounted the stairs with cautious ease, one hand against the wall. At the sound of voices higher up he slipped into the lavatory and bolted the door. The familiar acid smell assaulted his nostrils as he stood at the bowl. Someone had cut a newspaper into squares and hung them from a nail in the wall. He jerked down a sheet and noted that a man was being charged with the murder of a sixteen year old girl with whom it was alleged he had first had relations. Later, he'd cut up the body and tried to burn it in a furnace. Hanging was too good for them, Higney thought, ripping off more sheets until only the loop of string remained. Damn foreigners! Coming in and trying to take over the country. In Merrion Square a big brazen coloured man had taken a woman Higney had put his eye on. He'd stood there and raised his finger and the woman had turned away from Higney just as he was getting her down to his price and the two of them had walked off without a backward glance. Someone rattled the handle impatiently, seeking entry. Unhurriedly Higney buttoned his fly. He reached up and pulled at the length of chain. Water flushed noisily into the brown-flecked bowl and subsided gradually, the cistern gurgling and sighing. The door handle shook once more and there was the sound of feet jigging urgently on bare boards. Casually Higney pushed back the bolt and emerged onto the landing. A figure darted past mouthing obscenities and the door banged shut. Unconcerned, Higney mounted the stairs until he could go no further.

The door sloped inwards on one hinge. She had lifted it the night before into place but someone had come by in the early hours and now it drooped top-heavily inwards almost oppressing her as she lay there. On the landing below, the cistern gushed noisily, a door banged and the stairs creaked rhythmically under the pressure of ascending feet. Someone paused outside her door. Peg felt eyes watching her over the sloping edge and raised herself with difficulty to peer defiantly into the surrounding greyness.

'Get away,' she tried to shout but was betrayed by her phlegm-roughened throat. The boards creaked as weight shifted. A wheezing cough, instantly checked, reached her straining ears. It was Mick Higney, she knew it. 'I know yeh're there, Mick,' she screeched. The words sang in her mind as the silence stretched. Through the floor she heard the Molloys stirring. Children's voices thin and intermittent becoming shrill and strident as hunger gained the upper hand on sleep. Foot-steps on the stairs to empty slops and far below the distant banging of the street door as, flushed out by the house's stirring, Higney lost himself in the awakening streets. She lay and drifted. The walls telescoped, compressing her between ceiling and floor. Breathlessly suspended, forehead all but crushed, she hung there, a sickness behind the eyes, until the distant toning of the mass bell brought release. Ash Wednesday with its earthly reminders; no compromise.

Upright at last, dressing merely the addition of one more tattered layer, feet thrust into balding suede and over all the plastic mac. A last examination of some treasure stowed deep in the orange box, evidence of its bright cargo still adhering in strips to the rough surfaces. Java – an eternity away. Fingers made insensate by Rinso and Vim suddenly tender stroking the smooth plaster. Two shillings long ago at the Jesuit Mission at the Mansion House; half a day's pay. The screws in the remaining hinge wobbled when touched. A screwdriver was what she needed and would get at Mrs Breen's. She had seen a fine big one in a box under the stairs beside the hoover they would never let her use. At the same time she would ask Mrs Breen to ask her husband about her position in the house. He would know whether they could put her out on the street after eighteen years. Mrs Breen had assured her as she washed the step one day if ever she wanted advice Mr Breen would be happy to give it. For after all it was free and did not cost him anything. He was a big man not saying much ever except to forbid her use the hoover, but then he was a busy man with a responsible job in the Corporation. Every Wednesday, wet or fine, she went to their house in Iona Gardens, not far from the Bishop's Palace. Last time Mrs Breen had remarked it was too much for her, meaning Peg, but might have meant herself. Every second week would be enough, she'd said, while giving her the few shillings at the door. But Peg looked forward to her visit to the Breen's house, now the only house she could go to anymore. And when her work (was that the name for it?) was done Mrs Breen would give her a bowl of soup. Good soup in the art of which she excelled, made from a stockpot she kept bubbling noxiously on the stove day in, day out. The girls were big now Mrs Breen had suggested and should be encouraged to keep their own room tidy and the youngest, a lad of ten, was over the troublesome stage.

She tied a plastic rainhat over her black beret once the property of Mr Breen and went onto the landing. The door trembled against the lintel as, supporting it, she edged her way around. Something moved far below in the well of the staircase. Was it him lurking down there waiting to catch her as she emerged with his Fine morning, Miss Dinnegan and his Blessings of God on yeh and Ah, but yehr looking great, accompanied by his wide smile and ready wink. Do yeh think will it rain, he asked her on the step one day. It won't catch you unawares anyway, he'd said, eyeing her closely. Aren't you well prepared for the rainy day, smiling as at some private joke. He had mounted his bicycle heavily and pushed off, the children running before and behind, mindless of his warnings. She had not put any great meaning on his words but now she wondered if after all he was speaking of something other than the weather.

A door closed quietly at the back of the hall as Peg dealt

with the clutter of prams in her way. Someone had left their garbage in an empty go-car and over it a cat crouched, ripping the plastic malevolently with its hindlegs.

Outside the air was crisp, causing her to sink her chin deeper into her hand as, shoulders hunched, she crept along close to the railings. An airline bag, the markings faded and almost obliterated by long usage, hung from her other hand, a relic of her cleaning days with Mrs Daly whose daughter once worked in a ticket office in O'Connell Street. As she turned into Sherrard Street a man passed her on a bicycle, the smudge on his skin still visible beneath his cap. Children played hopscotch by the gates of the church. Were they the same as those forever trailing in her wake, chanting Ould Miss Dinn-egan has a pimple on her chinegan? Was that the ringleader now with her bold face at the head of the gang scattering at her approach?

'Go home to your Mammy,' she told them, sinking her hand in the font and dabbing at her face with holy water. They stared after her and silently resumed play when she had passed on out of sight.

The queue to the altar rails grew smaller as she trudged up a side aisle. Submitting to the swift dab at the temples, reminder of the fallibility of earthly expectations, she returned the way she'd come. The church emptied and only the regulars re-mained. On the altar the sacristan genuflected deeply and transferred the heavy missal from one side to the other. Kneel-ing, she was conscious of a hunger unrelated to food as she waited avidly for the ritual of the mass to begin. Ahead of her old Carney beat the bench with her rosary and called out. In slow motion the elderly re-enacted, as in some eternal charade, the stations of the cross, grouping, retreating, endlessly.

Staring into the winking candle flames on the many tiered stands her eyes were at first dazzled by the reflecting glimmers of gold. The fiery haze shimmered and shifted and she closed her eyes, retaining on her retina a myriad of leaping silhouetted tongues of flame. And when she looked again she seemed no longer distant from the blaze but to be a part of that white heat and then she was the light itself and from her extended long spears of dazzling blinding truth.

I am the resurrection and the life. Anyone who believes in me will have eternal life.

She knew and in her slack-jawed wonder wished to impart that knowledge to the world. The tinkle of the bell announced the priest's approach, recalling her with a sense of exaltation to herself. Stiffly she levered herself to her knees, white flecks occupying the space before her face, one hand on the bench. Facing the people the priest intoned his opening lines. Her lips moved, her prayer still that of childhood.

Introibo ad altare Dei – to the God of my joy and my youth.

She took her beads and let them dribble between her fingers. Old Carney stood on, beating her chest – a sinner – shaggy white mop thrown back, eyes rolling heavenwards. A man with the look of a child glanced around smiling and grimacing. A dog trotted steadily between the kneeling congregation, tail swaying always just out of reach. Near the doors a man went down on one knee, cap in hand, as the priest raised high the host.

'Now let us offer each other the sign of peace.'

At once began the extension of hands reaching forward

and behind. Brown spotted crepe engulfing and engulfed. Eyes averted, cold tips brushing aloofly, a duty done. Half-hearted dabs and tenacious graspings like drowning men, the only contact left in a life filled no longer with the holding and caring of happier days. Gradually a settling back into the closed circuit of daily existence, prisoners of self, until the next releasing words were spoken.

Outside the church the dog followed hopefully at her heels, nosing at her bag. She stopped and turned her head. Uncertain of his welcome he stayed where he was.

'Here, Major,' she called, and threw him a piece of stale bread rummaged up from the depths of the travelight. To her all dogs were Major. He sniffed at the bread but no more than that, tail faintly wagging. She moved on. A car horn hooted as, head down, she crossed the street.

It wouldn't take much to get the door off its hinges, Higney decided. He picked at a loose screw until it wobbled out into his hand. The door sagged lower. He eased it upright and slipped into the room. His foot trod on something soft and he recoiled before realising it was the edge of the blanket trailing the floor. He stooped before the plywood crate and carelessly tipped it over. No earthly treasures met his eye; no wad of dirty banknotes or scattered sovereigns to gladden his heart, only a jumble of scapulars and rosaries, a few statues; all the flotsam and jetsam of Christianity.

A spider ran up the wall and in disgust he let the mattress flop back. It was not as he believed. But could be, he told himself. He surveyed the room, then paced it out, his black boots eating up the inches. There was room enough for a cheap divan and a two-ring gas cooker. In Woolworths he could purchase a print of a woodland scene to hang over the bed. He saw himself knocking a few nails into the wall, maybe fixing a yale lock on the door. It was a room a bachelor living alone would be glad of or, perhaps, a couple of young ones fresh out of school. Either way there was profit to be made.

The gate to the Breen's house was open. She trod the path more swiftly now, if a snail can be said to be swift. She let the heavy knocker fall repeatedly but no one came. Passively she stood. If you have faith all things can be accomplished. Her head sunk on her chest, her arms hanging loosely from their sockets, the airline bag an extension of her wrist, Peg waited. Having come so far in the certain hope of a bowl of Mrs Breen's life-giving soup she was prepared to wait for ever, if necessary, to achieve her desire.

Against the orange and green frosted glass Mrs Breen saw her outline and retreated hurriedly on tip-toe. With infinite caution she edged around the scullery door and, safely off-target, relaxed. Lucky she had chanced to be in the front room and seen the familiar figure coming in the gate. A few moments more and she would have had her hat and coat on, descending the step. Now as Mrs Breen waited for Peg to give up and go away, she reflected on the incongruity of her position, mistress of the house, cowering backstairs like any housebreaker avoiding detection. But the alternative did not bear contemplation. It was just that the work was beyond Peg. Had she ever been up to it? There only remained to pass on the message, Mrs Breen had decided, tiring at last of cleaning everything twice over and of Mr Breen's constant complaints about the state of the broom cupboard; his particular bugbear being dirt and fluff in the opened polish tins. He'd laid a ban on the use of the hoover and his daughters refused to allow Peg in their bedroom. Mrs Breen had to admit they had cause. She still remembered the occasion she had been marched upstairs to view their unmade beds, on which was gathered like the start of some bird's nest heaps of fluff and dirty tissues, under-the-bed residue, fished for and then forgotten. Or rather abandoned in favour of a more rewarding mission; that of replacing with holy pictures torn from religious monthlies the sunkissed bodies of their chosen idols.

If Mrs Breen could have given Peg the few shillings at the door and barred her entrance to the house it would have solved matters but Mrs Breen believed in the dignity of human persons. Or so she told herself. Was not Fr Lynch always preaching about helping others to help themselves? How much better, he said, to give a person work to do for which you recompensed him than to give him charity which, unearned, eventually wears away his self-respect. In theory it was all very fine. Mrs Breen agreed wholeheartedly with her pastor but when applied to real life she would have gladly risked under-mining the char's self-respect in the cause of improved domestic relations.

For some time there had been no sound from the porch. Mrs Breen peered hopefully around the scullery door and was rewarded by unshadowed glass. Encouraged she stepped out, but with caution, to the front room where unobserved she could from behind the lace curtain review the outer scene. But she had reckoned without a betrayer in the camp. From the top of the stairs her name was called loudly and repetitiously. 'Mammy . . . Mammy, when are you coming up?' She had forgotten young Brian recovering from measles in an upper room. As though on cue the shadow loomed behind the glass and the knocker rattled triumphantly. Mrs Breen had no course but to open the door.

Peg trudged down the hall and pushed her way into the scullery. Mrs Breen, promising to run up to her child as soon as the opportunity presented itself, followed even more slowly. 'There's not a lot today, Peg,' she offered hesitantly, as the woman silently tackled the fastenings on her plastic coat. She stood shoulders stooped, the black beret pulled low over her forehead, the grey hair straggling from under it in greasy wisps. Geronimo or was it Witch of Endor? Mrs Breen took in a deep breath and tried to control, but without much hope, the situation. 'Why don't you . . .' she began, trying and failing to envisage some job that would not necessitate too much clearing up afterwards. 'Brush down the stairs . . . and when you finish I'll have some hot soup ready.' Like hot tea, the panacea for all ills. Even to her own ears the words placated. Peg would not be fooled by the task set her and might not even obey.

Disconcerted, Mrs Breen watched her rummage in the broom cupboard and come out bearing a tin of Vim and cleaning rags. She started to speak but saw no point. Peg would do what she wanted and always had. She felt a sense of hopelessness as the tattered lisle and split boots creaked away over the polished wood and began slowly to mount the stairs.

Higney fiddled with the remaining screw and caught the door as it fell. He propped it against the wall and wiped his face on his sleeve. In the gloom of the landing below, Mrs Molloy strained upwards in a listening attitude. 'Are yeh up there, Miss Dinnegan?'

Higney quickly slipped the screwdriver out of sight and stepped back into the room. He heard the flapping of Mrs Molloy's slippers on the bare boards as she came from below.

'Are youse alright?' Curiously she peered into the room, her expression changing at the sight of him. 'Oh, it's you. I heard sounds,' she said, by way of explanation.

Higney shook his head sorrowfully. 'Isn't it a terrible thing,' he sighed, 'no respect for people's property.'

At first Mrs Molloy did not take his meaning; to her the room looked very much as it always had but then her gaze encompassed the doorless hinges and travelled downwards to the orange box with its vandalised contents. 'My Gawd! Who done it,' she demanded, stroking her neck repeatedly while all the time staring fixedly at Higney as though he might at any moment surprise her with the answer.

'Who knows?' With a shrug Higney stepped around her. 'There's a lot of it these days.' He leant towards her insinuatingly. 'Yeh wouldn't want to go leaving your door ajar, Missus, not if yeh've left your purse lying about.'

He watched smiling as she scurried back to her landing, a slipper coming loose in her flight, and stood motionless until he heard her door slam shut.

A tin of Vim stood on the top step of the stairs, a danger to the unwary. Peg sat on the child's bed and fashioned a rabbit out of a handkerchief taken from Mr Breen's drawer.

'When will Mammy be back,' Brian asked fretfully, for how could you make a rabbit out of a hanky.

'She'll be back any minute . . . hasn't she to get the few messages.' Peg eased herself deeper into the bed, gnarled fingers twisting and poking the piece of cloth.

Mrs Breen, against her better judgement, had slipped out to the shops. Calling from the front door she had promised to be as quick as she could and to bring with her some books or comics on her return. As Peg made the rabbit, she repeated what Father Burke had said only the day before from the pulpit about the evils of drink. Men were spending their wages in the public houses every Friday and leaving their wives and families to go short. He'd asked them all to make a special effort to cut down on intoxicating liquor during the six weeks of Lent.

'It's a disgrace, that's what it is,' Peg said. 'They should be puttin' shoes on their childer and bread on the table. Alcoholics the lot of them.'

He stared at the seamed puckering of flesh on the underside of her chin and wondered what an alcoholic was. The skin of the old woman's angular face was of a hard grained texture bringing to mind a walnut or similar piece of wood. She had once told him she never used anything on herself but sunlight soap. It was good for everything, she had confided, even your teeth. All the others were a waste of money.

'Look, he's jumpin'.' She jerked the rabbit forward over the curve of her arm and laughed, showing toothless gums, at his alarm. He fingered the handkerchief petulantly.

'That's not a rabbit. Where's Mammy . . . why isn't she back?' He shifted restlessly, troubled by a strange unidentifiable and disturbing odour. She sat on, pinching and stroking the cloth, talking quietly about her devotion to this saint or that.

'St Martin's a good one but the best of them is St Jude. He's a great man for the bad cases. If yeh're desperate pray to him . . . and there's another . . . he's not a saint . . . not yet but he will be. Mark my words, Matt Talbot will be canonised, you'll see. I can ask Matt anything and he gets it for me.'

He wondered at the way she spoke as though the saints were people she met and talked with every day (and weren't they in a way?). It seemed as though she'd only to mention something to them and they would get it for her as easily as his mother was at that moment getting his comics. His interest aroused, he asked, 'Would they get me a bike if I asked them?'

'You can try,' was all she said, before going on to speak of the sales of work she often frequented. 'There do be great bargains. Do yeh ever get going yourself?'

'No,' he answered shortly, feeling she'd led him on about the saints. But he wasn't being strictly truthful for he had on occasion gone to the bazaars run by the nuns at his sisters' school.

'Yeh should ask you Mammy. Next time I'm going I'll bring yeh.'

Appalled at the thought of going anywhere with the 'witch' – the Breen sisters' name for her – he gladly leapt from the bed at the sound of the front door opening.

Mrs Breen opened her bag and handed her son a bundle of

comics. Within minutes he was back up the stairs and into bed, oblivious even of his mother's existence as he avidly read of Wilson of the Wizard and the adventures of Desperate Dan.

Mrs Breen had hurried back from the shops, unable to rid her mind of a fear that Peg, no longer under supervision, might take it upon herself to hoover the house. As she had waited impatiently at the checkout of the local supermarket she had seen as clearly, as though she were present, the woman pushing the hoover over large, indissoluble objects until, choked with debris, it inevitably gagged and died. So great was her apprehension that she had hurried away without her change and been recalled by a young packer hastily following on her heels. On re-entering the house she was relieved to find the hoover still intact in its shrine, and sagged thankful that Mr Breen's homecoming need not be marred by any distressing disclosures. She unpacked her shopping bag and, almost happy, placed the chops for the next day's dinner on a plate in the scullery. Going upstairs, her foot kicked against an object she found to be a tin of Vim. Of Peg there was no sign. Downstairs once more Mrs Breen was surprised to see the woman coming up the garden. Through the scullery window she observed her bending and scrabbling in a flowerbed. Well, she would get up to less harm out there compared to within, she thought, as she went to put the chops in the meat safe. But she was wrong, she realised, in the disillusioning discovery that the plate was empty.

Higney dismounted and propped his bicycle at the kerb. In a chemist's shop he stood at the counter waiting to be served.

An assistant in a white coat climbed onto a chair to take a box from off a high shelf, showing an expanse of snowy thigh in the act. Higney wondered if she had anything on under the coat and in his mind unbuttoned it slowly. He saw her standing before him in her underclothes and imagined her taking them swiftly from her body.

'Can I get you something?' She stood, regarding him expectantly.

He fingered a bar of fancy soap, still a prey to his thoughts. 'Outrageous!' he said on learning the price. 'Ah, I think I'll stick to the auld Sunlight. Doesn't it do the job and at only a quarter the cost.' He laughed, inviting her to share his amusement. She stood stolidly without expression. Stuck up little bitch, he thought, who does she think she is. 'Here,' he said, 'give us a bottle of disinfectant, Miss.'

She reached behind her and removed a bottle from the shelves. He cleared his throat. 'A small one,' he said, and watched her make the exchange. She placed it in a bag marked with the name of the chemist and rang up the amount on the till. Higney took out a handful of silver. He extended his hand, palm upwards, inviting her to take what she needed. As she selected the coins he leaned on the counter and said quietly, 'You look like you have a fine pair under your jumper. Will we go for a drink later on. What do you say?'

A red flush spread over her face and neck as Higney took the package and walked smiling towards the door. He threw a leg over the crossbar and glanced back through the plate glass door before pushing off. He saw her standing next to the chemist talking animatedly and was pleased. A good humping was what that one wanted. Wasn't it what they were all after. He pedalled strongly up the hill and turned into a street at the back of Mountjoy Square. Parking against the side wall of a house he rested his foot on the step and removed his bicycle clips. Then untying a bundle of rods from the crossbar he carried them to the porch and rang the bell.

Mr Breen came home at lunch hour each day. It was a time he liked especially. He looked forward to it as an oasis in a turbulent time-stretch in which he had to deal efficiently with the problems of inoperative street lighting or striking binmen. As soon as he put his key in the door he detected signs of the char's presence and knew it would not be the most tranquil of midday breaks. Frowning, he took out his handkerchief and, spitting discreetly into it, rubbed at the cream-coloured smears beside the letterbox. As he hung his raincoat on the hallstand his eye fell upon an open polish tin, on the surface of which sprouted like a fungus a dark matting of fluff. Another hallmark of *that* woman. Quickly he strode to the broom cupboard and looked in. The hoover appeared untouched, the flex looped in even coils the way he had ordained it should be. He closed the door and thought, not for the first time, how he must put a lock on it. While he sat beside the fire, listening with half an ear to the lunch-time serial, he wondered what his wife would put before him. He fancied a bit of brown stew or maybe a tasty chop with a rasher or two.

'What's this?' He pulled back from the table and stared down at his plate. 'Where's my dinner?'

Mrs Breen turned from adding a shovelful of coal to the

fire. 'That's it,' she said, 'a nice bit of cod.'

'Have you no meat? I fancied a bit somehow.'

Mrs Breen stared at him, the shovel hanging loosely from her hand. 'Meat!' Her tone was scandalised. 'On Ash Wednesday!'

Mr Breen was unaware or had forgotten the day it was. The smudge on his wife's pale skin had passed unnoticed, his wife too if the truth were known. Feeling hard done by, he tackled without enthusiasm the white mess before him. Mrs Breen, used to his ways, took a seat opposite and in a lowered voice told him he'd be lucky if he got meat the following day since the chops she'd purchased for his dinner had mysteriously found their way into the dustbin.

His hunger in no way assuaged Mr Breen irritably poked a wad of bread into his mouth and spoke over it, 'Is there any pudding?'

Momentarily deflected, Mrs Breen fetched a dish of prunes and custard from the kitchen and would have left him to get on with it had he not stayed her with his hand.

'Who did it?' he enquired, spitting prune stones into his cupped hand and dropping them on the bread plate.

Eagerly Mrs Breen resumed her seat. 'That's what I have been telling you. It was her . . . Peg . . . all along.'

'Is the woman mad?' Mr Breen dropped his spoon into the dish with a clatter. 'I always held it she was touched.'

His wife cast a glance towards the door in case of an eavesdropper and went on to relay how Peg, incensed at the sight of meat blatantly displayed in the house on the first day of Lent, had taken it upon herself to remove the impediments to the Breens' salvation.

Mr Breen stood up abruptly. 'The woman's a menace.'

He had not forgotten the time his magazines for men had suffered a similar fate. He wiped his mouth on his handkerchief and grimaced at the taste of Brasso. 'Don't have her here again.'

Mrs Breen, aware that she had confided too much or perhaps seeing her chance of sanctification receding, wavered. 'Ah, now, Paddy, don't let us be hasty. God help her . . . the poor creature . . . she's really a bit of a saint, if one was to know.'

Of his own mind Mr Breen smoothed his hair before the scullery mirror. He had little to do with saints but knew enough to know they were uncomfortable people to have truck with. 'Give her some money and tell her not to come again,' he advised.

Sorry she had let herself be betrayed into an unequivocal position with regard to the saintly one, Mrs Breen helped him on with his coat and watched him walk away. A glint of silver caught her eye and she bent to lift from the step a milk foil cap, so missing his farewell wave had he made it.

'Five pounds to clear the drain!' At the woman's incredulous tone Higney paused half-way in the door. He laid his rods against the wall and put his hands on the backs of his hips.

'A terrible price,' he agreed.

She stared at him suspiciously. 'The last fellah charged thirty bob.'

'Is that a fact, and when might that have been?' He waited, noting her sudden look of uncertainty. She was a well made woman he thought, wide hips and good strong-looking legs. She'd be good on a bicycle. He saw her in a pair of black shorts, her calves bulging as her legs strongly turned the pedals.

She shrugged. 'What does it matter . . . some time ago . . . he was a lot cheaper, that I do remember.'

'And now it's blocked again?' Higney said, intimating that in certain circumstances he might be prepared to settle for a lot less. 'You look like a woman of the world,' he suggested. 'You know how it is.'

The woman stared at him in disbelief. 'I'm a married woman,' she said.

Higney kept his eyes steadily upon her. He believed these things went on, he said, and no one was any the wiser. So long as the woman was willing. 'No one misses a slice or two off a cut loaf. D'ye get my meaning?'

To his surprise the woman became suddenly violent and threatened to call the police. Before he could stop her she had caught up his rods and thrown them out of the door with such force that several broke on striking the pavement.

'You get outa here and don't come back,' she shouted, lifting a plaster statue off a table and holding it up high.

Higney stared at her, alarmed. He moved quickly over the threshold. The woman was mad, demented, he told himself. He was lucky to get away unharmed.

At the door, Mrs Breen, her conscience troubling, changed the coins for a note. It would make it up to Peg, she thought, or rather hoped, as she put her on the long finger. 'Won't be needing any work done in the house for a while . . . maybe going away . . . better leave it till after Easter.'

Had she heard? The rainhat quivered. Was it in reproach?

At the gate Peg stumbled and would have fallen but for her outflung hand. Behind the front room curtain Mrs Breen doubtfully stood. Was it a sign? She felt the shadow of Fr Lynch and trembled.

Along Dorset Street children straggled from school. Close to the Palace wall Peg moved, shoulders hunched, the bag heavier now with Mrs Breen's sop to conscience; ageing seed cake and yesterday's tea scones. Her plastic mac and tie-on rainhat, donned like an additional skin, tempted the elements but perversely no rain fell. Towards Gardiner Street like a homing pigeon her feet strayed, hungry for the odours of incense and candlewax and the corridor confessionals of the Jesuit Fathers.

Higney went into the Big Tree and sat near the counter, nursing a whiskey. Despite various setbacks he was pleased with his day. Coming away from the house of the woman who had taken exception to his proposal, his rods once more firmly tied to the crossbar of his bicycle, he had been called to another house requiring the unblocking of drains. This time he'd been careful to keep any mention of cash out of the conversation until the job was done. Before closing the mantrap he'd requested a bucket of water to which he'd added a few drops of disinfectant before slopping it ceremoniously about the area. This was the difference, he'd explained to the mystified housewife, between chancers you'd get willing to do the job for a quid or two and someone like himself trained to the profession. He'd likened his work to that of a doctor, describing at length how the maze of underground pipes, invisible to laypersons like herself, could be compared with the human body. 'Have you heard of cholesterol, Missus,' he'd interrupted himself to ask. When the woman started to speak he'd hurried on, keeping a wary eye for plaster statues or other objects of defence. 'It's a terrible thing. Clogs the arteries and builds up a fatty wall about the heart. Now your drains are not dissimilar . . . abuse your drains, Missus, and they'll act up in the selfsame way. You wouldn't object to paying a doctor if yeh were stretched, amn't I right now?' In the end he'd settled for half and was glad he hadn't wasted more than a few drops of the Dettol.

'Bedad, yeh drive a hard bargain, Missus,' he'd said as he wheeled his bike away.

Now, in the light from the bar he examined a small object taken from his pocket.

'Would yeh say it's valuable,' he asked the barman as the man was removing a pile of bottles and glasses from a nearby table, holding it up for his inspection.

The barman glanced at it briefly. 'Couldn't rightly say. What is it . . . brass?'

Higney polished it on his sleeve and held it out for a closer look. 'Paid ten quid for it,' he said, staring hard at the barman, 'this afternoon.'

The barman ran a wet rag over the table and turned to go. 'You were robbed.'

Higney caught hold of his sleeve. 'Wait . . . take another look. It's an antique. D'ye know what it is, if I was to sell it now I'd double my money.'

'Why don't you then?' The barman moved away to serve a customer and Higney replaced the object in his pocket.

Perhaps a tenner was a bit steep, he thought. Next time he'd do better to suggest half and work up to it more slowly.

In the church the aisles were filled to capacity. Coming from the confessional she found a space and burrowed in. Light after darkness. Ten Hail Marys lengthily explored. I am the light of the world, says the Lord. Anyone who follows me will have the light of life.

'Do not come back so soon. There isn't need,' the priest had said, head drooping wearily forward, an image just discernible beyond the mesh of wire. Then silence. Was he asleep? But no, a frail hand upraised in benediction. 'Do your best. No more is asked of any of us.' One more approach sealed off with the clicking shut of the little wooden door. Do not come back so soon! One more contact with living breathing humanity severed, or at least discouraged.

All about the congregation stood close pressed, raising their voices to mingle with the leader.

Have mercy on us, O Lord, for we have sinned.

Youthful supplicant at the lectern confessing to offences only barely guessed at. What is evil in your sight I have done.

Oh, Lord, have mercy.

Higney finished his whiskey and went to the counter for another. A man propped himself on his elbow staring into his glass. Higney paid for his drink and stood beside him. He spoke quietly, asking if he wanted a room. He knew where one could be had, he said. Not cheap but not expensive either. He'd only to indicate, and for a little extra company could be had there too without further ado. The man seemed not to hear. Higney laid a hand on his arm. It only needed a coat of paint, he promised, and it would be a palace.

'Would you like to go and see it,' he persisted. 'It's not far from here.'

The man knocked away Higney's hand and expressed himself succinctly in a few sharp sentences. Higney drew back abruptly. 'Here, there's no call for that,' he said angrily. 'I was only trying to do you a favour.' The man turned his back on him. Aggrieved, Higney withdrew to his seat.

She struck her chest, aware of her concentration wavering, her breath laborious. Deprived of her share of oxygen by the too close proximity of the faithful she experienced a strange though not unfamiliar disembodiment. She might have been a saint of old in the act of levitating. That her only warning, and she was in it. Back arched, head flung sideways, strange sounds emitting from the larynx, she jerked and swayed. Was it ecstasy? The roof, how far away it seemed. How unyielding the tiles beneath the plastic rainhat. The implement of speech grown suddenly unwieldy, slipping and gagging in an agony of involuntary movement. Restraining hands and hushed faces curiously bore down on one who strived to communicate or perhaps resist.

Give her air. With the approach of one in authority the situation, fast deteriorating, gained not before time a sense of direction. *Loosen her clothing.*

The commands distantly heard set up an echo in the void of her consciousness. Eager to participate, the faithful moved in on her. But where to begin, the plastic mac a fortress around whose perimeter access vainly sought, deterred all but the most valiant. At last, Chinese fashion, each layer peeled away to reveal yet another until the prize was reached, surprisingly pale and young after a lifetime of hibernation.

Leaving the premises of the Big Tree Higney pushed his bicycle along the North Circular road. He'd like to have mounted but he wasn't sure he could keep his balance. After he'd had words with the man at the counter he'd gone back for another whiskey. 'Make it a double,' he'd said as the barman stuck a fresh glass under the Powers Gold label. 'Sure why not…isn't the evening young.' When he'd sat back in his seat he'd found himself going over in his mind what the man had said to him. There was no call for it that he could see. He'd spoken to him civil enough. What right had he to suggest that Higney was a pimp or, worse still, a gigolo? All he'd done was to offer him the chance of renting a room. 'Bloody cheek,' he'd said out loud and the barman glanced over, at once scenting trouble. 'Off you go now,' he'd urged, catching Higney's arm and pressing him towards the door. 'Time to go while you still can.'

At the intersection Higney waited for the flow of traffic to ease. Seizing his chance he swung his leg over the saddle and pedalled along Sherrard Street. A horn blared close to his rear wheel, causing him to wobble dangerously.

'Get out of it,' he shouted. Drawing level he rested his hand on the back window and peered intimidatingly in at the occupants. The car moved forward, landing Higney in the roadway. Surprised, he remained where he was until a fresh blasting of horns spurred him to his feet.

Shaken, he wheeled his bicycle around the corner and slowly made his way along the path. An ambulance stood at the kerb and from the lighted doorway of the church white-coated men carried a recumbent figure. Higney halted to allow them pass and something about the shape caused him to draw closer. Surely there was only one made in that mould? For a brief moment his eyes rested on the apparition, then it was slotted into place and the doors of the van slammed shut. Siren moaning, it sped away to Jervis Street with its aged captive; one more casualty not yet dust.

Within, the doxology continued, unaware of any drama other than that on the altar; transubstantiation. Without, her only other witness, the dog Major, nosing at fallen seed cake, the product of Mrs Breen fashioned in another age.

BUBBLES ON DARK WATER

MÁIRÍN O'CONNOR

The sun was hotter than it had any right to be in the middle of April. Sometimes, she'd been told, Easter would be warmer in the West than it would be in summer. It was so hot that she peeled off the heavy wool cardigan first and then the jumper, and sat in the deck chair clad only in skirt and blouse, looking up the hill. The grass around her was already long and silky, in need of cutting, but she couldn't find the energy for it.

'If we lived in a country where the sun shone all day, every day, we'd get nothing at all done,' she thought. It seemed crazy to waste a hot day in energetic pursuits. Sunny days were for being still, immobile, lazy. Beneath her chair the cat sought the shade but couldn't rest. A bumble bee whipped past his nose and he was up again, pacing through the grass, seeking cool.

They could both hear the lark but not see it. It trilled and sang small scales from somewhere over them. Through it the Wavin gutters squeaked and creaked in the heat and the voices of people talking on the other side of the lake floated clearly over to her. It was something you always had to remember – how clearly sound travelled in the country air.

Someone had got hold of gelignite for blasting rocks and as she looked to the north of the lake, two greyish puffs rose into the air, followed by the thud of the explosion. Sight was faster than sound by a second. Insects blew about and crawled on her legs. When the lark ceased, she could hear a lot of the smaller sounds – the whirring of wings, the buzz of flies. It was a drowsy pleasant sound and she welcomed it.

On the side of the hill the man spilled out the last of the 'slits' – the seed potatoes that should have been planted a fortnight ago. He wasn't young and his back ached. One more drill and he'd be finished. It didn't occur to him to shed his gansey and the sweat ran down his back. He spread a sack on the ground and lay down, knees cocked up and clay thick on his boots. His neighbours couldn't see him this side of the ditch so there'd be no smart remarks in the pub tonight about busy farmers. Still, he was glad he hadn't been tempted into taking the job at the factory like so many of them. Living alone he didn't need the extra money and he didn't think he'd bother getting married at this time of his life. Nowadays if you weren't married, or thinking of it anyway, they thought you were odd or something. In his young days lots of fellas chose not to marry for one reason or another – or none – and no one thought anything of it.

Below there at the bungalow he could see the strange woman sitting idle in her deck chair. There was no sign of the husband. There was a white cat prowling around the sleeping woman. With his good sight he could see she was about his own age but seemed younger. Her hands would give her away for sure.

'Twas hard to tell a woman's age nowadays with the old and the young wearing the same kind of clothes. His own mother, God be good to her, wore dark skirts and black shoes and stockings all the years he could remember her. The married women left the bright clothes to the young ones in those days. Not anymore.

He heard the blasting and could place it. They were getting a spot for sinking the septic tank above at the new house. Two blasts wouldn't do it; no, nor three. Gelignite was hard to come by these days. The slam of a wooden door seemed close by but he knew it couldn't be. The nearest cottage was four fields away.

The cottage sat in a hollow behind a shelter belt of sycamore and ash. The washing hung lazily on the line and by this the turf for the night was in, the hens fed and the daily jobs all accounted for.

The old woman was tired. Others, like the city woman stretched out in her stripy canvas chair, were doing nothing all evening. And himself above on the hill was lying down for sure, his job unfinished, idle and careless like his father before him. Her own old man had his potatoes down since Saint Patrick's Day, and he was ten years over the pension and plenty of life in him still. They had a long rick of turf and the walls whitewashed, the hedges trim and the gutters secure. He always said a good start to the day and the work got done.

She banged her door shut and retired to her bed. The old man was already asleep. An hour in the bed and they'd be ready for tea.

The sun had to climb down out of the sky sometime and the change of air wakened the farmer. He eyed the field from under the peak of his cap and thought he'd done a good job. He'd finish it tomorrow maybe. He was stiff and cramped and muzzy from sleeping in the sun. And he'd been dreaming. It amused him to think of himself out here on the hill lost in dreams. It was a secret world he rarely entered, and he chuckled to think what the cross old woman below would say if she could ever imagine having any thoughts beyond what he'd let out in the pub.

A jet had passed overhead and left a long white trail across the sky. The plane itself was barely visible now with its human cargo of travellers heading off for America across the ocean. They would be young and old, some of them emigrants, some returning 'Yanks'. He lay there visualising the inside of the plane. He'd never been in one but he was familiar with it from watching T.V. in the pub. It was a nightly entertainment for him and the programmes on foreign places and peoples were of far more interest to him than the news or political discussions. Some nights he would return to his cottage a disappointed man, but on others he would have had his fill of the wild behaviour of wealthy oilmen in Dallas, or the high adventures of climbers in foreign lands. He would sit, re-seeing the night's programme, and turn into bed with his head still full of this strange exciting world. But not until today had he dreamed of it in the daytime.

He stretched and gathered himself together, and the woman below, suddenly chilled as he had been, came awake and straightened up in her chair. She glanced idly about her and leant forward nursing her knees.

'I've been dreaming again, old cat,' she said aloud. The cat ignored her.

She thought back to the renting of the house for a month, now nearly over. The longer she stayed here, the less inclined she became to return to her normal life. She wondered if it might be possible to negotiate a further booking. The thought was so tempting that by this it was with her waking and sleeping. Her dream had been a vivid one – she was walking, or rather drifting, through a sunlit world with water sparkling beside her and enormous dandelions impeding her path. She recalled no fear in this dream, no foreboding.

If she approached her husband now, relaxed after a day of golf, perhaps he would be more partial to the idea of an early retirement. Surely he, too, must be sick of travelling and foreign cities and strange hotels. She had tired of it long long ago and generally during these last years had made her base the flat in Dublin. But he seemed compelled to push farther afield, chase business in the lesser known countries, endure heat and exhaustion to gain markets in unpronounceable places. He never explained the fascination of travelling, believing it to be universal; found it difficult to accept her boredom with it, her increasing opposition to his more distant projects. Would they spend all their days shuttling back and forth in the air from one side of the world to the other? Time was running out – time to stay still, to savour the delights of solitude and quiet. This short month had brought out all her repressed longings for another kind of life. As she watched her neighbour, the old woman in the cottage, she saw a woman going about her work at her own pace, competent and assured, whether feeding the hens or cutting her hedge, pegging out clothes on the line or working in the vegetable patch. The old man, her husband, complemented her perfectly, seeing to the animals, clearing the drains, drawing water for the donkey. They lived a sound, competent life with regular pauses for rest and nourishment.

While she had dozed and wakened and dozed again in the deckchair that afternoon she had heard the click of a spade, the rattle of a bucket. It came from the hill behind, where a man planted potatoes in brown flat-topped drills that wound around half-submerged rocks. The pattern of potato drills was repeated all over the stony peninsula and never failed to delight her. The brown earth, like a broad velvet ribbon, snaked up hill and around the rocks. Beneath half-closed lids she saw the man straighten up and look into the sky at the jet heading for New York. Then he lay down on the grass, blotted out the sun with the peak of his cap and rested. Her rest was not an earned rest; her back did not ache from bending and planting and her hands had been idle all evening. She could imagine a tired old body resting behind the curtained window in the cottage, breathing softly and puffing gently while the wrinkled face smoothed out in complete tranquillity. The quilt would rise and fall as regularly as the breathing. There would be no restless churning around, no nervous twitchings or sudden mutterings. The old woman would wake slowly when she was ready, yawn and stretch a little, roll sideways off the creaky bed and put on the kettle for tea.

Above on the hill as still as the rock he lay beside, the man stirred. The sun was sinking and she could feel the chill creep along her arms. She shivered and sat up. The same chill now touched the man. Effortlessly he uncurled and came upright, flipped his cap backward and stretched long arms to the sky. He surveyed the field, collected his bucket and spade and ambled out of her sight. He too would make tea and look back on his day, well satisfied.

When her husband drove up the road and blew his horn in cheerful salute he shattered the peace of the evening. He was not a man given to moods himself and failed to recognise them in others. He had driven off to the golf course, enjoyed a convivial game all afternoon and was at once cheerful, talkative and still brimful of energy. He thought his wife seemed quieter than usual but paid no heed to it. She was frequently more quiet than he could have wished.

She moved slowly and set about preparing a meal. Her pace was leisurely, to say the very least. He was hungry and beginning to resent the delay. He had left her after lunch, a lazy afternoon ahead of her, and yet now there was no meal ready. Silence fell completely between them. He left abruptly and showered and changed, felt refreshed and at ease again.

The meal was a simple one and the table set.

'Are you feeling all right, old dear,' he asked jovially. 'Not quite yourself, are you?'

She took time to reply.

'I'm fine, never better. That's why I need to stay on here for another month.'

'What on earth's got into you?' he protested rather than

asked. 'We're due in London next week, Kenya after that.' He felt shaken and had spoken sharply.

She looked away and out the window, to the ageless mountains, the steel-blue of the lake.

'I have to stay another while.' She spoke more to herself than to him. 'If I remain here, while you go on, I will have something to carry with me through the rest of the year. But if I leave now there will be nothing at all.'

He waited for a further explanation but it did not come. He felt an anger unusual for him. There was no understanding this statement, but a prick of fear held him quiet. After twenty years it was unfair to start talking in a language unknown to him. He recognised an ultimatum beneath the soft blur of words, cursed the day he humoured her wish for a month of living in the remote West instead of soaking up Spanish sun beside a hotel swimming pool.

Swiftly he weighed up consequences.

'If that's what you really want, m'dear, then that is what you'll have.'

The tone was chill and crisp.

She smiled. He patted her hand. He wondered how narrow his margin of safety had been, how many more concessions it would take to keep a good marriage going.

Sudden weariness enveloped him. For the first time in his successful career he felt threatened. She sat, relaxed and smiling, on the opposite side of the table, a quiet, well-preserved woman who had never before given him a moment's anxiety.

'You must suit yourself, m'dear.' His tone warmer, almost conciliatory.

He awaited her 'Thank you' and was made freshly uneasy when it failed to come.

He would remember this moment long after it was past and be bewildered by its significance.

TROUBLED WATER

MÁIRÍN O'CONNOR

The row – if such it could be called – was only the last in a series. They were all low key, undramatic and boring. He wished that just once she and her husband could have an explosive row–a row that would reverberate from wall to wall and room to room – a row to end all rows.

In town such a luxury was unthinkable, penned as they were within a flat contained by thin walls. Here in the isolated rented cottage, in the middle of a field, all things were possible, but the established habits of inhibited living that the flat imposed on them were with them here as well. She sat in her room wondering yet again why life nowadays was a continuing argument, sometimes acrimonious, sometimes not, always disturbing. And inconvenient. She could never be sure whether he wilfully provoked her when it was most distasteful to her to be provoked – as when guests were expected–or whether their life was so continuously fractured by disagreement that friction between them was inevitable, no matter what the occasion.

Take today for instance. They were due to leave shortly, booted and kitted appropriately, for a day on the Lough. They had met Fitz in the pub a couple of nights ago, had enthusiastically renewed an old friendship, and were to share a boat and a day's fishing with him today. At the time it had seemed like a splendid idea. The weather was cool for August and an outing on the lake would be a novelty. They had both jumped at the suggestion and were prepared to shed all city attitudes towards weather and discomfort for the joy of a day in the open, renewing an old friendship and probably catching a few trout as well. It had all been gleeful anticipation up to an hour ago. They were pouring over the map, working out the best route to the lake and calculating the time it would take to cover the twisting twenty miles on roads unknown to them. It had begun as a very small argument and developed along familiar lines to the point where she avoided shouting at him by banging the door instead and retiring in fury. There was no way they could cancel the trip. No convenient phone, no possible way to contact Fitz, probably already en route from his home to prepare the boat for the comfort of his guests. There was no time either for sulking or the licking of wounds. They would need to move fast now to make up for time wasted in unprofitable argument. She shrugged.

Fitz was waiting for them. Not idly. The impedimenta for the day were piled on the grass verge and he himself was climbing into his fishing outfit. He greeted them cheerfully, acknowledging that the day wasn't the best but dismissing the high wind and the squalls of rain as of little consequence. Separately and secretly they had fully expected the expedition to be cancelled as the weather hit them driving out of their sheltered valley, but neither had made any comment, and now none was required of them. They were here, the lake beyond the sloping field, and they were going fishing as planned.

Immediately she was at a disadvantage. She was trim and neat in slacks and flat shoes and a gay anorak. After a quick glance Fitz had thrown her a disreputable old oilskin, the legs much too long, the seat much too wide. She climbed into them.

The two men were easy and chatting, sorting out rods and plastic containers, rapidly establishing the old remembered relationship of college days. Even after a decade they had had no difficulty in relating to one another. They had gone their separate ways when qualified, Fitz choosing to return west, her husband sticking to what he knew best, the city.

She felt a complete outsider.

Laden with equipment they squelched down through the soggy field, disturbing a bunch of heifers that terrified her by both their size and their proximity. She felt mud oozing through her leather shoes, recognised her stupidity in not providing herself with wellers.

The boat, one of many moored at the water's edge, lay on its old tyres, moved gently with the flow of water. The engine was wrapped in heavy plastic but there were oars as well. She wondered about that but kept her ignorance to herself.

She had been given charge of the picnic bag and the blackened kettle and a plastic-covered cushion to sit on. Fitz was pointing out the repairs he had recently completed on the boat. A bullock had jumped into it and done a lot of damage. He mentioned it casually, his philosophic attitude to the accident amazing her.

She wondered briefly what her husband's reaction might

have been to a bullock jumping on his new car. The thought made her giggle. She sat on her cushion and held the sides of the boat while the two men pushed and heaved, up to their knees in water, and once afloat leapt in to join her. They glided out from the shore, faced onto a lake of choppy metallic grey water. Fitz knelt in the stern wrestling with the recalcitrant outboard motor, the boat bobbed and lurched, buffeted by threatening waves. It was a movement totally new to her, exhilarating and a little frightening. But as in the old days, Fitz was in charge, exuding competence, her husband content, as of yore, to leave decisions to his friend. This dependency on Fitz had once annoyed her. But not today. The man was obviously as much at ease on the water as he was on land. She shifted her position gingerly and looked about her.

The lake was dotted with islands. Out in the middle she could see the larger islands covered in bright green fields and specks that looked like sheep grazing on them. She would have questions for Fitz about this later on, but not yet. The engine was taking its time to catch, and he was preoccupied. The rocking of the boat seemed out of control. Her husband sat easily, relaxed and silent. She gripped the sides and was careful to conceal anxiety.

The engine spluttered into life, carried them down the shore and was then out. They drifted and fished.

The silence was something she grew to accept during the day. Conversation was minimal once the fishing had started. She was pleased to be given a rod and line, her 'dragon-fly' bobbed on top of the water and when it became sodden she lifted it off the surface as instructed to dry in the breeze. The fact that no trout rose to her fly bothered her not at all.

The two men were silently casting. Again and again the lines were cast, reeled in and cast again. Trying to remember the instructions about keeping her rod at 90° to the side of the boat, she sat sideways on her cushion, the wind boldly whipping waves up across the lake and the mist shrouding the surrounding mountains. When the boat was drawn too far from the shore the engine would be restarted to bring them back in again to shelter from the land. Gusting and galeing the day slipped by. It was not a day for venturing out onto the broad bosom of the lake and no boat but this had considered fishing. The sun occasionally burst out between banks of cloud but there was no warmth in it. A lone mallard winged overhead. Houses on the lake's edge gleamed whitely, cars skimmed silently by on the road above them. It was far removed from her notion of a day's boating but, as the day wore on, she adjusted contentedly.

They picnicked eventually on a small wet island, among scrubby small bushes and stunted trees backing onto a ridge of holly and sycamore. They were out of the wind and sheltered from the showers. The smell of wild mint growing among the stones was strong where they crouched on fallen branches, and drank strong hot tea and ate beef sandwiches. The meal had none of the niceties of a conventional picnic but charmed her by this very lack. The small black kettle served as teapot and the tea was scalding hot. Surreptitiously she lined her wet shoes with discarded plastic sandwich bags, pulled her wool cap inelegantly right down over her ears, and was agreeably enthusiastic about a further couple of hours drifting on turbulent water while casting changed to trolling and the catching of three small perch. The little fish with silver bodies blended with cinnamon stripes lay panting on the bottom of the boat, their geranium scarlet fins and tails startlingly vivid. Unreasonably and illogically she mourned them silently. The menfolk exchanged amused but tolerant glances and the silence that embraced all three of them felt warm and comfortable and wholly acceptable.

Only when the light had drained out of the sky and hope of further fish had died, did they consider coming in to land. The boat secured, the rods sheathed, the oars stored, they tramped back up the hill to drive to the nearest pub. Even here they shared a silence, uninterrupted by taped music or television – three tired, windblown and raindrenched people, at ease with themselves and with each other. The floor tilted and moved under her feet, the rocking boat still with her. Her face burned and her eyes drooped. The two men drank large pints and occasionally addressed one another.

'We'll get a better day for the fishing next year, please God. Pity we didn't get an old trout or two.' Fitz was apologetic. She reassured him. 'It was a marvellous day, the best of the holiday.' They smiled contentedly at each other. Her husband nodded agreement.

When they reached the cottage again she could hardly keep awake but there were perch to be cleaned and fried and no electricity, the ESB pole blown down somewhere by the gale. She used the gas ring, and the smell of fish permeated every corner of the house. The fish tasted like cod, firm and white.

Her mind turned over and over, like precious stones, the

strange small incidents of the long day. It had been an experience new to her in every detail. Nothing she had imagined came near to the reality. Perhaps she had naively anticipated sunlit water and a cool breeze, a picnic on a green sward and a lot of harking back to younger days when they had all been optimistic and vital and full of promise. Instead the churned waters, the tilting movement, the spray dashing and drenching, the lowering mountains and particularly the silence were what was left to her now. There had been no need or room for speech. Each had apparently been sufficiently rewarded with differing aspects of the venture. She knew instinctively that any attempt to analyse her satisfaction would be to destroy it.

It had been a day given to them, an extraordinary one, bearing no relation to any other day they had experienced together. Whether it was a beginning or an end, she could not guess.

Her husband chewed his way through the coarse perch, marvelling at her enthusiasm. Her hands were badly scratched from inexpert handling of the spiny fish but she presented them on a hot dish with a flourish. 'They'll be different, Bob. Quite different. Try some lemon on them.' Humouring her, he ate with care; so many bones, so little flesh. Had he misread her all these years? Would there be time to rediscover, reassess the woman he'd married ten years ago? If recent signs were anything to go by, the sooner he put his mind to it the better.

The prospect of all the energy and patience to be invested in rescuing a crumbling relationship dismayed him. Would his reserves of affection be adequate? Would he be of the same mind in the morning?'

Unloading his gear from the boot of the old car and changing into dry clothes was an unhurried ritual for Fitz. When he came into the warm kitchen his wife was waiting placidly for him.

'Well, how did the day go?' she asked.

'Hard to say.' he replied. 'We had rain and rough water and no trout.'

'A pity, that.'

She knitted a while and he packed his pipe.

'Did they enjoy it at all so?'

'I'd say they did.' He sounded unsure. 'They've changed a lot, d'ye see. They're quiet and easy-going now. Very little talk. Whoever told you they were splitting up was hard pushed for a bit of gossip. I saw nothing wrong with them.'

He turned on the radio for the news and stretched cold feet to the fire. His wife recognised a conversation closed and left it so. A great man for leaving out all the details and refusing to speculate, her husband. There would be nothing more to be got out of him. She got up and made the last pot of tea for the day.

'It can't have been a total disaster anyway or he'd have noticed,' she consoled herself and, grinning ruefully, poured him out a mug of tea.

Note: The 1983 award was shared by Jim McGowan (story on p. 185) and the late John Jordan, but as records were incomplete, the latter's story could not be identified. Its omission, consequently, is unavoidable, and greatly regretted.

FAIR AND FOUL

JIM McGOWAN

The three boys laughed. It was a glorious day, the sun still high in the heavens, the smell of Summer alive in their veins.

The heather was purple proud, competing with, complementing the wild yellow of the gorse. There was an energy in the air of this mountainy place. It met a response in the sinews of the three lads who regarded the disorganised industry of worker bees moving from clump to clump. It was good to be here among the sounds, the separate sounds of water in persistent argument with rock, the call and answer of linnets unseen in trees on the far bank of the river, the dissonant drone of the bees. To be silent was to hear, to hear was to experience the mysterious adventure of life.

Brendan moved in harmony with river, tree, bird and insect. He raced up the slope of the hill, bounding from rock to firm grass, skipping the squashy green terraces of yielding moss. He looked at the blue emptiness of the sky, filled his lungs with mountain exhilaration, roared a challenge to the puzzled-looking goat on the higher ridge. The goat eyed him haughtily, moved a few feet higher, looked again at the roaring youngster and finally trotted off with a muttering wag of his head.

Brendan raced back down to the river, couldn't stop, took a flying leap across the water, landing surefootedly on a spread rock, back bent, hands outflung, foiling expectant water. He wished he could fly, soar out over the edge, tease the fall of the river, mock the riveted trees in the valley.

He looked at the deep still pool on his left, placed his open hand in it, sensed the four formed tributaries move through his fingers, marvelled at the unity of it all. His spirit linked to Stephen and Larry, to the rhythm of water and tree, gorse and heather, goat, bird and skyblue liberty, he threw off his clothes, lowered himself into the shock of cold water.

Freedom stirred the mood. Larry and Stephen waded in. They flung water, sang their celebration, shot dead imaginary enemies, struggled to the bank, danced their victory. Dressed again, hunger called, ah, the good of tea and sandwich, yarns told of school and teachers, relived glories of yesterday's two-all game.

The bikes were three spitfires as they zoomed for home.

'So-long Stephen. See you Larry.'

Brendan was home. His mother laid the table for tea. His two brothers and his sister sat, chatted. The clock on the mantelpiece was stopped. Had been for ten years. There. The sound. The key in the halldoor lock. They stopped talking. Their father came in. He sat in his place. Opened his newspaper. Finished his meal. Took up his paper. He didn't speak to Brendan's mother. Nor to them. Never did. He got up, left the room, went upstairs, came down, went out. Always did.

Brendan went into the sitting room, shifted the curtain, looked out at the receding back, the fine manly stride. He went back into the dining-room, looked at his mother. His mother went into the kitchen.

MORNING

JOHN McDONNELL

This was one of his good days. The dragging heaviness in his stomach was still there but the pain was at a bearable level. He could think about things other than his own misery.

Pain was the problem. It not only tormented the body – it crippled the mind too. It killed objectivity. He often wondered how the martyrs had made their pain a prayer, how their minds had been able to stand far enough back from their pain to lift it up in sacrifice. Perhaps they, like him, had offered it up before it came or after it had gone. But the martyrs had been strong, he supposed. He was so weak.

He was able to admire the warm, calm evening now. The garden was not in the best of trim but the flowers were there, and the sweetness. He found himself thinking about poor Jemmy Donohue, who used to do the garden for him. Jemmy had died there in the garden twelve months before; he had sat on the seat under the apple tree one evening and slumped quietly into eternity. Again he asked the risen Christ to bring Jemmy up into glory with Him. Jemmy would be so much at home in paradise, among the flowers and the trees and the brightness and the innocence.

He walked slowly, marvelling at his freedom from intense pain, up the centre path towards the seat where Jemmy Donohue had died. He sat on it and gazed down on the village. What would he say to them in his sermon tomorrow?

Father Joe's sermons were always short, and he had only two basic themes – God and sin. Such a lot of nonsense was talked and written about religion these days! He had heard a fellow saying, unchallenged, in a radio programme a few days before that loving one's neighbour was the basic tenet of Christianity – despite the fact that Christ had said that this was only the second thing. Loving God was the first thing, and love of neighbour was only a tributary of love of God. It did not make sense in any other context.

Religion was like an iceberg: so many people were concerned with only the little bit of it that showed. How many of the people down there in the village really believed in God? Some of them, he knew, did not. They had said so. There they were, stuck like little limpets to a big ball of clay spinning in the middle of infinity and eternity, and they thought they had all the answers! But at least they were honest in their sad pride. If there is no God, we are only talking monkeys.

And what had happened to sin? Nowadays people were tailoring sin to their own desires. Conscience they called it. But conscience was the opposite thing: tailoring one's desires to the pattern of known right and wrong. He would talk about sin tomorrow. About the *big* sin, pride. Pride was the father and mother of all evil. If God was love, the devil was pride.

He shivered a little. The evening was growing cool. He was no good at all now in the cold.

As he walked towards the door he saw little Ellie Ryan coming up the avenue. Petite, shapely, golden-haired, miniskirted, she was like a doll. Wondering what she wanted, he waited for her at the door. She had never come to the parochial house before.

Perched on the edge of a chair, a beautiful sprite, she symbolised everything that was young and fresh. But her face was grave. She had greeted him with a half-smile and asked him if she might talk to him. He had ushered her into his livingroom.

'Well, Ellie, what can I do for you?'

Father Joe had not been involved very much in parish affairs recently. The Bishop had given him a helper, and Father Brian was doing all the work. The younger priest kept him well informed but Father Joe was not aware of any development in which Ellie Ryan figured.

'My mother said I should come to you.'

'Ah. And how is she?'

'She's fine.'

'And what's the problem?'

'It's about Tom. Tom Burke.'

'Tom Burke? From Kelly's Cross?'

'Yes. You see, we're…'

'He's your boyfriend?'

'Yes.'

'A fine lad. But what's the problem?'

The priest already had an idea of the problem. The old story. And as he waited for her to put it into words, he wondered why she had come to him. He could not solve such a problem.

He could only be compassionate. But he was a little surprised. Young people took that sort of thing in their stride these days. They did not come running to the priest; they sorted it out themselves, for good or bad.

Ellie looked at him and there was anguish in her eyes.

'He's going to die,' she said. And she burst into tears.

Father Joe could only stare at her. The effect of her statement was almost physical. Not only was it not what he had expected— it was so astonishingly unexpected that he could not take it into his mind at all for a few moments. And now, as he tried to grasp it, her distress seemed to transmit itself to him too and he suddenly felt weak and fearful. These days his mind and his body seemed to be one: mental distress would bring physical strain too. He sat there, tense, waiting for his pain to come searing back. It did not.

'What do you mean?' he said.

Tom had been feeling unwell for some time; everything made him tired. He had gone to the doctor, who had arranged tests for him in Drumreen Hospital. It was some blood disease. Tom had only weeks to live.

The specialist had told Tom's father and he had told Ellie's father. Ellie's father had told her mother, and she had overheard; they had not known she was in the house at the time. They could not deny it then and had told her the whole story.

'Are you certain about it?'

She nodded.

'I don't want him to die, Father. I love him.'

Trying to rationalise death was nothing new to Father Joe, but he was completely confused now. What could an old, dying priest say about death that would make sense to this lovely little princess of youth and life!

'Would you like a cup of tea?'

'No, thanks, Father.'

A little bit of irrelevant normality, he knew, sometimes helped to stabilise a situation, but he had not really expected it to work this time. What should he say? It was the great contradiction of the times that, although respect for life was at such a low ebb, there was a very poor philosophy of death. The no-tomorrow complex seemed part of the present phase of human evolution. Man was using only the top of his mind. But all that was irrelevant too. No philosophy could answer the heartbreak of this girl. He wanted to take her in his arms and let her cry herself to some sort of peace.

'What can I say, Ellie?'

'I know, Father. But will you pray for him? Say a Mass for him?' She took a little purse from a small pocket and opened it. He shook his hand at that, irritably, and she closed it again.

'Of course I'll pray for him. Of course I'll say Mass for him.'

He got up, crossed to the window and stood gazing out at his unkempt garden. Over to the right the blossoming apple tree stood like a parasol over the white seat where Jemmy Donohue had died.

'I suppose you know,' he said, still gazing out, 'that I'm going to die soon myself?'

There was silence.

'I know you haven't been well,' she said then.

'Soon. Very soon. So you see, I have been thinking a lot

about death.' He knew how she was reacting to that. He was old and had lived his life, but Tom, her sweetheart, was young and his dying was a different thing. The priest knew too that he could not expect a young girl to see the years between youth and age as merely a preparation for eternity. To her, those years were the blossoming of life, not a prelude to death. Nor could she appreciate now that those years would bring the healing of her heartbreak. All he could do was try to tell her what death really was.

'Ellie,' he said, 'I have before my mind, all the time now, the picture of a moment in history, the greatest moment in all history. It is morning, a bright Sunday morning . . . and there is a Man standing outside his tomb. A man who has just conquered death.

'This was a real moment, Ellie. A real moment in time. Jesus Christ was God, but He was a man. And He was not only a man – He was every man. And in that moment He was gazing into the future, a future without end, without pain, without death. He had a body that would never know suffering and a spirit that had power over time and space and thought. He was free for ever. And that was His promise to us. Can you see that picture, Ellie?'

'Yes . . . I can see it.'

She was blinking through her tears at him, seeing him only as a silhouette as he stood against the window of evening light. The interior had dimmed. An element of mysticism had come into the scene and she was a little afraid. The priest was only a figure, a dark statue. There was nothing now to show who he was, whether he was young or old. She could imagine him, as he spoke, being renewed, rejuvenated in body and spirit, being made powerful and free for ever.

He had gone a bit queer, she thought, and she was being caught up in it. She should not have come.

'God did not make us to die, Ellie. He made us to live for ever.'

She was a normal Catholic girl. She went to Mass on Sundays and lived generally by the rules. She was no better and no worse than the next. But she had never felt the real mysticism of religion before. Religion had always been part of her life; now it seemed to be primarily about death. Death was looming all around her – Tom's death, Father Joe's death, young death, old death, death. Even her own death did not seem so remote.

The priest came away from the window and as he moved out of the background of light she could see him in some definition again. He sat at the fire, across from her.

'It's myself,' he said, 'that I'm trying to help. I'm sorry. You came to me for help and look what I got up to! But you will get help, Ellie. God will help you. Of course He will expect you to do something in return – He will expect you to help Tom. Bear your pain for Tom. Offer it as payment for help for Tom. You see, there is always a balance sheet to be worked out. And it is Tom who needs help most.'

'He doesn't know yet that he is going to die.'

'No. The pain of knowing is yours. That makes it all the more valuable as currency. Make it your prayer. And remember too the old saying – where there's life there's hope.'

'There's no hope, Father.'

'Where there's death there's hope too. And that's the *real* hope, Ellie. That's the only hope that makes sense of anything.'

She was not crying now. He sensed that she wanted to leave, that her visit had not turned out as she had expected.

But what *had* she expected? A miracle? And all she had got was the added gloom of his own looming death. A great wave of compassion for her surged up in him. She was only a child, a child in years and in understanding. She wanted help that she could understand. Simple help. Simple hope. And yes, maybe a miracle – a simple miracle. She could not understand the pain of life, but she could understand a miracle.

She stood up.

'I think I'd better be going now, Father,' she said. 'You will pray for him, won't you?'

'Of course I'll pray for him. And I'll say Mass for him in the morning. Eleven o'clock. For a special intention . . . you know. Our special intention.'

'Thank you, Father. And I'm sorry about your . . . about yourself.'

He stood up, smiling.

'Oh, I'm an old man. I've had my time.'

He saw her to the door and watched her lonely little figure going down the avenue in the twilight. He felt so sad, so helpless. And he offered up the fear and anguish of his own death for some consolation for Ellie Ryan.

The pain was coming back. 'Dear God, help me!' he prayed. But he was grateful that he had been able to talk to the little girl.

He stood at the front door for some time after she had gone out of sight and gazed at the twilight world. The garden seemed utterly lonely now in the dimness. He could still see the white seat under the apple tree and thought it would be a nice place to die. But he would like it to be morning.

When he was stronger he used to do the garden himself. Wouldn't it be lovely if he could get up some morning now and bring his spade and rake and clippers into the garden and make the place trim and artistic again!

'Father Joe!'

His housekeeper was calling him to his tea. He went in, closing the door on the darkening world outside. Tea was only a formality, a little bit of pretended normality. He had no appetite at all. Indeed the little bit he might eat would distress him. Later, if the pain got worse, he would take a couple of tablets. Sometimes they helped and sometimes they did not.

Oh, it was all so unreal! A nightmarish half-life. He hoped his sanity would hold out.

After tea he would telephone his friend, Sister Veronica, the matron in the hospital, and ask her about Tom Burke. That too, he knew, would be only a formality. Doctors nowadays were rarely wrong about terminal illness.

He managed to eat his scrambled egg and sipped at his cup of tea for a while.

The pain had not intensified; it seemed to have receded a little; and he was able to think about Ellie Ryan again.

He should have been able to help her more. The poor child had come to him expecting something. But what could he have done? The only answer to death was the certain hope of resurrection – and he had tried to show her that. But that was the hope for Tom Burke and himself. Had that helped Ellie

Ryan? The hope she wanted was for now, for here.

What she needed now was faith – absolute trust in God– trust that transcended the greatest grief and pain. It was a tall order for an ordinary young girl, but it was the only thing. He would ask God to strengthen her in her faith.

No, he wouldn't talk about sin in his sermon tomorrow. He would talk about God, about faith. That was what all the bother boiled down to - faith in God. There had to be that absolute trust. There just had to be. And pain and death were the test. People were always saying that it was easier to believe in God when one was in great trouble, but that was all a cod. That was the time when it was hardest to have such trust.

Father Joe sat back in his chair, putting up his hands protectingly before his face to ward off the despair that was always there waiting to assail him at the worst moments. He closed his eyes and tried to make the bright Easter morning scene unfold in his mind again. The scene that meant everything. The risen Christ standing outside His tomb free from pain and death for ever. The sun was bright, the morning fresh. There were birds and flowers.

Now the risen man was Jemmy Donohue. Now he was young Tom Burke. Now he was . . .

But the old priest could not superimpose his own image on the scene. His imagination did not seem to have enough power.

'I *do* believe!' he moaned in his mind. 'I *do* believe!'

When the housekeeper came in to take the tea things off the little table and saw him slumped in his chair, she knew he was dead.

FATHERS

AIDAN MATHEWS

'In the lost childhood of Judas, Christ was betrayed.'

Graham Greene

I was halfway through my homework when my father put his head round the door.

– There's a good programme starting, old man. About the Nazi death camps and the Eichmann trial. I thought you might be interested.

The night before, it had been a special report on the fate of the white rhinoceros in Zambia; and on Sunday, a document-ary about the shanty towns in Rio. We'd had the television for six months, and my father still played with it like a new toy.

– I have this poem to learn the first verse of, Bill.

– I can give you a note, my father said. This programme's important. I want you to see it. Come on down.

He took his smock off as we went downstairs, wiping clay and crayon from his hands onto the tough cloth. He could never get rid of those stains. Even on holidays in the caravan, away from work, his fingers smelled of the studio.

My mother was doing her nails in the study when we came in. She held her hands in the air like a prisoner to dry them while my father fiddled with the contrast button and the vertical hold.

– I hope it's suitable, she said. I don't want him having bad dreams.

The voice in the television began to speak up.

– Eichmann is not however a satanist or sadist. His domestic life was both modest and moral. When he was promoted from Untersturmfuhrer to Hauptsturmfuhrer, his first action . . .

– Here it is, my father said. This is strong stuff, old man, but you have a right to know. The day your mother and I married, ten thousand children were gassed at Auschwitz. I went out that morning to buy flowers.

He stood at the fire and looked into it, working the dottle from the bowl of his pipe with a pipecleaner. Then he came over and sat down beside me.

There was loud music. A man appeared. It was a map of Europe on which shadows were spreading like inkstains to show where the armies advanced. I glanced at my father. He was stroking his beard and nodding his head. I looked above the television, then beneath it; at the knobs; at the screen.

A boy was holding a model train in front of a soldier who struck him with the butt of his rifle so that the boy fell down and lay in the road. The voice was saying dates and places like the names in the Brothers Grimm. Heidelburg, Bucharest, Birkenau. My father put his hand on my knee.

– And you see the people standing round? he said.

Two soldiers were dragging a man by his collar along the pavement. They passed an old man who took off his hat. Then they let go of the one they were pulling, and they kicked the old man until he kneeled down.

– Bravo. Bravo.

My photograph was on top of the set beside the Madonna my father had made. I looked at the picture of me in my Communion suit, and at Mary taking her breast out of her blouse to give it to the baby on her lap. I did not want to see the rabbi in the snow with his face burnt.

– Would you look at that?

– It's not fair, said my mother's voice. He's too young.

My father waved his pipe at the television. I had not seen him so upset since the programme about the baby seals.

– No man is an isthmus, Mark, he said. No man. On the Last Day, it won't help to conjugate a Latin verb. Did you feed the starving? Did you visit the prisons?

A woman walked into a yard where soldiers were smoking and lifting box-cameras. She started to take off her clothes, wobbling as she pulled her dress over her head. When she opened her stockings, she fell down, and curled up like a baby with her stockings bundled around her feet.

– If not, then to Hell with you. For saying it was none of your business. For saying Pass the salt.

My father tugged his beard like a bell.

– Are you finished? my mother said. Shall I pass the plate now?

– Mark understands, said my father.

He went out in a bit of a huff.

My mother began to fix the cover on the couch, working it down into the edges, straightening the pattern.

– He's not content to be a father. He's not content to be a husband. He's not content to be a sculptor. He has to be a Good Man.

My father was working with a blowtorch when I went in. He kicked the plug, and turned up his goggles.

– The soldier fought bravely before the city walls, he said.

I thought.

– *Fortiter miles ante urbis muros pugnavit.*

– Father and son went up the mountain quickly to the altar.

That took longer.

– *Pater atque filius in monte celeriter progressi sunt ad alterem.*

– Fair enough, my father said.

He pulled his goggles down and started the torch. I sat on a box and watched the fantail from the white jet. He shouted at me over the noise.

– What do you think?

– It's lovely. What is it?

– It'll keep the wolf from the door, he shouted.

– And the roof over our heads, I called.

The Stations for the school chapel were in a pile beside me. Jesus Falls For the Third Time and Jesus is Comforted By The Women. The parents had complained and said it was their money because Jesus was naked except for the thorns and you could see everything. My father's picture had been in the paper but it was before he had his beard. One parent had come up to me and said he respected my father and would I tell him, and I told him yes.

– Bill, I shouted.

When he took off his goggles, there was a mark on his forehead.

– Yes, old man?

– Just Bill, I said.

I couldn't settle down to sleep. Whenever I closed my eyes, I saw the old rabbi and the corporal who was striking a match to set fire to his beard. Another soldier had given him a bucket of horse manure to put out the flame, but the rabbi would not do it. He kept shaking his head.

I started to look at the stain on the ceiling which was like a map of Italy, and I named the cities, the rivers, the churches. When I closed my eyes again, I smelled sulphur. I didn't breathe, I went deep in the bed. A floorboard creaked.

It was my father. He was lighting a cigarette on the landing outside, listening to hear if I was asleep, standing in the darkness.

– In the name of the Father and of the Son and of the Holy Ghost, Fr Wilson said.

– In the name of the Father and of the Son, I said. I was looking at the poem we had been told to learn.

Fr Wilson leaned against the blackboard, inspecting his shoes.

– Today promises well for Fr Wilson, he said. Today is a fine April morning, and each member of this class knows his poetry. Isn't that so, Colin my friend?

– Yes, Father.

– Would you subscribe to that, Andrew?

– Yes, Father.

– Fine. The first three verses, Andrew. The first two verses, Andrew. We were all in bed an hour ago, and it wouldn't do to tax the mind. I know you've made a special effort not to disappoint poor Fr Wilson for the third time running.

I knew better. Andrew Masterson had been warming his hands on the hot pipes before class, wrapping them round the bars till the tears ran down his good eye.

I was right. He got through seven lines and came to a stop.

The class was silent. I stared at my desk lid, at the cartoon of the Nazi goosestepping on the cover of my jotter where someone had written: Sieg Heil, The Sculptor's Son.

Fr Wilson parted his lips so they made a sad sound.

– Andrew falls for the third time.

– I tried, Father.

– Are you stupid, Andrew?

– Yes, Father.

– And lazy, Andrew? A lazybones?

– Yes, Father.

- What does that make you, Andrew?

– A stupid lazybones, Father.

The class laughed.

– Our Lord died on the Cross for you, Andrew. And you can't learn three verses of a poem for Him.

Fr Wilson nodded his head up and down in patience, side to side in disbelief. He held up the note for the Dean.

– Goodbye, Andrew.

– Goodbye, Father, said Andrew Masterson. He walked

up the aisle; and the boys tittered, moving their satchels to let him pass. When he took the slip of paper from Fr Wilson, he got down on his knees. But he was only tying his shoe.

I didn't know that I had stood up until I saw the class turning to look at me, a rush of white faces like underneath leaves when the wind blows them back. There was a shadow coming in front of me. I saw the map, and Bill's face, the rabbi knotting his bootlace, and Andrew curled on the ground with his pants at his ankles. What was an isthmus?

– You're a bully. He can't help not knowing, and you knew he wouldn't get it right. You knew.

Bill. Bill.

I felt the touch and grasp of hands pulling me down into my desk. Then the hands stopped. I saw mouths opening and moving, Fr Wilson speaking, gesturing to Andrew Masterson, and Andrew sitting down, staring at his book without moving his head; and my nails with biro marks on them: a small hair, an eyelash, on the second nail.

– . . . to have an intercessor, Andrew.

– Yes, Father.

When I looked up, the bell had rung, Fr Wilson had left the classroom without his books, and the boys were looking at me, taking their books for the next class out of their satchels.

I waited after school until all the boys had gone. Then I walked to the bicycle shed. I was afraid I would meet Fr Wilson, and he would be ashamed. I wanted to be home so that I could tell my father everything that had happened from the beginning. He would look at me then the same way he had looked at me the night before when he had pulled down his goggles and I had said: Just Bill.

As I put my bag on the carrier, I heard the noise of twigs. Andrew Masterson came out from behind the hedge. Colin Dennis and Mick the Nose were beside him, each of them trailing a stick in the gravel.

– Hello, Andrew Masterson said.

– Hello, I said.

– Hello again, he said.

– What do you mean?

– We want to help you with your homework, he said. The three of us want to.

He flung his leg over the bike and sat on the saddle.

– I love your bike, he said.

Dennis and Mick the Nose were marking zeros and crosses in the gravel with the sticks.

– I wish my bike was as nice as yours, he said. He rocked it with his weight so the front wheels strained against the iron prongs in the wall.

– Go easy, I said.

He stood on the pedals and leaned over.

– I hate to say this but I think I might have warped it.

He pressed down on the handlebars until the front wheel buckled in the iron bracket and a spoke stuck out.

– Butterfingers, he said.

He bent down to open the valves on the tyres.

– It'll be easier for you, he said, to wheel it home.

They were killing a pig in the yard behind the handball court. I could hear its cries peak, like a fast car braking.

I began to cry.

– I forgot what I came for, he said. It was to say thanks.

I sat down on the gravel and curled in a ball at their feet. When they saw I was ready, they started. But I felt far away. I felt I was behind the hedge, watching.

Their boots rose and fell.

– It's about the rain forests of the Amazon, my father said. And the ozone layer.

– I have to work, Bill.

– The serious student, old man. The serious student.

– You can tell me about it later.

But he came back a moment later.

– I don't think I'll bother, he said. I'll work for a while. Keep the old wolf from the door.

He stood, waiting. I looked at the bits of a horsefly on my wall.

– And the roof over our heads, I said.

Then he was happy, and bounded down the stairs, taking them two at a time.

I put away my Latin. Below me, I heard a hanger clatter in the wardrobe as my father got his smock out; the rasp of a match on an emery board; and the dull whoosh of the torch as he pressed the footswitch.

I had to go down.

– What did you do tonight? he said.

– The subjunctive.

– No less. Do you know, he shouted, if you keep learning like this, I'll be more of a hindrance than a help soon.

I watched the flame peel from the jet of the torch and drop in pellets on the floor. Quick droplets of bronze glistened.

– I might have been warned, I said.

– *Monitus fu . . . monitus fuerim.* Is that it?

– I don't know, I said.

– This is my beloved son in whom I am well pleased, he shouted.

– You do it, Bill.

– I've forgotten everything I knew, old man.

He stopped the torch and slung it in its harness.

– You must be tired, he said. It was hard luck about the puncture. Did you think of locking the bike?

– It's safe.

– Trust in God and tie up your camel, said my father.

I lay in my bed and looked at the stain on the ceiling. I wanted to think about the churches and the squares my father said you could not see for the first time without having to cry. But when I closed my eyes, the woman fell over her stockings and lay on the gravel with her bottom showing; and I stretched out my hand to touch it.

I got up and went across the landing to my parents' bedroom. In the pitch-black, I groped along the chest of drawers until I could crouch at their door, feeling the draught on my ankles. I had to be sure that my father was all right, that he was breathing.

– Cut your nails first, Bill. It hurts.

Bill's voice: my father's voice.

– O Jesus.

– Honour us with a verse or two, Andrew, Fr Wilson said. Unless Mark objects. Do you object, Mark?

– No, Father.

Masterson fought his way down twelve lines, and collapsed. I had been afraid he might finish. Before class, he had smiled at me as he doodled with a pencil, tracing a coin through tissue paper. But I had kept myself to myself.

– What do you write above your exercises, Andrew?

– What, Father?

– The Latin, Andrew, the Latin.

– *Ad Maiorem Dei Gloriam*, Father.

– Indeed. Translate that into modern English for the sake of the uninitiated.

– To the Greater Glory of God.

– A bold claim, Andrew.

Fr Wilson inspected his shoes.

– Homework, he said, is not much to write home about. It's small stuff, by and large. It's not staffing the missions or tending the sick or touring the prisons. But it pleases God that you should do it for Him. To say that you're doing it for Him, and not to do so having said so, is to do what, Andrew?

– Father.

– It's to commit the act of a bounder. The act of a cad.

He held up the note.

When Masterson had left the class to go to the Dean, Fr Wilson called me. I was studying my desk-lid, not looking at anyone.

– The next verse, Mark. I'll keep time on the tin whistle.

The class was uneasy. Everybody laughed.

– Go on, said Fr Wilson.

The seat clanged when I stood up. I thought of the woman with the stocking. I wanted to be with her. She would take her breasts out of her blouse and set my head on them; would cover my face with her hair.

Then out spake brave Horatius,
The captain of the gate.
'To every man upon this earth,
Death cometh soon or late;
And how can man die better
Than facing fearful odds,
For the ashes of his father,
And the temples of his gods.'

From the floor below, I heard the splashing of the strap. For a moment, I was sorry for Andrew Masterson, and sorry that the heating had been turned off that morning so that he had gone to the Dean without burning his hands.

– Fathers, said Fr Wilson. Ashes of his fathers.

– Fathers, I said. Fathers.

EASY TARGET BY RUNAWAY LAD
OUT OF SHADY LADY

PHIL FEIGHAN

Sister Kieran glides over to the brown-painted cupboard and removes a pile of copies from a shelf. There is a sudden hum of expectation in the classroom.

'She's giving back the compositions!'

'I hope I got a star. It'll be my fifth.'

'She'll kill me. I only did half a page.'

'She'll probably read Ann Byrne's out again.'

Sister Kieran returns to the rostrum. 'Mary McDermott wrote a very good composition this week.'

I look up, surprised, and my glance crashes into the stares of the other girls who in disbelief have turned around in their desks. Above their heads Sister Kieran smiles encouragingly at me.

'Yes, Mary, it was very good. Shall I read it out for you, *a chailíní*?'

Oh, please, God. No.

'Yes, Sister,' chorus the girls. Their curiosity is making them itch. Sister Kieran clears her throat. ' "My House",' she begins. 'I live in a big house in a garden full of flowers . . .'

She has a special voice for reading aloud; all her words are slow and separated, and she speaks like we have to do when we are doing poetry. It doesn't seem like my composition any more.

I turn off the sound and stare at the back of Josephine Kelly's jumper. It's purple with white stripes at the bottom and around the neck. Her mother knitted it for her. Her mother knits all her jumpers, and Patrice Kinsella's mother makes all her frocks. I look down at the ragged sleeves of my jumper and the patched, stained skirt which has long since grown too small for me.

'. . . I have a bedroom all to myself. It reminds me of a rose, because it has pink wallpaper, a fluffy pink carpet and in the centre a big yellow bed. When I go to bed at night, I feel like Thumbelina sitting in the petals of a flower . . .'

On the wall hang pictures which we discuss in *Comhrá*. My favourite one is just beside the statue of Our Lady. It shows Áine helping her Mammy in their bright, shiny kitchen, while Peadar helps Daddy outside in the garden. Everyone in the pictures has round cheeks and they are always happy, even when they are going to school. I close my eyes and step into the picture. I help Áine's mother in the kitchen. Together we sweep and shine and polish. Then I go out into the garden and play with Áine. We are best friends. We play skipping and Áine lets me use her rope for as long as I want. Then we play with Bran, the dog, before Áine's mother calls us for tea.

When the voices of the children are heard on the green
And laughing is heard on the hill,
My heart is at rest within my breast,
And everything else is still.

'. . . I am very happy in my house. It is only a dream house, a house in my head where I like to live, but it belongs to me.'

Sister Kieran looks up. 'That was very good. *Buala bos* for Mary, girls.'

There is a hesitant ripple of clapping and the smell of danger in the air. I'm going to be in for it when we get out to the yard.

I am hungry by lunchtime. There was nothing for breakfast this morning, as Ma doesn't get paid until tomorrow, so we just had a sup of tea. Ma washes dishes in the café at the far side of town. She works nights, because that's when the café does most business, when the cinema, dance hall and pubs have finished for the night. If there's any fish or chips left over, Mrs Casey lets her take them home, and if himself is not in, we all get out of bed while Ma heats it all up in the pan, and eat the lot.

There is a lunchroom at school, across the yard at the back of the cookery room. It has two big windows at each end and in the winter they steam up something terrible. It is freezing cold in there and we all sit at high, shaky tables eating our lunch with numb fingers while the rain streams outside and the window-panes stream inside. Those who have brought their own lunch, parcelled in Kelly's Bread wrappers, swop what they have with each other: a rasher sandwich for a jam; a tomato sandwich for a cheese. Lots of us, though, get bread from the Convent. Every day Sister Gertrude brings over four loaves, fresh from the bakery, and two pounds of butter. In the winter when the butter is hard she slices it up and puts the plate over the Burco boiler for a while. Then she plasters the half-hard, half-runny butter over thick slabs of hot bread. We get cocoa, too, served by two girls from my class from big enamel jugs. I always sit in the corner with my two sisters, Maisie and Julia, who are much younger than me. Maisie is eight and Julia is only five. Between them and me are three boys who go to the Brothers'. Sometimes Sister Gertrude stops by us and tells us that she is praying for us and our poor mother. We just nod and answer 'Yes, Sister,' like Ma told us always to say. There is no sign of the nun today, and over at the far side of the lunchroom I see a crowd of girls from my class huddled together, whispering and looking over at me.

'Come on,' I tell Maisie and Julia, 'we're going outside.'

Silently, they follow me, and we take our usual seats in the corner of the shed where we watch everyone play skipping, tig, or hide-and-seek. Maisie nudges me and I look up to see a crowd of girls walking over to us. They stand around in a circle, blocking out the light of the low sun. I can't see any of their faces in the shadow they cast – just black shapes with the sunlight around the edge of their heads, turning their hair into bright gold halos.

'Mary McDermott wrote a very good composition,' mimics one. I know by the voice that it's Vivienne Clarke, the ringleader. There is a burst of laughter.

'But Mary McDermott will also have to go to Confession, for she is a dirty, wicked girl,' she continues in Sister Kieran's voice.

'Yes, you don't live in a house – you live in a caravan.'

'A dirty caravan.'

'A filthy caravan.'

'A pig-sty.'

'You're full of airs and graces, Mary McDermott.'

'Who do you think you are?'

'You are a liar, that's what you are.'

Then they all chant together:

'You liar, you liar,

Your house is on fire,

Your tongue is as long

As a telephone wire,'

Over and over again. Julia is sobbing into my sleeve and Maisie, who has never cried in her life, clenches her fists, her face white, but her eyes like hot coals, burning into the girls around us. All of a sudden I feel old and tired. I am fourteen years old and still in sixth class. Ma keeps sending me to school here because we can't afford for me to go to the secondary and because she wants me to mind the other two until they can cope on their own. I am older than the lot of them, yet I feel big and stupid.

'I'm not a liar.' I say it quietly, because Ma says there's no point in starting a fight, especially when someone is aching for it. 'Keep your dignity – it's all you've got,' she tells us nearly every day, for fear we would forget. Sometimes, I think that it's herself she's reminding.

'What did you say, Mary McDermott?' There is a silent intake of breath by the whole group. The atmosphere is taut as they move in for the kill. I can feel it, smell it. It has been in my nostrils ever since Easy Target won the Grand National years and years ago.

'I said, I am no liar.'

'But you said you lived in a house and we all know that you

live in a mouldy old caravan.'

'That was my dream home. I mean, you are always talking about marrying a prince and living in a castle. I just want to live in a nice house, that's all.'

There is an insecure silence. They have lost their foothold on me. Finally, Patrice Kinsella breaks the deadlock. 'Come on, let's play tig.'

Indecision. Some begin to move away, but Vivienne Clarke is not about to lose her audience so easily. She raises her voice.

'How's Johnny Burke these days? I bet your mother has been looking after him real well ever since your father walked out on you.'

Gasps of shock at Vivienne's nerve. A thrilled horror shudders through the group. I feel my throat is melting; my chin quivers and I can't control it. My eyes get sore and down spill the tears, hot and silent on my cheeks, dripping into the neck of my jumper.

'Come on,' shouts Patrice Kinsella. Silently, the group moves off and moments later I hear them screaming and laughing.

Far, far away Maisie is muttering curses and threats, her voice thick with pain, and Julia's sobs have turned to hiccups. I hardly hear them anymore. I have gone into my head again and am floating down, down through soft silent green fields, alone and free.

When the voices of the children are heard on the green,
And laughing is heard on the hill . . .

After school, Sister Kieran calls me aside as the class is leaving.

'Do you like writing compositions, Mary?'

'Yes, Sister.'

'Good, keep it up.'

'Yes, Sister.'

'Do you like anything else?'

'Poetry, Sister.'

'What?'

'Poetry, Sister,' and I pull the book out of my bag.

'William Blake. But where did you get this?'

'Me granny gave it to me for me birthday when I was young, Sister.'

'I see. There must be a bit of the poet in you, too, Mary,' and she smiles at me.

'Yes, Sister. Thank you, Sister.'

In the summer, when the weather is warm, we take a short cut home through the fields, but in winter they are wet and soggy, so we have to go home through the town. Up the street we go, past the road that leads to our old house, past the women standing at their doors gossiping. They stop talking as we approach, then wait until we have passed before making comments. Grey women, with grey tight perms and grey tight lips.

Up past the shops, also grey in the disappearing daylight; small, mean shops with fancy names on signs overhead. Gibbons, the butcher, calls himself a Victualler; John Flaherty, who owns the sweet shop is a Newsagent; Tierney's chemist is a Pharmacy, and Hughes, the bookie is a Turf Accountant. Strange trades, hostile and unwelcoming to the likes of us.

I have many memories of Hughes. When I was Julia's age and older, Ma used to send me down there in the afternoons to bring Da back for his tea. I'd stand inside the door, peering through the smoke for him, while men, old and young, filled the shop, silently watching the races on television. Cigarette butts on the floor, the grim rays of a lone bulb overhead. As soon as Da would see me, he'd hunt me outside and tell me to wait there for him. And there I'd stand, patiently waiting and wondering which face he'd be wearing when he came out. The broad smile, the rubbing of his hands together, the tenpence for me – that was the more infrequent one. 'Run on home,' he'd tell me, 'and tell your mother I'll be back shortly. I'm just going to have one pint in Casey's to celebrate.' And we wouldn't see him until midnight.

If he lost, he'd emerge with a look of complete bewilderment on his face. He would raise his cap on two fingers and scratch his head with the rest for inspiration. On these occasions, which grew more and more frequent over the years, he would not return until midnight either; his credit in Casey's was always good, until he lost his job and then our house.

As we pass Keating's grocery we hear someone calling us. We turn around to see Mr Keating himself beckon to us hastily. He ushers us into the shop, fills a brown paper bag with broken biscuits and pushes it into my hands.

'Good girls,' he says, looking around in case his wife appears. 'Bring those home with you now and don't eat them on the way. Run along now.'

We have stopped outside the shop to examine the contents of the bag when Maisie tugs at my sleeve. 'Look, there's Da.'

I spin around. He is coming out of Hughes, cap raised, scratching his head. He sees us staring at him and quickly turns his back. I begin to walk on, but Julia breaks free of Maisie and runs down the street after him, shouting 'Da! Da!' She hurls herself at his legs and sobs into his trousers. Startled, he looks down at her.

'Whisht there, child of grace, or you'll have the whole town thinking I'm after beating you or something,' but Julia, her arms wrapped around his hips, doesn't hear him. Maisie and I walk back down to drag her away before she disgraces us all.

'Hello, Da.'

'Eh, hello, hello. Look, could you do something with this child? She has me wringing wet.' Da calls us all 'child', because he can never remember our names. We prise Julia's arms off and stand there for a moment. Da looks up and down the street as though he were searching for an escape.

'Are you being good children?'

'Yes, Da.'

'And are you going to school and doing your lessons?'

'Yes, Da.'

Silence. He looks different. The red flush is gone from his face, his eyes aren't glassy any more and he has lost weight from around his belly.

'You're looking well, Da.' He looks at me, surprised.

'Is that so, now?'

'Yes, Da.'

Silence again. We turn to move away.

'Just a minute, Ju – , Mais – , Mary.' I walk back slowly.

'Yes, Da?'

'Is he still staying with your mo-, is he still there in the caravan?'

'He is, Da.'

'I see.'

We stand at an angle, both looking away. 'Well, goodbye – ' I say.

'Listen, tell your mother I'm off the drink. Tell her I'm off it these past four weeks and that you thought I was looking well.'

'I will, Da.'

'Don't forget now.' He roots in his pocket for some money, but pulls his hand out empty. Again he lifts his cap and scratches his head.

The road narrows, rising sharply up over a humpy bridge. If we look over it we can see the single railway track stretching endlessly into the distance. We are nearly home. Maisie and Julia have forgotten about Da and play at being two of Mrs Morgan's geese we've just passed on the road. Old Mrs Morgan likes to let her geese roam free, and every day they chase us, hissing like snakes, long necks stretched forward to nip our ankles. It is the only thing I know of which frightens the life out of Maisie. But the gate into the yard was closed today and we got our own back. We stuck our heads through the bars and poked sticks at the gaggle inside. The geese flapped their wings, hissed and squawked, their eyes blazing with hatred. We were gone by the time old Mrs Morgan could get to the door.

Once over the bridge, the road swings sharply to the left and leads downhill to our caravan, sitting like a fat, blue bubble at the side of the road. Its tow hitch rests on a rusty milk crate.

'I'm going to tell Ma that we got biscuits,' shouts Maisie suddenly, and races down the hill.

'That's not fair! I want to tell her,' and Julia chases after her. Down they run ahead of me, coats flapping open in the cold wind and their hair snaking around their heads in rats' tails. I have some news for Ma myself: about my composition being read out in class and about Da. If I don't hurry too, they'll have told her everything. I notice that the big black bicycle is nowhere to be seen. Good. I step inside.

The caravan looks no worse than usual; perhaps it's the commotion I caused today in school today over 'My House' that makes me see it with different eyes. An occupied mousetrap greets me at the door. Over in the far corner the trash can stinks. A saucepan of stew bubbles on the stove and directly overhead swings a rolled-out fly-paper. The windows are grimy and the big one at the end is covered with a blanket to keep out prying eyes. My real house.

'Hello, Ma.'

'There you are. I'll get your dinner.' She shuffles in burst slippers over to the stove and spoons some stew onto a greasy plate that one of the boys probably ate from. She puts the stew on the table in front of me. In the gravy floats some cigarette ash. Maisie and Julia slurp down the last of their dinner and go over to one of the beds where they begin their homework.

The baby is playing quietly in her pen, an old wooden tea-chest. Her face is livid from teething and her mouth dribbles saliva, mixed with the traces of something black. I go over to check what she has been eating.

'Where are the boys?' I ask Ma.

'Gone hunting rabbits. They should be home soon – it's nearly dark.'

'Where's himself?'

'God only knows.' She moves back to the table and sits opposite me.

As I eat I watch her from the corner of my eye. The bruising around her face and neck is turning to yellow. Her hair hangs limply into her eyes. Now and then a shaking hand rises to draw the cigarette away from her lips. She has grown old and thin, with skin like that of a dried-up lemon and a voice like rusty nails.

'Maisie was saying you got biscuits from Mr Keating.'

'Yes,' and I pull the crumpled bag out of my satchel. Within seconds I am surrounded by shouting, pushing children. The boys appear from nowhere and join in the struggle, grabbing the bag and strewing the contents around the floor. The baby starts to howl and Ma sends Julia over to her with a bit of a Ginger Nut to ease her gums. A few half-Digestives lay on the table. I shove them over to Ma and get up to wet the tea.

'We met Da in town today.' Although I am standing with my back to her, I can sense her stiffen. She gets up and begins to clear the dishes away with a clatter.

'Is that so? Drunk was he?'

'No, he was sober.'

Ma gives a loud, dry laugh. 'Ha, that'll be the day!'

'Honest to God. He told me to tell you that he hasn't touched a drop in fou-, five weeks. He's looking shocking well, Ma.'

Ma's mouth is so tight the cigarette is almost flat at the tip. I try again.

'At least he never raised a hand to you, like Johnny Blake.'

'No, but it's thanks to his gambling that we're in this mess now. We had a house, respectability, food on the table. He's thrown it all away, and us with it.'

'He wanted to know if himself was still staying with you.' Ma sits down again, leaving the table half-tidied. The fight left her long ago.

'God help me, God help me.'

I think of us all alone with Johnny Blake when she goes out to work, of the way he beats us to keep us quiet, of the way he terrorises Ma by threatening he'll leave her one of the days. I hate him. I hate his black, greasy hair, his sweat of him. Once I found his good trousers hanging up in the airing cupboard over the stove. I shoved them right up against the chimney and burned two holes in the leg.

'Ma, you could always tell him to go.'

'And what then? A woman with nine children needs a man, Mary. You don't understand that yet. A woman needs a man in her life. God help me.'

'Da was looking very well, Ma, and he hasn't touched a drop in six weeks.' But she isn't listening any more.

When I go into my head, I often return to the times when we all lived together at Granny Dargan's, when I was the best in the class and had loads of friends, when Da used to pinch Ma's bottom and whisper things in her ear. I remember Granny Dargan pushing the boys in the go-cart while Ma and Da took each of my hands and swung me high into the air: 'One, two, three, oops-a-daisy.' I remember how Granny used to say Da had Ma spoiled and that she'd never make a housewife. But it's Ma's laughter I remember most. At the weekends, when we were sent to bed, she and Da would sneak down to the pub as soon as they thought we were asleep. I would creep out of bed and stand behind the lace curtains, watching them on their way down the street until they disappeared into the darkness. Then, like a trace of perfume lingering in the air, I would hear the soft laughter floating back to me.

> My mother taught me underneath a tree
> And sitting down before the heat of day,
> She took me on her lap and kissed me.

I remember the day that Da won the Grand National. The night before, he had scored three bullseyes at darts, and Easy Target seemed to be the horse to back, even though it had odds of fifty-to-one. Easy Target by Runaway Lad out of Shady Lady. I can still see that day in the kitchen: Da, face white, ear glued to the loudspeaker, while the man in the radio droned out the positions on the track; then, as Easy Target broke loose and made for the post, the man's voice growing louder and higher, and Da shouting into the radio, as if the horse could hear.

He won five thousand pounds that day. Ma got a suite for the parlour and we all got new clothes.

'Sheila,' he said to Ma that Sunday as we paraded down to Mass, 'I have the feeling that I was born under a lucky star. Easy Target has been the start of something new for us. A few more bets like that and we're home and dry.'

It's ten o'clock. Ma has gone to work, the children have their homework done and are in bed. I turn down the gas light and get undressed as fast as I can before he comes home. He's not back yet; he might be out all night; maybe he won't come back at all. I hear a snigger from the boys' bed. They're peeping again, and I turn off the light altogether before taking off the rest of my clothes.

My vest and knickers are cleaner and more decent than my outer wear. Every now and then Sister Aquinas takes me out of class and brings me over to the convent for a bath. I slip and slide around in the huge tub and look for spiders lurking in the corners of the high, high ceiling. I look at the hairs growing under my arms and on my bottom, and I feel the little rings forming around each breast. And sometimes I just float and dream and watch the bubbles rising to the surface of the water when I fart.

Sister Aquinas comes in afterwards to comb my hair and put it in a plait. Once, when the girls in my class had been mean to me, I cried and she took my head and clasped me to her big, low bosom. I curled up snug against her softness, breathing in the smells of beeswax and talcum powder from her habit.

'You poor child,' she said as she rocked me to and fro, 'your sad situation has made you an easy target for the mockery of cruel, ignorant people.'

Easy target, how right she was. Easy Target by Runaway Lad out of Shady Lady, with odds at fifty to one against ever winning this race.

It's warm in the bed beside Maisie and Julia. I pull the

blankets and coats over me and, as I shape myself into Julia's back, the smell of unwashed bodies fills my nose, a warm smell, familiar and somehow comforting to me.

I listen for the sound of regular breathing, and when I am sure that everyone is asleep I reach across for my frock and pull three nearly-whole biscuits out of the pocket: a Ginger Nut, a Morning Coffee and a Chocolate Wafer. If I chew them slowly they will last me half an hour. And as I linger over the sweetness of each bit, I enter a field on fire with poppies and chase down to a gap in the hedge which leads to green plains, stretching on endlessly.

Sleep, baby, sleep,
Our cottage vale is deep;
The little lamb is on the green
With woolly fleece so soft and clean
Sleep, baby, sleep

While far, far away there's the sound of a bicycle being thrown against the side of the caravan.

A CLEAR NIGHT

CATHERINE COAKLEY

One night in early September he walked away from her. She could not remember what they had fought about. He walked quickly across the road. The traffic lights turned from red to green, and over the shining roofs of cars she watched his thin shape disappear over the bridge, his arms and his coat swinging. She stood there while people passed and then she decided to walk by the river. Lights shone from shop windows, neon signs flashed, and across the river under the bright street lamps houses of red, brown and grey faced her. The river looked cool and smooth. It was a still night. Soon she left the shops behind and walked by red-brick houses with small, shadowy gardens. She felt excited and frightened. She might walk all night, to places in the city she had never seen before. She might just follow the river as far as she could go.

Time passed and the streets emptied. She grew cold and tired and nervously watched approaching headlights. When she saw a clock tower showing twenty past twelve she felt a panic rise. He would be home, waiting, his temper cooled or at least controlled. She remembered passing a guesthouse and she knew she had enough money to pay for one or two nights. It was late but she could invent a story. She rang the bell. The woman whose tired face appeared in the doorway seemed more annoyed than curious and simply said, 'You'll have to pay now,' and taking the money led the way to a room on the top floor.

She locked the door and sat down. She could hardly believe she was doing this and felt she wanted to catch her breath as if she had been running hard. She went to the window. A clear night; in the distance lights shimmered like low stars. The roof-tops beneath her shone smooth and grey under the cold moon. She switched off the light and began to undress. There were no curtains on the window. The sound of footsteps passed and grew faint as someone walked quickly under the trees below. That, she thought, could be me walking home. But the sound of the footsteps faded and then nothing. She was amazed by the silence of the night. She thought of him in their heated bedroom, a room filled with his silences. They were not like this cool, dark silence, she thought as she lay between the damp, white sheets.

The first thing she saw when she woke up was a tall red-brick chimney in a blue sky. A bell rang and children's voices drifted up from the road. While she dressed she watched a slow line of traffic pass below. Suddenly she felt unsure. What would she do now? The thought of meeting her landlady this morning, or even other guests, frightened her. At the foot of the stairs, when she was hoping to slip out quietly, she met a young girl wearing an apron. They looked at each other and the girl said, 'Breakfast is in here,' and pointed to an open door. The room was empty and she sat at the nearest table. As she was pouring some tea a man came in. He seemed not to notice her and sat with his head down. His shoes looked new. His trousers were neatly pressed. On his hand she was amazed to see four large blue letters, one on each finger, spelling LOVE. She looked at his face expecting to see the face of a boy. But his face was thin and hard looking.

She suspected that her husband would go to work but still she was nervous going back to the house. The kitchen table was littered with crumbs and used dishes. She took her bank book from the drawer. She went upstairs and put some clothes into a bag. It occurred to her that he might be worried. At the very least he might report her missing and the police might look for her. So she wrote a note saying, 'Don't worry about me, Peter. I'm sorry but I won't be back. There's not much point saying anything else. I'll be in touch sometime.'

This is what I want to do, she told herself as she gathered together the few things she wanted. There seemed to be so few things she wanted that she was suddenly shocked by the emptiness of her life. She sat down and looked around her at the familiar objects to which she felt no attachment. She saw a letter on the sideboard addressed to her. It was her sister's handwriting. She took it and left the house. On the bus she examined the small card the landlady had given her. *The Riverview Guesthouse*, 27, North Quay.

It was noon when she stood again on the steps of her new home, her few belongings upstairs in her room. The sun was warm on her face when she lifted it to watch the seagulls that flew overhead. The school doors opened and a large group of children ran onto the footpath, talking and laughing as they passed her. The feeling of bright activity pleased her. She battled her way through the blue-uniformed tide and headed towards the city.

'Dear Irene,

Hello and how are you. You'll be glad to hear that Sean has passed his exams and now he's looking for a job. It's not easy to get anything around here so we thought we might come up to the city for a few days and look around. Sean is not the world's greatest genius but there must be some decent kind of a job that he'd do well at. Anyway, we thought we might come up next week and stay with yourself and Peter for a few days . . .'

Irene put the unfinished letter into her pocket, finished her cup of coffee and left the restaurant. She had spent most of the day walking around the city. Tired, she returned to the guesthouse at six o'clock. To her surprise the dining room was full. She shared a table with two girls and listened to them talking about their jobs in a department store in the city. The room buzzed with the sound of talking and eating. She tried to compose a reply to her sister but she could hardly think of words to describe what she had done. The day of aimless walking had filled her with a kind of emptiness, as though she had walked all feeling out of herself. In her room, she watched the tall chimney disappear into the darkness. In the distance a grey church spire pointed crookedly towards the evening moon. Lights came on in the buildings around her. People were eating, talking, sitting, walking up stairs, facing into an evening with purpose. Was it really, she asked herself, only one day that had passed?

'It was by chance really that I got the job,' she told Mrs

O'Mahony, her landlady. 'I just happened to be passing the cinema when I saw this notice looking for new people and I got the job. It will keep me going and I'd like to hold on to the room for a while, if that suits you?'

But there was more she did not tell her landlady. Almost three weeks had passed since that night she left Peter and she had begun to lose hope of ever getting a job. She had not worked for many years because Peter said it was not necessary. She tried shops, hotels and restaurants. That afternoon she was on her way to a hotel when she saw Peter walking towards her. She looked around for some place to hide. Just beside her was a cinema and she pushed open the glass doors and went inside. She watched him as he passed. She leaned against the wall, her heart pounding. The girl in the ticket office looked at her. She had often imagined meeting him and had planned to be calm and distant.

'The picture is half over,' the girl in the office said. Irene bought a ticket anyway. Inside the dark auditorium she waited for someone to show her to a seat. After standing for some time, and when her eyes grew accustomed to the darkness, she sat down. Her eyes wandered to the screen but her mind was filled with the image of his face passing so close to her on the other side of those glass doors. He had been staring straight ahead like an actor crossing a stage.

When the lights came on again she got up and caught the eye of the man she had seen that first morning in the guesthouse. He nodded to her as he passed and her face grew red at the thought that he might have seen her coming in to the cinema so late and fumbling for her seat. Rain had started. Irene hung back to shelter and it was then she saw the notice saying, 'Usher/ette Wanted. Apply to Mr Green.' She thought for a few moments and then went back inside.

The following night she started work. The cinema was small but busy. Mr Green was a gentle, middle-aged man. He ran the cinema and worked in the projection room. He told her that the owners were planning to sell out soon. On that first night, Irene looked out anxiously for familiar faces, and when the lights went down and the film started, she went with relief to her seat in an alcove. She faced the audience, not the screen. In the flickering light she watched them, the couples as they moved towards each other under cover of the dim light and the larger activities on the screen. As the night passed, she relaxed.

Irene bought curtains for the window in her room. She bought a radio and an electric fire. Sometimes she sat with her landlady, watching television or drinking tea. Mrs O'Mahony grew more friendly. Her sitting-room was full of small ornaments on the mantelpiece and in glass cabinets that lined the walls. When Mrs O'Mahony crossed the room a slight tinkle rose from the china cats, dogs and other animals, as though they were responding to her. She spoke of her dead husband and her absent children. She never asked questions and Irene sat contented among the bright flowers of the narrow couch. Mostly Irene spent the time happily alone, watching the boats sail up the river, the swans flying in the evenings and the smoke hanging low over the city.

Late one night she was sitting in her landlady's drowsy room when they heard the front door opening. Mrs O'Mahony rushed towards the door. Irene caught a glimpse of a startled face as light from the room filled the hall. The door closed again and she could hear low voices in the hall. When the older woman came back into the room she asked, 'Have you met Mr Walsh?'

Irene said, 'No,' and added that she had seen him around the guesthouse and once in the cinema.

'That doesn't surprise me, since he doesn't have a job. I don't know why I keep people like him. Nobody else would.'

Irene wanted to ask about the tattoo on his fingers but Mrs O'Mahony began to rearrange her brittle animals on the mantelpiece and Irene felt it was time to leave.

Later that week he came to the cinema again. He smiled at her as she led him to a seat. When she left that night he was waiting for her, standing under a street lamp with his hands in his pockets. She said hello and they fell into step together.

They walked in silence for a while.

'Did you enjoy the film?' Irene asked.

'I suppose,' he replied, shrugging his shoulders. 'It was OK'

'I don't really enjoy them any more. You know, looking at the same one night after night.'

'You working there long?'

'About a month.'

'What did you do before?' he asked her.

'Nothing much,' Irene smiled. 'I suppose I was a housewife.'

'Got any kids?'

'No.'

'Got a husband?'

Irene shook her head but said nothing. She hoped he wouldn't ask her any more questions.

'Want to go for a drink?' He turned towards her. Irene guessed that he was in his early twenties. He was very thin and less well dressed now than when she had first seen him. 'There's a pub near here that I know,' he continued. Irene agreed and immediately regretted it. The bar was crowded and everyone there seemed very young. She looked around anxiously. She couldn't hear what he was saying to her. The loud music made her feel dizzy. There was no place to sit down. He was asking her what she wanted to drink. She asked for a glass of orange juice.

She watched him standing at the bar, joking with a dark-haired girl. Then a young man came over and the three of them were talking and laughing. Standing in the middle of the bar, alone, Irene tried to decide whether to walk over to the group or leave. She turned and left.

She lay awake for a long time that night. Each time she heard the front door closing she wondered if it was him and if she should get up and apologise. A few days later she met him again, in the dining room.

'Don't worry about it,' he said. 'First I figured you had gone to the toilet. Then I thought maybe you were sick or something. I met some old buddies anyway. It's no hassle.'

'It was just the noise and the heat and everything, I did suddenly feel a bit sick. I'm not usually like that. It's just difficult for me.'

'Yeah, well, some other time maybe,' he said and left the dining room.

She wasn't really surprised to see him waiting for her when she left work that night. They went to a quiet bar, though it was almost closing time. They walked slowly back to the guesthouse. When they got to the front door he said, 'You go in without me. I have to go see somebody.'

Irene went up to her room and undressed. She thought about how each day and each new thing she did carried her further away from the things she had left. Sometimes she felt weighed down by so much unfinished business but she pushed it aside.

They met regularly after that, hardly ever by arrangement but often he would be waiting for her when she left the cinema. Irene felt relaxed in his company and they laughed a lot, but still she felt she hardly knew him. She knew he was from another city and that he was looking for work here. Sometimes he was quiet and moody. But their detachment from one another suited Irene.

One morning he knocked on her door. He said he had borrowed a car from a friend and asked her if she would like to go for a drive. They drove out of the city. Because it was winter, the countryside was bare and empty. He drove fast along the narrow roads. They drove up a hill and soon she was looking down into the valley. They had passed a dam and the valley was flooded. Here the river spread out like a long lake. She asked him to stop. Across the river she saw small farmhouses. Clouds moved quickly across the sky and light spread across the water. She remembered that this was the same river she watched from her window.

'Isn't it nice,' she said, 'to think that this is the same river that flows through the city. I can see it from my bedroom. It looks so different.'

He looked at her.

'Sometimes I can't make you out.' He shook his head. 'You're always saying things like that. It's nice you know. It's different. I like it.'

Irene smiled.

'It's just, it's hard to explain, but my whole world has opened up lately. Just to be sitting here. It's like another world, really.'

The car rocked gently in the wind. He leaned towards her. Every sound seemed so loud, even the sound of his hand against the fabric of her coat. She rested her head against the back of the seat and closed her eyes. The wind carried the distant sound of a machine, a moan rising from across the river.

Later, when they came back to the house, he followed her to her room. She turned off the light and they lay on the bed together.

After they made love Irene slept for a while. When she woke up she saw that Brian was awake also. They began to talk.

'I used to think that I was too young when I got married,' Irene said. 'Now I wonder if it makes any difference what age people get married. I was twenty-one. Have you ever been married?'

'No, I was never married but I have two kids. They live with their mother and they have nothing to do with me.'

'That's sad,' Irene said.

'Not really,' he shrugged. She looked at his thin shoulders. He was sitting up, leaning against the wall. 'They're better off.

I'm not cut out for that business.'

'We never had any children. I suppose that was part of our problem. Peter was very set in his ways when I met him. He was in his thirties. He was living in his parents' house. They were dead. In the beginning I was sorry that we couldn't have any children. But later on I was glad. Because I found out that I didn't really love Peter. He wasn't a bad person or anything, but sometimes I used to think that he was dead inside. And he wouldn't have been able to love children. I don't think he would. I think even the day we got married, I knew it was the wrong thing to do. After we left the reception I cried for most of the train journey. He was so embarrassed. And he hadn't a clue how to console me. I was only a child.'

'I was eighteen when my first child was born,' Brian said. 'I didn't want a child. She didn't either. But I hung around. She was living with her mother. Then the next year she had another baby. And I took off. I couldn't handle it, you know?'

Irene was thinking about her sister. She had written to her trying to explain what had happened but she didn't send her the new address. She knew her sister would be shocked. She knew that if they met it would be an awkward and difficult meeting.

'How did you get those letters on your hand?' she asked him, tracing them with her fingers.

'Oh you know, just kids messing. You do these things.'

'Do you regret it now?'

'Well, I'd prefer if I didn't have them. But what's the use in regrets. That's a waste of time.'

After that evening, he came to her room often. Soon Mrs

O'Mahony stopped asking her in for tea. Irene suggested to him that they find a place of their own. He agreed but always put off looking for a flat or a bedsit.

'Things are getting a bit awkward here,' she said to him. 'The way the landlady looks at me. She hardly gives me the time of day now.'

'She still takes your money doesn't she? And mine too,' he replied.

Just before Christmas he disappeared. They had arranged to meet outside the cinema but when she came out he was not there. She went home to bed. She watched for him in the guesthouse over the next few days. She didn't want to ask the landlady about him but she learned from the young girl who worked in the kitchen that he had left without paying what he owed.

Irene felt angry, then worried. She thought of all the nights when he was not around and wouldn't tell her where he had been. He had talked about getting a job but that had never happened. His room was cleaned out. Irene found a cardboard box outside her door with his clothes in it. The box sat in the corner of her room, the clothes sadly familiar. There was nothing else in the box.

She walked around the city looking at the Christmas lights, watching out for him. Then two weeks after he had disappeared, she got a letter from him. At first she could hardly take in what it said. He was in prison. He was asking her to visit him. That night she couldn't sleep. She didn't even know where the prison was. She tried to imagine what it was like for him. She worried about going there.

The following day she took a taxi to the prison. She rang the bell and waited outside the huge metal gates. The door opened and she stepped into a dark entrance. The guard directed her to a waiting room. It was crowded with people, women and children. The walls were bare. They all waited for a long time. The children were bored and restless. The women's faces looked tired and resigned. Irene listened to the sound of gates banging and voices calling. Then she was called to the visiting room. This was a long room with a wide counter dividing it. There were no chairs. One side of the room was crowded with families, and on the other side stood men, leaning against the counter. There was a lot of noise.

Then she saw Brian. He was leaning on the high counter, his elbows resting on the surface. He was staring straight ahead. His face was expressionless. She walked towards him. She though how young he looked. He smiled when he saw her. She reached across to hold his hand.

'No touching,' said a voice behind her.

'Thanks for coming,' Brian said.

Irene said nothing. In the silence that fell between them she heard the voice of the girl beside her. 'Of course I'm sure you don't think I'd make up . . . '

In the crowded room people had to shout to be heard. It was getting hot.

'What happened, Brian?'

Brian looked over at the guard sitting in the corner. Then he looked back at her.

'Why are you here, Brian? Tell me.'

'All right. Look, I'm sorry for dragging you up to this place.

But I don't think I'll be here for long.'

'But what did you do?'

'Look, Irene, you don't know me very well. When I met you first at the guest house, I was just out of prison. And because I wasn't from the city, the social worker put me up there. Trying to help me out. I'm not a big-time criminal or anything. I was done for robbing. Robbing a shop. They caught me in the act. It was pretty stupid.'

Irene looked at his hands, clasping and unclasping.

'Robbing,' she said in disbelief. 'What would you be robbing for?'

He laughed.

'Money of course. What else?'

'We had plenty of money, between us, didn't we? I could have given you some.'

'Oh, I don't know. I met these guys and I just went along with them. It's fun, you know? Sometimes you're lucky, sometimes you're not.'

'Why didn't you tell me any of this?'

'Listen, I was trying to make a go of it this time. I was thinking to myself that things might be different. Hoping to go straight and all that. I thought things could be different. Meeting you and everything...' His voice trailed off.

He lifted his arms off the counter and stood up straight. Irene looked around at all the people, leaning toward each other across the wide counter, heads huddled together, trying to get a few moments of privacy.

'Look,' said Brian, shaking his head, 'I knew you'd feel like this.'

'Like what?'

'Like you'd be annoyed. Like you wouldn't understand. We're different.'

'Well, I don't understand,' Irene said. 'I don't understand how you could be so stupid. And me too, I've been stupid. I brought you some cigarettes.'

She opened her bag.

'They're in here somewhere,' she said, leaning over her bag. She began to cry.

'Jesus, don't start crying,' Brian said, looking around him. He put his hands in his pockets and half turned away from her.

'Just leave the cigarettes at the front gate on the way out. You're not allowed to give them to me here anyway.'

A cold wind blew against her as she made her way from the prison. One of the packets of cigarettes fell from her open bag. She had forgotten to leave them at the desk. When she got home, she called the cinema and told them she was sick. She thought about calling Peter, then laughed bitterly at the idea. It was four months since she had left him. She thought about the dark streets she had walked that night. She felt she was still walking them.

That Christmas week Irene put up the Christmas tree in the lobby of the cinema. Around the city people looked busy and happy. On Christmas Day she went to Mass in the Cathedral. The guesthouse was quiet. Many people had gone home for the holidays. Later, she drank a bottle of wine in her room. She ate the food she had bought for her Christmas dinner. She fell asleep watching the television.

The week after Christmas, Brian wrote to her. His writing

was childlike. She was moved by the letter. It was sad and loving. It seemed to be easier for him to write down his feelings. She didn't go to visit him again. It was easier for her also to write 'I miss you' or 'I send you my love'.

In one of his letters he suggested that they find their own place together. Irene thought about this and then set about finding a flat. Eventually she got a small two-roomed flat quite close to the guesthouse. She moved all her things in and wrote to Brian. 'When you come out this time, you'll have your own place. I'm doing it up as best I can to make it homely. This time things can be different for you. I can't wait to see you again. I think about you a lot. I think I can help you now, to make things better for yourself when you get out.'

In March he came home. Irene stood speechless in the doorway. She had been getting ready to go to work. The flat was messy.

'What are you . . . how did you get out so soon?' she asked.

'I don't know,' Brian laughed. 'They just said to me "Pack your kit. You're going." And I didn't argue.'

He pulled her toward him and began to kiss her. He had been drinking. She tried to pull away from him.

'I'm just going out the door to work, Brian.'

'Work!' Brian laughed. 'Forget that. I've just been locked up for three months. Here I am.'

'It's so great that you're out. It's just that I wasn't expecting you.' She moved away from him and began to tidy the room.

'Forget that. Leave it. Come on, let's go out. We'll celebrate.'

Irene looked at him. This wasn't the kind of homecoming she had imagined. She had pictured herself sitting, waiting happily. Food on the table.

'I can't ring them now at the last moment. Why don't I go to work and we can meet afterwards? Then we'll celebrate.' She put her arms around him. 'We'll celebrate together, in our new flat.'

He picked up his coat again.

'Are you coming or not?' he said angrily.

'Look,' she said. 'Don't be disappointed. Maybe I could . . .'

But before she could finish, he had turned and left.

She walked slowly to work. Maybe, she told herself, I could have tried to get the night off. They don't really need me that much. Maybe, she told herself, I didn't really want to. Who does he think he is to come breezing in and expect me to drop everything? She had to admit to herself that even though she had been happy to see him, she had been frightened too.

When she left work, he was not waiting. She decided to go home in case he was there. But then she remembered he didn't have a key.

Later he knocked quietly on the door. She got out of bed and let him in. He followed her to the bedroom and sat on the bed. He seemed calm. She sat beside him.

'I'm sorry about tonight, Brian.' She took his hand. 'We can start again now, like you just came in the door, like you're just arriving.'

He looked at her. She could tell by the look on his face that he was very drunk.

'OK Here I am. Home from prison.'

He reached out and touched her breast.

It was morning. Irene could hear rain falling. When she opened her eyes she saw Brian sitting by the window. He was sitting quite still, the only movement was his hand lifting a cigarette to his mouth. It was a graceful movement. The smoke drifted up into the morning light. He was wearing a trousers and vest. His bare feet were resting on the window ledge. In the harsh light, with his feet bare and his thin arms bare, he seemed exposed. He was not aware of her watching him. He was staring off into the distance, down into the city with a frightening look of sadness on his face.

He turned and saw her.

'Couldn't you sleep?' she asked, raising herself on one arm in the bed.

'I've done enough sleeping in that place.'

'Do you want to talk about it?'

'About what?'

'About prison, what it's like. I often wondered what it was like. I tried to imagine.'

'Talk,' he said, turning away from her again. 'I'm just out of the place. Why would I want to be talking about it? I just want to forget about it.'

He got up and walked over to the bed. He sat on the bed.

'I've made plans,' he said. 'This city gets me down. I think we should leave, maybe go to England. I know some people there.'

He waited for her to say something.

'Actually I've even got a ticket.'

He pulled it out of his trousers pocket and handed it to her. She put it on the bed beside her.

'When did you get this?' she asked him. 'You only got out yesterday.'

'They gave it to me at the prison. The social worker got it for me because I told her I wanted to go to England. I told her I had a job there. So she fixed me up with the ticket.'

'But why do you want to go there?'

'I just have to get away from here. I'm just going to get into trouble if I hang around. I know I will. Look, there's not much for you to hang around for either, is there? You won't have to be watching over your shoulder all the time, wondering if your husband is around. Keeping your head down in the street.'

'But that's just running away,' Irene said.

'So what?' he shouted, lighting another cigarette. 'So what if we run away. I can start again. You can too. I can get a job. We can get a decent place to live. OK I was only in for a short stretch this time. But I'll end up doing longer. We can do better. I was talking to a bloke up there, who was in London for a few years. He did pretty well there.'

'Why did he come home then?'

'I don't know. He had some reason. But I know he was making good money over there.'

Irene got out of bed and began to get dressed.

'I don't know, Brian. These last few months have been hard for me. Like my whole life has turned upside down. Everything's changed. Half the time I think I don't know what I'm doing. I think am I crazy or what and how did I get here? I'm just trying to get used to something, and then something else happens. Like suddenly I'm working in a cinema and suddenly I'm in a prison and then . . .'

She looked at him and smiled. 'If you saw what I came from you'd laugh. It's like a different world, Brian.'

'OK So you've done something different. So things have changed or whatever. Well, this is just one more change. Just one more thing and then we can settle in and have a decent life. It's just like one more step, you know. What have you got to lose? Nothing. You've got nothing. Just like me. So what's the big deal?'

'I'll think about it, Brian. Just let me think about it for a while.'

It rained every day and Brian sat in the room like a trapped animal. When he did go out she worried about him. She wondered where he was and who he was with. By the end of the week she had bought a ticket for the boat and they were packing. At the cinema she said goodbye and left as quietly as she had come there. She thought of writing to her sister but decided to wait until she got to England.

On Saturday morning they left the flat and went to the bus station. The bus crawled through the busy traffic. Brian sat on the edge of his seat, nervous and quiet. When they reached the quay they got off the bus and crossed the car park to the terminal. They walked slowly through the bare, hut-like buildings. There was a queue. Irene felt the wetness seeping through her clothes. She could hear the rain drumming relentlessly on the roof. Through a dirty window she could see the huge side of the boat.

'Brian.' She tugged urgently at his sleeve.

'What's wrong?' he asked, looking for his ticket. 'Did you forget something?'

'Brian, come over here for a minute.' She tried to pull him out of the queue. She walked away a few yards. He followed her.

'We're going to lose our place,' he said impatiently. 'What's wrong with you now?'

'I just can't go, Brian.'

He stared at her.

'Why not?'

'I don't know. I just can't. I just feel like . . . I just don't know if it's the right thing to do. I mean, did we really think it through enough?'

'Come on. You can't be serious. You're saying this now. We're at the boat and you're saying this.'

'I know. I'm sorry. I'm really sorry. But I'm not going, Brian. Not now anyway. Maybe you should go and maybe later I can follow you but I don't think I can face it now. It's just too much.'

He gripped her arm.

'Come on, Irene. You must come with me now. I want you to come. I thought we had settled everything.'

Irene looked at him. His hair was wet and flattened against his head. He looked like a child. She looked down at the cement floor, at the dirty pools of water gathering there. He still held her arm and shook her slightly. Then he let go and turned and walked onto the boat.

Irene found herself walking by the river again. It was a long walk from the quays to the city but she didn't care. The huge cranes by the warehouses were still, like mechanical creatures at rest. She touched the key in her pocket. She should have spoken sooner, she told herself. She told herself that she knew all along she wouldn't leave. It was true she had little to stay for. You can still go, she told herself, but she kept on walking. When she got back to the house she knocked on the landlord's door and told him she wanted to stay in the flat. Then she climbed the stairs and let herself in. She went to the window. She couldn't see the boat of course, but looked across the rain-soaked city. She took off her clothes and got into bed. Later, the sound of a ship's siren floated up the river, a lonely haunting sound.

CASUALTY OF 'CASUALTY'

MARY McENROY

It was fortunate for Helen that the car, instead of crunching her beneath its wheels, threw her up on the bonnet and left her dangling there shouting 'Stop, stop,' until she flopped down on the road, by which time the vehicle had ceased its violent, headlong dash into the night.

The driver was concerned about her. He took off his coat and tucked it around her. The little group of commuters waiting at the bus stop gravitated towards her, attentive.

The driver wouldn't let her move. The commuters wouldn't. They addressed an occasional remark to one another, desultory comments, the *modus colloquiendi* of strangers who have no intention of becoming acquainted. Helen knew what they were saying: 'She's too old for this . . . too old to be knocked down . . . too old to be carried on the bonnet of a car . . . too old to be thrown down on a hard road . . . '

'Like a flying saucer,' she'd have appended had they included her in the conversation.

Was it a concrete road, she wondered, or tarmacadam, turning her head to investigate the nature of the surface. They pounced on her. She mustn't budge. She might exacerbate her injuries – although Helen knew that she had broken no bones.

They could allow her satisfy her curiosity without deleterious consequences. But they meant well. She was grateful for their solicitude, if somewhat irked by it.

The ambulance was coming, they told her, they had telephoned. The gardai too, they added, were on their way. In a little while the sirens would rend the air and startle the birds in the nearby wildlife sanctuary. She wished the ambulance would come. Not from any desire to discommode the fauna but from a great longing to be taken from the hard, cold, inhospitable road. The paramedics would move her with impunity. They'd handle her deftly, expertly, speedily. In the ambulance she'd be safe, secure, and above all, warm.

Helen was less cold for the coat. It kept the sea breezes at bay. She was relieved to find that she could still appreciate a good, impromptu pun. 'Accidental' you could call it. Now, how did she hit on such a pertinent word? Enjoying the joke, she smiled a little. The merriment alarmed the onlookers. It wasn't the place for skittishness. Old ladies who plummet from moving vehicles don't engage in joviality. They exchanged apprehensive glances, with the casual disquietude of those aware that they never learn the sequel of the events they are witnessing.

The man must be frozen without his coat. Helen was visualising him standing there in the petrifying December twilight with only a suit for cover. Unless he had an Aran jumper. There was no use trying to establish how he was clothed. They'd only restrain her again. Perhaps fretting about her would render him oblivious of the cold. The Bard, himself, had referred to that phenomenon: 'As fire drives out fire, so . . .

something . . . something.'

Wasn't it a mercy that it wasn't raining or snowing. He'd have been saturated and the coat soaking. He wouldn't be able to put it on when the ambulance came and she had no further need of it. She'd have been drenched herself, too, and the bystanders sopping. Or would they have retreated to the bus shelter? The devil in her made her wish for rain so that she could personally observe the ensuing reactions, run for cover, stand their ground and gawp, or hold open umbrellas over her. Whichever option they'd plump for they wouldn't have long to indulge in it. Already their numbers were dwindling as the appropriate buses whisked them citywards.

To the city. Where she should be now, at the cheese and wine party. They wouldn't have missed her yet, she calculated. Later her friends and acquaintances would wonder why she hadn't come. 'Strange that Helen is so late,' they'd say, 'she's usually so punctual and reliable . . . loves those functions, too . . . still at her age. Of course I know she's spry and capable . . . and so light-hearted. And what a sense of humour she has. Bet she's cracking jokes now, wherever she is.' And they'd nibble another canapé.

Her mouth watered for a canapé. She was feeling peckish having skipped her evening meal to whet her appetite for the party. She now regretted not having taken a light tea. But, she'd survive. This sorry business would soon end. The hospital would see at once that she wasn't seriously injured. She'd be home and dried before her folks heard about the accident at all. Accident indeed. Incident, more like.

She hoped they wouldn't ring her house from the party to

enquire why she hadn't turned up. It would be a disaster if that was the way her family heard the news.

Helen's knees hadn't been straightened for a long time. There was too much arthritis in them. But the paramedics couldn't secure her on the stretcher until her body was in perfect alignment with it. The limbs had to be flattened. That required much force. It occasioned much pain. Maybe some day someone would design a stretcher to accommodate misshapen, agonising, rigid joints. Meanwhile . . .

They slotted the stretcher into the opposite niche in the ambulance, fastening the straps with skill and speed, rendering her safe, secure, comfortable almost, if the knees were disregarded. It would have been tragic if she had been seriously hurt and have to stay in the hospital. One night there and they wouldn't leave her a leg on stand on. The way they'd bulldoze the clothes under the mattress and tug at the sheets until they'd smoothed the final pucker. And pulverise everything between them. And if that happened to be a pair of rickety knees . . . 'So what?' as the nudist said to the sewing machine. There are rules for adhering to, regulations for complying with, regimes for abiding by. Crippled humanity, apropos neat beds and tidy wards, ranks low on the list of hospital priorities.

The ambulance zigged, zagged, zoomed to avoid the cars. Why would it swerve like that except to circumvent the cars? What were they dodging if not cars? Except buses or vans or bicycles? She could only surmise. She couldn't see or hear. She was cocooned, corralled, in a dungeon, with light in it. But a dungeon because she couldn't look beyond its walls. It was a crypt, more terrifying for the darkness outside, for the deep, forbidding, ominous night.

All that hurry, that mindless, needless hurry. Because she wasn't maimed. Trifling injuries don't demand immediate attention. But they had to make haste, to be on tap for other accidents, other emergencies. Additional exigencies were, even then, arising. Hence the hustle.

Externally Helen was securely anchored. Inside, everything was loose and leaping. Her stomach was surging and seething, her bowels bounding and bouncing, her liver lurching and lunging. And then there was pain. It struck without warning. It zigged through her, zagged, zoomed through her. It zipped her into a strait-jacket, a jacket of iron, of lead. It was a tourniquet, turning, twisting, squeezing, crushing, kneading the breath out of her. It was worse than pain. It was all the cramps of the world compressed into one. The discomfort in her knees could not compete with this torment. But soon, soon, they'd relieve the pain, let her respire again.

This must be the hospital. That was a gentle arrest of motion, as if they intended stopping, not like that hurtling around a while back. The time her innards had somersaulted entirely. The time she had overhead them saying 'That was a close one,' the way drivers refer to 'near misses'. As if she hadn't enough on her plate without a supplementary contingency. She hoped this was the hospital.

It was. They were undoing the trusses with the same rapidity that had chained her in. At long last it was the end of the agony, curtains for the cramps.

Trolleys in lines, in rows, in columns. Stretchers on the trolleys. Forms on the stretchers, fitted to them. Human forms, outlines, silhouettes. Beings, bruised, bashed, broken, lassoed to stretchers, on trolleys, cluttering the corridor...

Persons were coming in, persons were going out. Opening doors to come in, opening doors to go out. Breezes coming in with every entrance, breezes coming in with every exit, breezes coming in between entrances and exits. Because they left the doors open. Voices calling out 'Close the door'. Someone closing the doors with a bang. Someone coming, someone had to, the demands of the job. They couldn't close the doors for they'd things in their hands, things for the job.

Helen was colder, her distress deeper. People were passing, walking at running pace. Nobody paused, nobody lingered to lessen the pain. Yet, they knew how bad she was. They had written it down...so long ago they might already have mislaid the information. 'Taking the Particulars' they had termed it. At least the 'Particulars' would ensure that they'd know who she was, (had been), when they came and found her dead of suffocation with piercing gales gusting around her. She'd be satisfied with a breath, a little breath, half a breath, any bit of a breath.

It was dawning on Helen that they were a lousy lot in that hospital. It was asinine of her not to have been aware of that very obvious and elementary fact from the start. 'Particulars Taker', she recalled, had been terrible, burly, brusque, boorish, cold, callous, a negation of nursing. 'Is there a Christian in the house?' she'd have inquired, had there been an ear to listen, a tongue to respond. She was dying to sit up and see if the deaf mutes that periodically shunted the trolleys had any ears at all on their skulls or tongues in their buccal cavities.

Beyond the door towards which the trolleys had been inching they were unloading the merchandise. Helen kept her fingers crossed. They might have someone kind, compassionate and considerate here. The finger-crossing ritual was a dismal failure. It was Dracula again.

'Strip off,' snarled the harpy. Snap, crackle, pop, she yanked the straps from their buckles. 'Off with the duds, get into this.' How did one 'get into' a dressmaker's paper pattern? And then she was gone, without a word about the pain. For all the cognisance that harridan took of it, Helen's distress could be a four letter word or a figment of the imagination of little green men.

Helen would never have divested herself but for the aid of the two young assistants or whatever they were. But the youngsters couldn't have fully understood the procedure. Naturally, at their age, they were too inexperienced to appreciate that an old lady, even an old lady in the pick of health shouldn't be left shivering in an icy cubicle with only a sheet of tissue paper and a single blanket to shield her from the elements. 'Wait here,' they instructed her, bundling up her garments and departing. Wait! What the hell else did they think she could do? Streak around the place and frighten the horses!

Helen panicked. Suppose the bosses outside didn't realise that she had insufficient packaging to safeguard her from frostbite. What if she were abandoned here for a very long time! Hordes, she fantasised, may have perished in this manner, in this place, and the world may never have heard what became of them. Soon, very soon, she herself would be another statistic, Helen Ryan another item on the long list of casualties of

'Casualty'. Even now she might be in the initial stages of hypothermia.

There are chillier places in the world than draughty corridors or freezing cubicles and Helen had just made the acquaintance of one of them – an X-ray table. And then a great wave of comprehension enveloped her. This gradual lowering of the patient's temperature was, in reality, a benevolence. A normal, warm-blooded organism couldn't withstand contact with this fiery slab of ice. Perchance years ago, when X-rays were infants still, medicine had not attained its modern finesse and this cooling technique was as yet unthought of, myriads might have, from here, decamped for sunnier shores.

Whither trolley? To what further horrors were they whirling her now? 'Ride a cock horse to?' The cubicle of course, there to tarry, paper-suit-and-blanket clad, colder, hungrier, her request for a warming cup of tea deferred.

Helen wasn't shivering any more. She was jumping up and down with cold, the trolley vibrating in unison. She'd have given a lot now to have the man's coat. It was such a lovely warm garment. She wouldn't be well enough, now, to go home that night. She'd have to stay and let them play havoc with her knees in accordance with the vagaries of their profession. She wished someone would come soon so that arrangements could be made and she'd get into a ward or some such. Anywhere would do. She hoped the bed would be heated.

Suddenly a light blazed at the end of the tunnel. They couldn't abandon her here to cross the Jordan, alone and unaided. Simply because they'd have to return for the stretcher and trolley. They'd need them, the cubicle too, for, judging by the blaring of sirens since she'd come in, they'd had a busy night. What o'clock was it? She couldn't see without her glasses.

When they came they were carrying her clothes. Whatever for, she wondered, since she wouldn't need them until morning at least.

'You're a lucky woman, Mrs Ryan, no damage done. Get dressed, you may go home.'

All along Helen had felt in her bones that a mistake was inevitable, the daft demented way they were all dashing around. Would they recheck? They'd have to recheck. There must be another Mrs Ryan. A Mrs Ryan who could breathe without unease, who could walk and talk.

Remonstrations, protestations, pleas, entreaties, supplications submitted and ignored. Helen was seated on the cubicle bed and abandoned to fumble with her accoutrements, the physical discomforts now ancillary to the far greater numbness of shock. Her tears were warm on her cheek. She wondered why they weren't blobs of ice. Not to worry. The scientists would have little difficulty in proffering an obscure and incomprehensible biological explanation. Some day, if she survived the present ordeal, she'd investigate the phenomenon.

The person approaching her across the cubicle was the living image of Maeve. She could be her twin sister. They must have relented, after all, and sent someone to help her dress. Indeed they had sent two, for now a second young lady had entered the arena. 'The sooner to get rid of you, Red Riding Hood.' She felt she wasn't doing anyone an injustice in expressing that sentiment, except the Wolf, maybe, misquoting him.

The girl was sniffling. The brazen effrontery of them

sending a girl with a cold. As if she hadn't enough on her plate without going home with a barrelful of bugs to boot.

But beggars can't be choosers and she was in dire need of a succouring hand to help her disentangle her innumerable items of apparel from the assemblage at her elbow. (Since the onslaught of the inclement weather she had taken to wearing layers of garments, the 'onion look' they had called it, in good-natured raillery, at home).

'Mam.' Helen started with surprise. Pain from the effort seared her bosom. Was this agony ever going to plateau out? The girl that was so like her daughter had addressed her by the term of endearment used by all her children. Oh, rubbish! It was 'Ma'am', of course, she had in mind. Maeve couldn't be here. Helen had been uncommonly careful that the story would not filter home. She had lied about the phone, and so far she hadn't met any friend or acquaintance. Besides, even if someone had recognised her, the urban grapevine is exceedingly fragile.

'Ma'am, are you all right, are you all right, Ma'am?'

The girl was speaking as if Helen were one of her own. Perhaps she had not yet contracted the nonchalance of the dispassionate professional.

'We have been waiting for hours,' the voice continued. Helen abandoned a battle with a button and strove to wipe the mist from her eyes, the more effectively to scrutinise the speaker.

'Maeve . . .' White-hot rivets in her chest arrested the words. It wasn't sniffling, it was crying.

Maeve and companion assumed what her questions would be, anticipated her queries. They endeavoured to unravel the mystery for her, to clarify their presence in the hospital. The telling was complicated. It was tedious. It was protracted by irrelevancies. Julie was a neighbour, residing a few doors from the Ryans. She had been at the bus stop.

'Wasn't that the strangest coincidence, mam?'

Had Helen recognised her, noticed her, could she now even recall having seen her? Were they going to insist on answers and set the Catherine-wheels spinning in her breast again?

Helen indicated that she had followed the narrative up to and including this point.

'And she waited till the ambulance came, wasn't she very good, mam?'

It transpired that Julie, having verified Helen's name and address and determined the destination of the ambulance, had gone home and apprised her parents of the incident. Whereupon they had done their good deed for the day and driven Maeve to the hospital.

'And here's Julie, mam, and her parents are outside. Wasn't she great to recognise you, mam, and weren't they very kind to come, and wait so long, weren't they, mam?' Maeve would no longer forego acknowledgement.

But at this juncture the pangs, steadily increasing in ferocity and frequency, forestalled any reply at all. Perversely, Helen was gratified by this development. It was a vindication of her moans and groans. The big wigs and chief bottle washers in this throbbing heart of modern medicine would have to concede that she might kick the bucket without further ado if the tender loving care they had been heaping on her for the last four or five hours were suddenly withdrawn.

Maeve and Julie, separately and individually, and even prior to their surreptitious exchange of nods, winks and glances, were inclined to the same conclusion. They were unanimous, all three of them: Helen must overnight at the hospital.

'We'll see the doctor,' they chorused, 'that's the ticket.' There would be no more parley, no more palaver, no nonsense from nurses. They'd call in Julie's parents for support if needs be. This was no longer a one-woman war.

Doctors under duress are redoubtable, dauntless, indomitable. Sisters seldom surrender. These two simple and irrefutable facts and their devastating consequences were, that night, disclosed in unmitigated horror to our determined trio. The inadequacy of Maeve's nursing skills, the problems that a rheumatic, (worsened by a toss on the tarmac, plus the knee-neatening exertions), might encounter with certain unmentionables in the smallest room in the house, the persistence of the pain, the inability to inhale, the offer of remuneration for a bed – all dismissed, disregarded, ignored or rejected as their specific demerits warranted. Nothing had been accomplished except that Helen, and the night, were farther spent.

'Was a cup of tea still on the cards?' That tiresome girl was carping again. If she had the cards, she'd play Patience. Helen relished the riposte, though vexed she couldn't voice it . . . yet! The tea could be considered 'on the cards'. A welcome 'consideration'!

The vessel that contained the proffered fluid was a teacup. The cup was the main evidence of the identity of the liquid! Even if Helen's stomach were not already sick, had she not been retching before she beheld the stuff at all, she couldn't have partaken of the wretched watery, tepid, beige infusion with its garnishing of little black specks. She returned the beverage untouched.

Likewise she handed back the prescription for palliatives, not because she didn't need the medication, but that she required it there and then, that midnight, not eight hours later when pharmacists were available for business. Meanwhile, through the night, the long, dark, pain-filled night, she'd evaluate the efficacy of Aspirin.

No broken bones . . . no beds! That had horrified Helen. No ambulance if alternative transport available, transfixed her. Those knees of hers, never amenable to travelling by car, would not, following the abuse they had just received, permit her to stoop that low at all.

Helen tottered, teetered, toppled to the car. They were carrying her, nearly, pushing her, pulling her, dragging her. They had to pause when they hurt her too much. The car door gaped, they couldn't open it any further. (They'd have needed a mechanic to take it off altogether!) It was a small car, it was very hard to bend down that far. They had to manoeuvre her in, to joggle her, to force her. They couldn't avoid hurting her.

The car had to hurt when it was moving. Because the road was full of lumps. Every lump had a hole of its very own. The car went over all the bumps and into all the hollows.

She wished the Nolans would stop saying they were sorry they had come at all, that she'd have been better off if they had stayed at home, that she'd have been far more comfortable in an ambulance. If they'd have sent one, even then.

It would be the same all over again at home. They'd have to extract her from the car. They'd have to ensure that Maeve would be able to take on the nursing. They'd have to hoist her into the bed. See if she could manage the little jobs one performs behind closed doors.

Speaking of which reminded her that all through the endless hours in the hospital she had not been asked if she needed to use 'the facilities'. It was lucky she could go without, or there might have been an accident. And imagine the state her clothes would have been in then. All the party finery and everything. Though a mishap might have been a blessing in disguise. For in that state they'd have to deliver her by ambulance, they could hardly expect her to re-attire herself in sodden (or worse) garments. They might have sent her wrapped in a blanket, H-Block style. She'd stop bothering about it. Agatha Christie couldn't predict how these Florence Nightingales and Mother Teresas would mastermind the operation.

Helen's knees were disabled for a long time after. Long after the spasms in her chest had ceased. Long after the bruises on her buttocks had faded away and she could again sleep comfortably in her accustomed position. Long after her friends and neighbours and acquaintances had stopped asking her if she had recovered from her ordeal. Long after she had last recounted the hardships in the hospital. And that was a very long time, for she had told the story to multitudes.

And for every listener who had the same experience in similar circumstances there was another enthralled with the treatment there. The first group and the second concurred on many points. For instance, that the world should be instructed that it is not inhumanity but the possibility of subsequent anaesthesia and surgery that prevents the administration of food, drink, tobacco or other drugs to patients awaiting diagnosis. It was also agreed that hospitals should scatter the cantankerous, the churlish and the condescending members of their staff over a large number of rosters instead of allowing them to function in disharmony in the same place at the same time. But no one in group one could pardon, and no one in group two could justify the discharging of a patient in pain without an anodyne for the night.

THE LAND OF OZ

LIZ McMANUS

With acknowledgement to Philip Larkin

I felt the moment of impact when your plane touched down. It felt like pain through a nervous system, or a seismic wave traversing the globe. A silly romantic fallacy of mine, I know. After all, I have time-zones and distances so mixed up in my mind that I hardly know what time of day it is. The clock on the wall is working but it doesn't tell me the real time. It doesn't tell me *your* time. But our bodies have their own clocks, and yours and mine their own synchronisation and I have no reason to believe that time alters those time-pieces. When rubber tyre hit concrete runway in that upsidedown world that you now inhabit, all I can tell you is, the umbilical cord snapped.

Let us have done with it.

See me? I'm the grumbling, grey-haired, menopausal woman crouched on her hunkers in the kitchen, and using housework as therapy. I'm disembowelling kitchen cupboards, sweeping corners clean, scraping traces of jam, that are sticky with dust and stale crumbs, out of the crevices. Unearthing junk I haven't seen for years: bent forks, plastic boxes from forgotten picnics, an old school tie, Christmas cake decorations. That's when I find the book lodged behind a pile of old cake-tins. Your teeth-marks are still on the cover, a funny habit you always had, chewing on the corners of books, and suddenly you're here in front of me, all gawky arms and legs in your school uniform and looking owlish in your new glasses, your nose crinkling up at this choice of book. *The Wizard of Oz.* Do you remember? It was the favourite book of my childhood, and I urged you to read it. You thought it was tedious. I could see it then, in your nine-year-old eyes, the shadow of disillusion. If this is the object of love, you were thinking, what does it make the subject? In that instant, I understood that Dorothy and the Tin man and the Cowardly Lion and the Wizard were merely human creations and that this was the beginning of the end of my mythic stature in your life.

Now you are in that lucky land of Oz and I shall not tell you where I am. Diminished and shrivelled up and closer to death, that's where; lessened and weakened and crushed. I shall not tell you because I do not want our parting to be calamitous and bitter.

Never were hearts more eager to be free.

You are always so far behind me that I keep losing track of the distance. When you were a child I used to talk to you as if you were an adult. Any barrier to our communication was ephemeral, as if we communicated through veils of gauze. You talked in riddles and so did I, but we had an absolute understanding. Now you're as big as I am, you wear the same kind of clothes. And you raid my wardrobe, steal my clothes and wear them. *Stole* my clothes and *wore* them. When will I get the tense right? It's easy to misjudge the gap between us now, but it has not been changed by circumstance. The only difference now is that you are looking forward and I, despite my convictions, am beginning to look back.

In the past

There has been too much moonlight

and self-pity.

Maybe, after all, I'm just jealous – of youth, and opportunity, of the world opening out to take you in. Long before you were born I was on the move. It took me years to settle here in Ireland and years to shed the evidence of my displacement. Even the words that I used betrayed my origins. Occasional bum notes sounded in the making of an opus. *Barrette* instead of hair-slide and *moostache* and *salade*. In everyday talk, the words surfaced to mark me out as a foreigner. It took me years to learn how to say lettuce instead of salade. Lettuce. Let us...

Let us settle. In Australia, the Irish settled and established a squattocracy in a place that is touching Paradise, if you can believe Gay Byrne. A masculine country. I've never known such a place for phallic symbols; every building punctures the sky; every mountain swells tumescently; every thing pushes and jerks and penetrates and explodes. Your husband will be happy there. It will suit his temperament. He wants to be where the traffic moves and there are no queues in the banks and the sun shines and where he can make lots of money. Don't we all . . . the prevailing wisdom dictates. He who does not, let him have the first stone cast upon him.

I don't want much. My child reared and settled and happy. More or less, what I have. It's what every mother accommodates to, in the end.

> *We are husks, that see*
> *The grain going forward*
> *to a different use.*

What a role to be cast in!

That's not what I want at all. Starting out with such extravagant desires I end up with only one, and that is to be able to open my wardrobe to find that it has been raided again and that half my good clothes are missing.

To begin at the beginning. I had my doubts about immortality. 'Of that of which nothing should be said . . .' Until the continuum of life was expressed, not on the enscribed page of an ancient testament but absurdly, between my legs, in a mess of blood and mucus.

You can't get more rudimentary than that. Vixen-care, cow-love, henpecking, mother-smother. The occupational hazard of single motherhood. As far as I was concerned a man would have only got in the way. I was unmarried, and therefore untrammelled and unbowed. At the moment of your birth a bald-headed, wrinkled little Wizard gave me everything I needed; courage and a heart and a way back home and an unexpected capacity for love. If I had invested in a man one-tenth of the time that I invested in you it would have been considered a magnificent obsession, the kind to inspire literature. Invested . . . what an ugly word, implying that there is a profit to be made on the transaction. Which, of course, there is.

There is regret. Always, there is regret.

How many times? How many million Irish mothers have gone before me, mourning and keening? I don't want to be part of their distress but if I want out now I should have made that decision long ago. Instead, I had a daughter and you assured me my immortality for, despite any rupture that you or I may experience, the line is set. There will be grandchildren and great-grandchildren of whose history I will form a part. Forever. Bold and burnt-brown is how I imagine them, boys and girls with Aussie voices. *Yers, Gran.* We always imagine that our children will be like us but they can only be like themselves. On visits home, yes, to establish their roots, and discovering instead, for themselves, this solitary tuber. Scenes at airports, or ferry terminals, hugs and kisses, I can envisage them already but these aren't the times that I'll begrudge you, not the occasions pumped up with excitement and tears. It's the ordinary moments that I'll covet, the minuscule advances that go unnoticed except by women who live out their lives at the threshold.

That which I cannot have.

You can see how parasitic life has made me.

It is better that our lives unloose.

Better for you and for all these grandchildren that I have bequeathed upon you. And probably, in time, better for me. I have my own final migration to consider. And better, I have no doubt, for Australia. Look at what a ragbag of convicts was able to create in the lucky land of Oz. Now it is our brightest stream that flows through the seas of the world, towards its shores.

The seas of the world . . . that, at least, is something we have always shared. Ever since you learnt to walk, the pair of us, Summer and Winter, went swimming at the little stony beach at Sandycove, remember. We made quite a sensation. There goes the French hussy and her bastard daughter flouting God and His elements. Both of us reaching delightedly, back into the womb, as we slipped and rolled like porpoises through the waves.

Strange that we should both keep the ritual alive even now, when we are so far apart. Daily, in the magical tides of Bondi beach, your young tanned shoulders are preparing to support a dynasty and each day too I stand and withdraw my feet from the cold colourless ocean at my door and think of you. We live in different climates, different seasons, different worlds, different differences. The warm sea that is cradling you there is the same body of water that touches me now, but here it is different; here it curls my toes to ice.

Abroad on that sea we travel like emigrants do,

with their courses set.

AFTER THE MATCH

MARY O'DONNELL

They burst into the reception hall at Old Woodleigh, fists raised in triumph, the growing *waaahh* sound which had been audible from a distance now deepening, distorting their faces as they fell *en masse* through the double doors. The opposition had been trounced in a stunning display of muscle and airborne muck at the Leinster Schools Rugby Final.

Helen stood with Doreen and Katy, the wives of two other Bellemont teachers. *Waaahhh* . . . The women shifted uncomfortably, taking pointedly casual sips from their drinks as they watched the boys close in around the two trainers. Helen studied Adam's face. He was in seventh heaven. This was the moment when all the extra time spent training the young beasts – the late nights, the pep-talks and sessions which had intensified during the last, vital weeks – suddenly added up. She was pleased for him, the happy glow on his face some sort of pay off.

'Isn't it marvellous for them!' Doreen giggled over her G and T, adjusting a frothy pink blouse at the neck as the tangle of cheering bodies suddenly shifted in their direction.

'Absolutely!' Katy agreed. 'You must both be thrilled skinny.'

'Oh it's great to see them win. As a mother I know just

what it means to the boys,' Doreen said, eyes shining with pleasure.

'Aren't you thrilled, Helen?' said Katy again, more for something to say than in true speculation.

'Delighted. Delighted,' said Helen, distracted by the whooping and back-slapping.

'Of course it's your first time so it'll seem very new,' Doreen whispered. 'But when Adam has worked with Patrick and brought them through like this a few more times, you'll take it all in your stride. I know when Patrick started training I was so nervous you wouldn't believe it. I mean you want them to win, you wish so desperately for everything to work out.'

'Well it has anyway.' Helen was vague, uncertain of her humour.

Patrick and Adam were hoisted shoulder-high, good-humouredly tolerating the heaving and jostling. The parents of the players mingled with the group, not quite at the centre of the knot of bodies but near enough to be hugged and kissed by sons who were out of their minds with joy. One of the boys forced the cup, a well-dented trophy chased in silver and gold, into Adam's hands.

'Ah, lads, I can't balance!' he shouted, raising the cup unsteadily. They roared again and took off at a lumbering gallop around the hall.

'Easy now lads!' Patrick called. Nobody heard. He was older than Adam, his face finely-lined, more assured.

Flustered helpers tried to seat the jubilant mob. Waiters and serving women signalled, ignored until a few of the parents and most of the teachers made their way to the dining area.

The boys followed untidily. Helen groaned as one of them started the school rallying song again. It was rapidly taken up as they filtered through. She was starving. The afternoon on the terraces at Lansdowne had been freezing, hail and wind whipping in under the stand till they were drenched. They were proper ninnies to have taken so much trouble with their appearances, she thought, observing the other women. Like fresh, dewy flowers, individually not so interesting, but as a group colourful and strangely expectant. Like girls at their first party. The older ones were muffled in furs and fine wool. Because it was a day which had promised victory, she'd had her hair plaited, and wore a new navy and green dress bought specially for the occasion. It had cost too much but she liked it and Adam would find the effect exotic and interesting among all the matrons.

'*Womba, womba, womba,*' the slow chant began. She tried to look benevolent and pleasant as she took her seat and watched the team and their followers crash their way down along the tables. '*Ing-gang-oolie-oolie-oolie-oolie,*' they growled, reminding her of visiting rugby teams from New Zealand whose ritual dance was intended to intimidate the opponents. One of the boys grabbed a seat opposite her and sat down, panting.

'Jaysus!' he gasped, blinking in her direction, but she realised that he wasn't looking at her so much as drifting in and out of some hallucinatory and highly-pleasured dream. '*Ing-gang-goo.*'

To her right a restless middle-aged man with lightly-tanned skin shifted continually in his seat.

'Hello, I'm Helen Kilroy.' She introduced herself, decided she'd best make an effort and be sociable. The bane of her life.

Being sociable. Making an effort for the sake of civility. He looked at her for a moment, surprised at her presence, not expecting to be addressed.

'Oh. How d'you do? McElligot. Jim,' he mumbled, extending his hand.

'You've a son on the team, right?'

'Wrong. Nephew,' he said, looking over her shoulder and waving at somebody.

'Good man Delaney! Knew you'd do it, ya bloody hound!' he bellowed, taking a slug from a glass of wine. '*Chow-chow-chow*,' the call went, its barking rhythm strengthening. Helen tried again. For Adam's sake she must make an effort to be amenable.

'Oh yes, I remember the boy – Ciaran McElligot is your nephew.'

'Got it in one!' he said, before stopping suddenly. 'But . . . but . . . my God, I've just realised who you are!' He sat back, absorbing her from head to toe as if she were a vision.

'I do apologise Mrs Kilroy . . . Helen, that what you said? . . . The way things are today, I don't know what's happening. Super isn't it, you must be so proud of Adam, delighted with yourself, what?'

'*Womba, womba, womba.*' She wondered how to counter the flood of hyperbole. How pleased did she have to be, how could she convey her pleasure, that yes, it was wonderful?

To her left, Doreen chattered to somebody's father. She was cut out for it, Helen thought, remembering the chocolate eclairs and apple-tarts which Doreen had ferried to the team the evening before every match. 'I really feel for them,' she was saying, staring wide-eyed at the man. 'It's so hard for them in a boarding-school. I find they really need something to remind them that we all care, that somebody really, really cares.'

'Oh you're quite right, quite right,' the man replied.

The poor bugger was bored stiff. Helen peered over Doreen's shoulder and into his eyes. He caught the look and in the flicker of an instant almost responded, stifling a smile. She looked away then. No joy there. *Homo domesticus* if ever she saw him. Common-or-garden species. Widespread in the British Isles. Sheds its inhibitions only during summer migration. Likes the company of its own sex. Probably saves his charm for the rugby tours. Miles away from solicitous wives. Still. Best not start messing. For Adam's sake. Best behave and keep her talents for the home front or circles where they wouldn't be misinterpreted. This was no place for wit and irony. Or so much as a hint of sex. '*Yak-yak-yak-yak-yak-yak-yak,*' the boys roared. '*Come on, Bellemont, win it back!*' The '*Waaahh*' sound rose again as they finally settled down, plastic chairs scraping and hacking on the wooden floor.

Adam and Patrick sat like young bulls, penned off at the top table, surrounded by priests, the headmaster and various significant supports, including the priest who had once found her bathing naked with Adam in the school swimming-pool. Adam had been raging afterwards. Hadn't he told her not to strip, but no, she'd insisted, determined to tease, and had even tried to rip his swimming-trunks off, just as Goggle-face walked in. The thought of it made her suddenly splutter with laughter. The McElligot man scrutinised her.

'God but it's a tremendous occasion,' he muttered to her,

as if testing her sanity.

'God but it is,' she replied glibly, giggling again in recollection of the priest's bland face as she'd waded to the side of the pool in an attempt to conceal her flesh. Word inevitably got around. A black mark. A man who couldn't control his wife in certain situations was open to question.

During the meal, people were absorbed in the post-mortem: the earnest dissection of every moment of play, comparisons with previous finals leading to disputes, jokes, noisy debate. She could think of a million and one more interesting topics, even if it was their special rugger day. Hadn't she shown interest in other people, even in the brat sitting opposite, hadn't she tried a variety of conversational options, from current affairs to UEFA and British soccer hooligans, the Olympics? Of course it wasn't necessary to say anything to that lot. She glared balefully at her soup. More a matter of making the right sounds, little-woman chat. She listened to Doreen.

'Well of course education is important, it's one of the most important things any parent can give a child!' she was saying with vehemence.

'Quite. The wife and I like to take certain decisions too. All in all some guidance is needed and the discipline which rugger adds is damn well unbeatable,' the man beside her said.

'Discipline?' she cut in over Doreen's shoulder. 'What do you mean by discipline?' she asked, putting on an interested face, hand curling under her chin. The man looked extremely surprised.

'Aaaah! Discipline? Discipline's discipline any way you look at it: the boys have to be ready to forge good careers, stand up for themselves, go for it in a tough world, that type of thing . . . '

A waiter slid a plate of turkey and ham before her, then another slammed a heap of mashed potatoes and liquidised sprouts on top of the meat.

'You mean externalised discipline?' Helen asked, determined to be awkward.

'What? Beg pardon?'

'The ability to kow-tow to authority and suchlike – a bit like doing things without asking why?'

Doreen nodded her head in agreement and Helen was suddenly aware that she was listening intently.

'But what else is there?' Doreen asked.

The man started to hum and haw.

'Asking why isn't always such a bally great thing, young woman,' he commented, focusing at a point beyond her.

'You'd drive yourself crazy if you were constantly questioning things, Helen,' said Doreen.

'Is that so?' said Helen.

'Yes, and the long and the short of it for me is that they get such a lot out of the experience. It stands to them, makes . . .' she searched for the word, '. . . it makes men of those boys.'

'Well said, well said.' The man applauded quietly with manicured hands.

The meal was over. There was, she thought, little to say which would have made the slightest difference. She glanced along the length of the table, making no effort to conceal an expression of boredom. Katy was chirruping with some guy from the IRFU, Doreen was flirting with the disciplinarian, McElligot brayed joyfully over his wine, his nephew smiled like an imbecile and the muscular boy opposite, who told her he was a hooker and laughed, expecting her not to understand what the term meant, rocked backwards and forwards on his chair, spooning trifle into his flaccid mouth. Adam and Patrick sat in the sanctuary of the top table. Thank God Adam wasn't a yob, one of those aleckadoos. At least the whole thing was a game for him, a sport. Rugby was rugby was rugby and if people didn't know the difference between Phase One and Phase Two possession they could forget it. Not for him the ribald tribalism that emanated from their opponents' dressing-rooms prior to every match as trainers bullied mercilessly and told the team they couldn't generate a pint of piss between them. That wasn't Adam's style. Instead, Patrick had been persuaded to adopt Adam's half-baked meditation techniques, picked up as a result of some cursory reading and a trip to Bangkok some years back. The Bellemont boys had been ribbed mercilessly, with 'Bellemont Boys Levitate' and 'A Try for the Maharishi' lashed across the evening papers. All the more satisfying to prove them wrong, Helen thought, to see Adam have his glory. She was nothing if not loyal.

McElligot wheeled back in his chair as the speeches began. He had reached the point of no return, and lit a cigar, his hands unsteady. The place was noisy: boys and fathers shouted and catcalled across the room; wives and mothers smiled in complicity, the *waaaahh* sound threatening to erupt again until the headmaster raised his right arm in a plea for silence.

'*Sieg heil!*' somebody shouted from the back of the room. The whole place exploded.

'Dear colleagues,' he finally began, 'Reverend Fathers, parents, staff and – of course – students.'

They yahooed long and loud. Tables were hammered, floors pounded with heavy feet.

There were at least five separate toasts and a few broken glasses. Helen's hands were sore from clapping. Nobody cared. This was Happyland. She knocked back her fifth glass of wine, face slightly numb, wanted to crawl into bed. Any long, wide, spacious area would do, somewhere she could wiggle her toes and open her bra. She helped herself to another drink. The red was good, fair dues to the priests. The headmaster was blathering on about history and the future, the importance of the Bellemont tradition and the splendid good fortune they'd had in their trainers.

'Hear, hear!' she called in a full, confident voice.

Doreen looked quizzical, then tittered.

'It's all right – I'm not pissed, just pissed off!' Helen whispered loudly. She waved at Adam. His attention was held by McElligot's nephew who was at that point unbuttoning his shirt. She tutted with impatience, as it came to her that her husband was as remote as he had ever been, perhaps as he had always been.

'But there are two people we especially want to mention, to whom gratitude is due for their unstinting support, without whom much of what we achieved today might not have been possible.'

He beamed down at them, his face radiating good intentions and assurance. There was a slight hush.

'Would Mrs Patrick Watson and Mrs Adam Kilroy care to stand and make themselves known?' he said in mock seriousness.

Doreen hesitated, then stood, beckoning to Helen.

'It's us, stand up!' she hissed uneasily. People applauded half-heartedly. Helen stayed sitting, her face pounding as two smirking boys waltzed down the length of the hall carrying bouquets. '*Waaahhh*' came the sound again as they were jeered on their way. The smoke from McElligot's cigar was cutting the back of her throat. Someone slapped her on the shoulders from behind and told her she must be proud as punch, as the flowers were plonked at her place.

'Well done, well done indeed, my dear,' said McElligot.

'Congratulations! A wonderful day for Bellemont!' someone else called.

'Thank you,' she said with what dignity she could summon.

Flowers. She simpered bitterly to herself. '*Ing-gang-oolie-oolie-oolie . . .*' Flowers for those who selflessly support the great endeavour. For rugger-hugging ladies. Healthy activity ze old rugby, she muttered to herself. The city hotels were flooded with women on the rampage during internationals, hungry for Frenchmen, Welshmen, Scotsmen, any man who'd take them, willing to do or die for a life of leather balls and pungent socks. Good at the old rucking too, just like the lads in their own way, in for the kill. '*Womba, womba, womba.*' Doreen looked pleased with herself, poked her face into the flowers time and again, saying wasn't it lovely of them, so thoughtful to think of such a thing, sure they'd done nothing to deserve it.

'When you make the sandwiches and cakes, that's what you get,' Helen snapped, then checked herself. Make an effort.

McElligot was reminiscing about his schooldays to nobody in particular.

'It's very nice of them all the same,' Doreen insisted.

Helen was about to contradict her but stopped. What was the point when Doreen was so humble? Flowers. She didn't want anything. Being rewarded wasn't the point. The point – she took a deep breath – was that everybody pretended that the women were necessary to the scene, and the truth was they weren't. Which was fine with her but, by God, they needn't expect her to feel grateful.

'I wonder why everybody goes through the motions of thanking us?' she asked.

'Oh they're not just the motions, Helen!' said Doreen quickly. 'It's well-meant, it's their way of saying something to us.'

'Yeah, like fuck off, girls!'

Doreen raised her eyebrows, her jaw falling open.

'Sorry, sorry Doreen,' said Helen. Oh Jesus, here we go again, apologising when there's fuck-all to be sorry for. The McElligot man cut in.

'They're saying thank you for putting up with this,' he said in a wavering voice, his eyes moist and sentimental.

'Yip. It's a lot to put up with, isn't it?' said Helen.

'Ah now, ah now, it's not that bad.'

'It's very important, Helen,' said Doreen. 'That's how the system works and it's very important for the boys.'

'Of course it is, of course it is,' Helen replied, folding her arms.

'There's no point resenting it, my dear,' said McElligot. His lucidity surprised her.

'I don't resent it,' she said lightly.

279

'But my dear lady, you've sat here all evening on sufferance. Mean to say, what are you, some sort of feminist or something?' he spat the question. She swallowed hard.

'Helen has her own ideas on everything,' said Doreen in jolly tones, trying to smooth the atmosphere.

'I don't know how to answer you,' said Helen. Her face was blotched, even her neck and chest felt hot. She caught a glimpse of Adam. Nabbed by yet another adoring mother ingratiating herself for a ray of his attention. Lapping it up. Both of them.

'Of course I'm a feminist,' she responded, not knowing whether it was a lie or not. Weren't most of them ball-breakers anyway? McElligot raised his eyebrow in amusement.

'But I don't resent rugby. I just think it's given too much importance.' She was hamming it up. Sounding resentful.

'In what way, my dear?' he asked, taking a puff from the cigar, his lips making a wet smacking sound as he inhaled. She could have shoved it down his throat.

'To enhance careers. Old boys network, that kind of thing. It has damn all to do with sport.'

'I see. But you're a feminist too – I don't meet too many of those – thought all that kind of thing had faded out in the early eighties really.'

'No.'

'Thought they were all lesbians too if you don't mind my saying so. You're not one of those, are you?' he chortled.

She laughed, because otherwise she might have wept.

'Ah well, I'll leave you to it, my dear. The wife's over there waiting; got to get home y'know. Nice meeting you, don't take it all so seriously.'

He was gone, leaving a whiff of aftershave and cigar smoke in his wake. Reason and honesty didn't make for satisfaction when dealing with his sort. But neither did outrage. What he'd possibly expected. At her age she knew a few things. One of them was that most men would follow a ball or a pint across a roomful of naked sylphs, much like the joke said. The other was that, unlike the men, women were solitary hunters. They split the pack, then conquered one, and one only. When she felt sour it showed. Men could sniff out womanish discontent and rebellion wherever it lurked. Doreen seemed spot on. For the umpteenth time she wondered why the hell it mattered what men thought about women. And then again maybe she'd been codding herself. Look at Doreen. A decent skin. A nice woman who worked hard at keeping Patrick happy, doing what she thought he wanted.

'*Womba, womba, womba.*' There it was again. The boys formed a train and shuffled Maori-style around the two trainers. '*Ing-gang-oolie-oolie-oolie-oolie-oolie.*' Gathering her bag and jacket, the green one borrowed from her sister to match the dress, so that she'd look well on the day, she stared at Adam. He was like a god to the boys, even looked like one, a colossus, in command, the glow of victory on his smooth brow. Patrick was more avuncular, a sort of tribal chief. If this were the Amazon jungle, she thought, the rites of passage would be somewhat different. Circumcision with a piece of flint. A bit of vine-swinging. Ritual raping and pillaging instead of socialised aggression. A time for the elders to pass on the wisdom of their sex, the lore of centuries. They were getting their lore today, all right, messages in abundance. How to live. Entitlements. An inheritance.

She turned in disgruntlement to Doreen. 'How did Patrick enjoy Paris?'

'Had a ball, won all their matches – didn't Adam tell you?'

'He did. Just wondering how Patrick found it.'

Patrick had drunk himself footless one night, the gendarmes eventually prising him from a restaurant into which he'd staggered, wearing a balaclava, shouting something about *un petit hold-up.*

'It's all right Helen – I know what happened,' said Doreen.

'What?'

'He rang me up in the middle of the night singing the Can-Can.'

'Oh.'

'Count yourself lucky that at least Adam's no boozer,' she added. The tables were turned. But Helen didn't mind. It was common knowledge. She was used to it. Adam's French floozie. Adam's bonbon, sweetmeat or whatever. He'd told her himself, full of boyish remorse.

'Men,' she said grimly.

'Bastards.'

'Have you been drinking?' Helen asked, unaccustomed to Doreen's directness.

'Two G and T's. It's such a load of shit, isn't it?'

'Wish I'd never set foot in the place.'

It was a kind of truce, an acknowledgement of some essential base-line failure on both sides.

'Would you look at them!' Doreen spat in outright mockery.

'Boys will be boys as they say!'

'*Chow-chow-chow.*' In this setting, she didn't recognise Adam. This was what he escaped to, like all men in flight from women. He looked innocently past her, certain of his life, its correctness. Through it all, she did not exist.

'Are you staying, or d'you want a lift?' she called to Doreen. Let him find his own way home.

'I'll come: God knows where the carry-on'll end tonight.'

'*Yak-yak-yak-yak-yak-yak-yak.*'

'Your hair's gorgeous,' she said companionably.

'Oh, look the flowers – '

'Leave them,' said Helen. The sight of them renewed her irritation.

The crowd had dispersed slightly. The atmosphere was damp and beery, like a hotel after a hooley. Forlorn. She stood at the exit and searched for the car keys. It was drizzling. Outside, daffodils wavered. But the night was spring-like despite the needling cold. And the season was over. Her husband would gradually shed his inattention. He would be hers again in some limited way. He might want her, might learn that she was more than a sanctuary of peace. He might actually desire her. That was what mattered. It was why so many women turned out in force. Hanging on to men they loved in some quirky way. '*Yak-yak-yak-yak-yak-yak-yak,*' the sound faded as the two women hurried across the carpark. The main road was blocked with traffic.

'Will we go somewhere?' said Doreen, straightening her coat as she sat into the car.

'What? You mean not go home? Entertainment?'

'I wonder what Bad Bobs is like?'

'Full of men. Have you any money?'

'Cheque book,' said Doreen, opening a bottle of perfume and spraying both wrists.

'That'll do. Let's go,' said Helen, her expression set.

She fastened the seat-belt, listened for a moment to the distant '*waaahhh*' sound and revved up. She was ready for anything.

SWING DOORS

MARIE HANNIGAN

I'd been knocking about Gora taking stick all day, and I was fed-up with the lot of them. From the lorry driver who lifted me outside Castlecove, to the geezers on the pier who looked at me as if I'd just landed from outer space.

The lorry driver cackled when I told him the crack. 'Good-lookin' blonde like you aboard a boat? Not a chance darlin'.' I had my feet wedged against the dashboard trying to brace myself as my friend booted the lorry into the corkscrew bends. When he deposited me at the end of the pier, I said my first grateful prayer in a long, long time.

The pier wasn't much bigger than the slip in Castlecove, just long enough to take the dozen half-deckers that were tied up along one side, with a high wall breaking the force of the Atlantic on the other. There were clutches of old bucks hanging about and they nearly went hysterical when I asked about the start, shaking their heads at the absurdity of a woman asking for a berth.

I'd left Castlecove after a row with my father. There was no way I was going back to admit that he was right. I kept pestering everyone in sight until eventually one old boy mentioned a name, and I was away. 'Pol Francie? Who's that?' I asked.

'Young fella lives in the big house above the lake. Got his whole crew livin' with him.'

'Aye,' someone muttered. 'There be's all kinds of rare ones comin' and goin' in that house.' They were still laughing as I walked away from the pier.

I found Pol Francie leaning up against the bar of Charlie's Roadhouse, with a couple of other young fellows. The minute he turned to look at me, I took his measure. Weather-bleached hair and wide green eyes. Watch it, I thought. But he didn't laugh when I asked him for the berth. 'You been out in a boat before, Valerie? Ever been seasick?'

'Sure. Been a bit queasy, but no big deal. My father skippers McStrancher's Bride.'

'You're Owen McStrancher's daughter? Okay, you're on,' he said.

One of the others gave him a look, but he just shrugged. 'We're shorthanded. She'll be as good as the young fella anyhow.'

The young fellow looked hurt. He didn't have the weathered look of the others. I knew I'd be better than him.

I showed Pol my rucksack. 'Will I stow my gear aboard the boat?'

'No need. You can kip in the house with us.'

The house was a surprise, a massive old place, bang in the middle of a golf course. As Pol led me through, he could see I was impressed by the space of the rooms and the wide bay windows, built by the gentry, he told me. 'Those old landlords had taste,' he joked, dumping my rucksack onto a wide bed. 'This room belonged to my grand-aunt. Take a good look at it now. We'll be fishing nights, so you won't see much of it.'

We shot in the dark, dozing through the night by a paraffin heater. At dawn we hauled in, hand over hand, and my gambler's heart jumped to see the brightness of the salmon breaking surface.

That first week I watched the young fellow retching over the side, holding back my own bile till I thought I'd die. The net hauler was broken. We pulled in the slack quickly with the dip of the boat, holding fast as she rolled onto her port side. Only the kid tried to haul against the heave of the half decker. At the end of the week, I bound up his raw, blistered hands.

'Don't haul on the rise of the boat, Jason. You'll kill yourself pulling against her.'

'How come you know about fishing, Valerie?'

'It's in the blood,' I told him.

The row with my father had brought it to a head. He needed a crewman, and I'd asked him for the berth.

'Haven't you got a job already.' He clucked his tongue.

'I'd make more money fishing than I'd ever see pounding a typewriter for "Silver Sails". What was the point of all that navigation you taught me, if you didn't want me fishing?'

'You're a girl,' he said. End of story.

No skipper in town would take me on when my father wouldn't do it. So I just took off. I told myself I was well out of the stinking place, though every fisherman worth his waders knows Castlecove is the only place to be, on this goddess-forsaken shamrock shore. Factoryless, pollution-free Gora will never be fishing port of the year.

But you can still smell the salt of the sea here.

My presence in the house has sparked off some speculation. When I'm buying groceries in the village shop, Maya, the owner, passes some remark about me living alone with all those men. 'Maybe you'd need one of these,' she jokes, holding up a slide bolt. I don't take it seriously at first, but later, as I'm getting into bed, I pull a heavy trunk from a corner of the room and drag it across the doorway.

Sometimes when I catch Pol looking at me, I remember the foreign girl who was fishing on a trawler in Castlecove. She had worked on the deck as well as any man, until two of the crewmen fell out over her. Whenever I catch Pol giving me the eye, I turn the other way.

The morning sun is climbing into the sky by the time we land our fish. It intrudes through the south-facing window above my bed. In the beginning everything kept me awake, the light on the high ceiling, the snores of the others, the swans below on the lake. Now I could sleep through the Big Bang.

Saturday and Sunday we are forced to lie ashore, chafing at the vigilance of the bailiffs who patrol the pier, enforcing the weekend fishing bar.

Jason is a music student. He practises his violin in the study. Mick and Jimmy squat in the sitting room playing blood and guts videos. Pol is heavy into some black blues singer. He stays in his room, his stereo turned high to drown the rest out.

Every night we're ashore these different sounds fight for air-space till I think I'll go mad in the head.

We were fishing for a fortnight when Pol gave us our first sub. There would be no square-up until the end of the season.

I had a couple of pints in Charlie's with the boys and came home early. Soothed by the emptiness of the house, I took a can of wine to bed and lay back, wallowing in the silence. At this stage, I was tired of dragging that trunk across the floor, but for some reason, before dropping off to sleep, I hopped out of bed and barricaded myself in.

Hours later I drifted up from sleep to hear the clatter of footsteps on the stair as the boys landed home, well tight. Everything was quietening down again when I heard a rattle at my doorknob. The door was pushed inward, jamming as it met the resistance of the trunk.

The next day, when I was picking up the groceries in Maya's shop, I dropped a slide bolt into my wire basket along with the grub. Maya picked it up and examined it as she was doing up the till. 'I see you're taking my advice,' she smiled. I smiled back at her. That trunk was breaking my back.

There were other intrusions on my sleep. Once I woke to find a man looking over the brass bedhead. I swear, smiling down at me. I closed my eyes, waiting for the smiling mouth to come down on my neck and suck my life's blood from me. Five terrified minutes later, I opened my eyes – to nothing. My man had drifted out through the bolted door again.

One night I heard a girl crying, bawling her little heart out. Another ghost, I thought. But when I went down in the morning there was a long silk scarf lying across the back of a chair. I waited for its owner to appear for breakfast. But she never did. Pol had turfed her out some time in the middle of the night.

The others were such pathetic cooks, I ended up doing the

lot. I was boiling my sheets in a pot on the range one Saturday morning when Pol tumbled a bundle of laundry at my feet, 'You wouldn't shove mine in as well,' he coaxed.

'I wouldn't,' I said.

But I did. After all, the man did give me a chance. So now every Saturday, Jason helps me to light a huge fire and I spend the day hanging over the ancient bathtub.

Five weeks into the salmon, coming to the end of the season, Pol told me to order an extra load of grub for the boat. 'We'll chance it out Saturday evening. The bailiffs are after the Fanad men this weekend. We should get away clear.'

It was perfect salmon weather, a gentle breeze to ruffle the water, and a light continuous mizzle of rain. With none of the other boats out, we shot away clear in the best patch of water and settled by the stove to wait. We hardly spoke or slept all night. At sun-rise my pulse jigged as we hauled in one hundred and eight-three salmon.

We were making for shore when a voice came crackling over the radio. Pol put his ear to the set. 'It's Charlie. The bailiffs are on the pier. There's a load of them heading out in the motorboat. We'll have to make for the estuary and drop anchor. Charlie will pick us up in the punt.'

'What if the bailiffs catch up on us?'

Pol pointed to the bundle of gaffs at the bottom of the boat. 'There's one for every man.'

I looked at the vicious hooked instrument. Then I thought of the catch, the best we'd had in the season. I picked up a gaff and gripped it hard.

Pol navigated the boat, keen as a blade into the estuary.

We'd just settled ourselves into Charlie's punt when we saw the enemy rounding the Point. We'd be long ashore by the time they reached the empty half-decker.

Charlie had brought two bottles of whiskey with him, and we sat in the house through the morning, toasting the defeat of the bailiffs. There was no urge of sleep on me. As the others drifted off to bed, I was left alone with Pol to sip the remains of the second bottle. He talked about his grand-aunt who had come back from America, loaded, and how he had come to live with her when she bought the house. The eldest in a house full of sisters, he was barely eight years old. 'I felt like I was dumped.' He was lost to me for a moment, caught in the past. Then he smiled, 'I did alright out of it. She left me this place when she kicked the bucket.'

He wanted to be straight with me, he said. Now the season was nearly over, they'd be starting the lobsters. He only needed two crewmen. 'Jason's going back to college soon, but I'd like you to stay on in the house. With me.'

He kept a steadying arm around me as we mounted the stairs, standing close as I stopped by my bedroom door. 'Well? Will you stay?'

I hesitated for a moment, then I remembered the silk scarf. 'I'll think about it,' I said, and went into my bedroom alone.

Mick and Jimmy came into the kitchen as I was cooking the Sunday joint that evening. 'We weren't going to say anything . . . but after last night . . .' Mick halted over the words.

'He's not going to give you the full share,' Jimmy blurted. 'Yourself and Jason are getting a half.'

Mick turned away from the glare in my eyes. 'We know the

young fella took a while to learn. But you worked as well as any of us. And you looked after us well in the house.'

There was a council of war around the kitchen table when Pol came in. He squared himself at the scent of mutiny.

'So you're planning to snooker us,' I said.

'It wouldn't be fair to the experienced crewmen to give you the full share.'

Mick spoke. 'The experienced crewmen don't mind.'

'I mind. And I own the boat, so I make the divide.'

When they left for the pub that evening, I rooted in my bag for the telephone number my brother had given me before going off on his last contract, took half a bottle of wine from the fridge and slowly punched out the long Saudi dialling code. Manus answered the phone, and I told him the whole story, talking as the minutes tick by, and the hours, clocking up a massive telephone bill for Pol. I didn't put the phone down till I'd finished the bottle of wine. Then I picked up my rucksack and started thumbing home.

I stood outside Gora for two hours in the pissing rain while all these sleek cars splashed by, skiting water up my jeans. As darkness fell a dilapidated van pulled in beside me, front passenger door opened and a girl stuck her head out.

'Hop in quick before you get drowned.' She's young, with a nice round face. The lad behind the wheel looks hardly old enough to be driving. 'Where are you headed?'

'Anywhere, just to get out of the flippin' rain.'

At this stage my teeth are imitating a pair of manic castanets. Though there's water dripping off my clothes all over her, the girl laughs, handing me an apple as if the drenching doesn't bother her at all.

'What are ye doin' out a night like that?' the boy's voice booms in the closed space of the van.

'I'm going fishing. I've a berth on a boat in Castlecove.' I was always good at lying through my castanets.

The boy grins, flashing a black hole in his mouth where his own back teeth should be. 'That's a rare carry-on for a girl to be at.'

The young one looks at me as if I'm away in the head. The idea is too weird, or too boring compared with what she has on her mind. 'We're only married this two months.' She beams across at the boy behind the wheel, who bares his gappy smile at her. 'We've a caravan in the car park fornainst the big disco in Donegal town.'

I take a good look at her again. 'You're very young to be married.'

'I'm sixteen. Himself is eighteen.' The look passes between them again, uninhibited pride and joy in it.

'Were you ever inside that disco?' she asks.

'The Starlight? Sure. Every Sunday night without fail, till I got a bit of sense in my head.'

'They've a balcony, an' a big round ball like a mirror an' coloured lights that makes your clothes all shiny in the dark.' The girl has it all of.

'You go dancing yourselves?'

'I be askin' ones comin' out what it's like. You can hear the music in the caravan at night. I be tryin' to get himself to dance with me.' She giggles. The lad shakes his long hair out over the steering wheel, doing his folly of women bit, but he can't help taking another look at her. They're so indecently crazy about each other, it would make you want to cry.

They drive twenty miles out of their way to leave me in Castlecove and when they drop me off, the girl sticks her head out of the van window and waves. I picture them in a couple of years, up to their ears in crying babies.

Maybe some day they'll push their way through the swing doors of the 'Starlight', and maybe it will be as they imagine. Not the way I remember it – married men touching you up, drunks falling over you. Every Sunday night I knew what it would be like and every Sunday night I went back. I could never resist the challenge of those swing doors.

I took a long walk around the pier to cheer myself up. One of the mackerel boats had just landed. There were forklifts zooming backwards and forwards like demented ants. Over-loaded lorries were pulling out, leaving a wake of blood and fish. I stood watching the men working. They were huge and bulky in their hooded orange suits. But there was nothing clumsy about them. Every movement was rehearsed, pared back to the ultimate efficiency.

Coming up the town a couple of fishermen called out to me. 'Where you been, McStrancher? Fishin' in fucken Gora? Welcome back to the land of the livin'.'

I head into the 'Harbour' with them and order a round of pints. It was worth going away, I tell them, for the pleasure of coming back to this filthy, smelly town – to the energy, the blood and the life of it. I lift my pint and drink to all of us, to our diesel-scent and leathered skin, to our scarred hands and blackened fingernails, each at the mercy of variable skippers;

all of us chasing the one dream.

Some day I'll skipper my own trawler, and the first time I fill her up, I'll take her into Gora and berth her up beside Pol's half-decker.

Only that vision got me out of Gora without gutting Pol Francie.

Out in the harbour, a Nigerian ship is pulling in. I can see the slim black figures running up and down the deck, putting out ropes. I could watch them forever, delaying the moment I have to face back home. The old doll will tell me that's life. My father won't bother; he knows what I'm like. I'll keep on pushing my way through swing doors, barging through, half-knowing what's on the other side. It's the unknown half that lures me in, the half that calls to the part of me that wants to make everything different.

ACROSS THE EXCELLENT GRASS

CHRISTINE DWYER HICKEY

As a child she believed that the racecourse was in another country. So strange it seemed from her home just twenty minutes ago. Each suburb passed was a city crossed, each mile a thousand covered. It was as though she had been on a day out with Mary Poppins and button-booted had placed her tiny foot upon a chalk-drawn scene, watching it melt into the pavement as the picture grew to life about her. Losing its flatness and its silence, making her part of a mystery that was not her own.

And this is how small she was then and always walking with the left arm raised and the left hand held by a power greater than hers, that guided and pulled and shrugged her through the crowds and coming face to face with nothing except for handbags square and smooth or binoculars, badges bunched, swing-swong, from their straps. Flutter – 'I have been here'. Flutter – 'I have been there'. And no one to see their gold-cut letters save the child that tagged behind.

And then her head would be skimmed by a dealer's stall, sloping downwards, and fruit upon fruit laid out on sun-sharpened cobbles. And it could have been the roof of a Catalan house. And it could have been a Spanish voice that cried in words harsh and unfamiliar, *'APPLEANORANGE* AND *ORANGEANAPPLE . . . '*

And then the arm could come down and wrap itself around her and she would be raised legs loose, little stork, eyes squealing silence at the two bubbled toes of freshly whitened sandals. Flying yet higher for a moment in a soar so glorious. And then swing and then swoop. And how would they land? Please not on the bars of the iron-cruel turnstile or not so the dust rises over their straps. Veer to the concrete, clean and hard and the spark that shoots up through the legs won't matter. Just keep the white white, little stork. Keep the white white.

And then the loud grunt beside her head.

'She's gettin' big, Ed. She's gettin' big.'

'Aye, I'll have to be paying for her soon.'

Sometimes the crowd, so sure before, would hesitate and stop and the drum of hooves would come from behind the trees, passing in a string so fast they might be caught in a photograph, so fast no individual movement could be seen.

'Quick. What was the first number you saw?'

And quick, she would lisp the first number that came into her head, never really being able to pick out any one in the streak of saddle and flesh and the long bright blur of colour mixed.

'What did she say? What did the child say?'

And for once you could be heard and welcome, face puffed pink from your own importance.

'Ah yes. The luck of the child. Number 3, did she say?'

'What's that in the next race? Ah yes. The child brings him luck.'

But he kept a black man in the back of his car for that. Not a full body, just a head and a neck. He said he lost his legs at the Curragh and his hips at Fairyhouse and his arms and his chest at Cheltenham and he could have lost his willy anywhere. Longchamps maybe or Ascot. He wouldn't be the first fella to lose his willy at those places. Now all his luck was in his head and his brains were in his neck. She said he must have been very small for a man anyway even when he had all his bits and bobs. 'Ah, but you see,' he said, 'his mother was a pygmy and his father was a jockey and it was bound to be so.'

And so the head as small as a fist came everywhere, an eye on either side and cut like a tadpole and being able to see east and west at the same time. Able to see you no matter which side of the car you were on. And there were cuts without blood on the pointed chin and across the mushroom nose where the luck had chipped off over the years, and she must chip off more and graze her hands raw if need be, so important it was to the day. Feeling his hard head on her palm when, after her father, she would rub her hands in rotation, roundy roundy, and copy the chant that extracted the luck. She was afraid of him. The little black man that was in charge of the luck. For yet she might see those elbows sharp above her rise and move like scissors in the air and yet she might see fall like confetti to her feet the slow, coloured speckles of torn up dockets drop disappointment on her day.

And she would think of him now, his mean black head stuck inside the tyre where she had left him, upside down. How angry he would be. How spiteful if he chose . . .

But the horses past now and the men in grocers' coats flip

back on either side leaving a gap for the feet to move through. And the crowd begins to spread itself apart leaving spaces where she can see now the familiar and the wonderful. Here on the right and penned in by shining fence, the ring of careful grass and its outer ring of clay scuffed like brown meringue, where delicate hooves have tipped themselves upward on parade. And here, too, another brim with stool after tiny red stool, the exact amount of space from each to each and the spongy seat tight clung with artificial leather. But not hers now. Not yet. Now a bottom droops loosely over each one. Later on, when the spots and flowers and the salad of whirls of female colour have taken themselves off, and later on when the men in straw or donkey-brown hats have led the way to celebration or condolences. Then. Then they would be hers, to spin like tops or talk to as her pupils. And she can watch them from the seat that travels around the tree amongst the green and the quiet and the dots of tickets, thin as tissue and as useless now. She might eat a bar of chocolate while she waits, square by square and slowly, like on the television. Or the other one, the one that runs in pyramids down a pale yellow tube of paper and foil, the points of chocolate catching on the roof of her mouth at first, then melting softly with almonds and honey and secret crunchings. So long the tube, it may take all year to eat it. So long.

But that would be later on and now is now and her father's thick warm hand is ever pulling.

First walk up to the little house in the middle that looks like a wooden tent, the one whose floorboards moan beneath the feet, and the woman with the white fluffy hair and the chalky lips, penicillin pink. And waiting. Always waiting for the talk to stop.

Up in the air and only some words heard 'claiming this and carrying that and ground too this and proved form here and no chance there and Barney Chickle in the long bar says sure fire certainty from the brother's yard and sure fire certainty of losin' if that eejit's tippin' . . . and . . . '

Oh hurry up. Hurry . . . and she grabs the cloth of his trousers, making ding dong bells from the baggy bits behind his knee.

Turns on his heels and nearly knocks her.

'Got to go.'

'Good luck.'

– Good luck.

Now at last outside and there they are. Up above and skirting the balcony, cloaks red and navy hanging across shoulders and more navy in the hats neat as bricks on top of their heads and raising instruments like golden toys from the raw knees squeezed up from woollen socks to pursed lips that push and pull sound into shape for the crowd below. And making a change to the mood too and the step, the men a little looser at the knee, the women a little heavier at the hip. And hoop, a flash of brass stands up and caws and here and there a human hums in recognition. These are the Bold Boys. The boys from Artane. The boys who look no one in the eye unless he too wears a cloak and an instrument. Who will come down the wooden steps and march red-necked and eyes down before the off, to point their brass to the sky and herald den den derran . . . the horses are coming, they are coming, here they are.

And it must be easier to go back when the crowds have

another spectacle. It must be easiest going up the steps when you can look upwards.

Oh what did they do that was so bold? No one tells. Is it as bold as her bold? Is it as great? Could she end in a place where the devils roam free and sins are kept secret under the fall of a cloak? Could she play music so sweet?

And now turn to the clock standing like a giant's watch with hands so long and spear-tipped pointing at lines. No numbers. Behind it the bushy tails of the Garden Bar peep green through fragile lattice where women move and stop, move and stop, faceless under brims so wide. Except for lips pink and orange and red, one rosebud on each plate.

And more knees stop to greet and more possibilities to be swapped and sometimes stoop and, 'My she's getting big' and 'That can't be her – I wouldn't know her, so big.' And a child could be a giant before the day is done and a child could wear the watch that is a clock with lines. No numbers. But the child smiles tiny through one eye and dips the other scraping off the trousered-leg she knows.

'And do you want to go wee-wee, love?' Mini's rosebud asks and lowers down a hand with fingers knotted and striped with gold, stretching nails she's dipped in blood.

And no one looking down to see her shake her head. No wee-wees.

'Take her Min', as sure as J she'll want to go in the middle of the race.'

So unfair, big fat lie, she never would. She never did. She can go by herself. Big girl.

'See you in the Weigh-Inn.'

'Right so, Min, thanks.'

And turns back to Mini's husband, little man, leprechaun face. Used to ride himself before, now he talks his way over every furlong to the winning post. Min never says a word when they're alone. Just pulls. The trinkets at her wrist tinkling softly. A fruit basket, a star, a moon, two little balls on a chain. Always talks and buys her crippsanorange, crippsanorange, when daddy's there.

Only one woman in the ladies room looks different. Only one of so many. She wears a coat like a pillow slip with a zip up the front and her hair like a woolly hat pulled around her ears. She is always busy opening doors and handing out pins and eyes looking slyly through the mirror at big brown pennies drop into the ash tray.

They line up by the sinks and all their twins line up in the mirrors and all the while pencils and puffs and brushes touching on this and that on the upturned faces. And silence. Mostly silence. There is nothing to hear but toilets clear their phlegmy throats and tick-tack heels move and stop, move and stop. And 'Thank you, Ma'am, thank you' as the pennies drop.

She hates the smell. The pushy perfume smell. The clouds heavy in the air. It makes her want to vomit. She is afraid she will be too sick for her chocolate. Her eyes sting because of the smell or because she wants to cry. She doesn't know which. Min comes out plucking at her skirt. There is blood on her heels where feet forced into reluctant leather have been gripped so fiercely that blood has been drawn and cakes between the creases, tough and brown. Min asks the woman for a plaster. She takes out a foot that is big and mushy and spreads the band-aid onto the wound. Min doesn't say thank you. Nor does she wash her hands. She puts on more lipstick though and then they leave. Min doesn't notice that she hasn't done her wee wees.

They walk into the garden of the gnomes. Her father sits amongst the furrowed faces of the little men. They all stand, feet firm and legs in archways like plastic cowboys. There is no laughter now. Just talk. From earnest mouths that still manage to hang a tipless cigarette from one corner making it dance with words.

Everyone owns dark brown bottles. Some held, some tilted, some left standing for the light to shine through. Her father points his upside down into a glass. He makes black porter rise and leaves a tide of cream loosely on the top. Through his lips he draws black upwards. Ahhh, the tide falls down to the bottom of the glass and clings waiting to be melted. The little men have funny names. Nipper and Toddy and The Pig. The Pig runs messages for her father, slow winks and wise nods. They pass rolls of money and whisper. Later he will laugh. When her father laughs.

This place makes her think of the city at night when it should be dark, but it is not. The balls of light hanging from the ceiling like street lamps and the crowds that shove at each other, unafraid. Her father stands up. He is as tall as the highest shopfront.

'I'll go up so and take a look at this one.'

He fingers through his pocket and takes out a note. He points it at The Pig. 'Get a drink for the lads,' he says. The Pig is nodding at each one and asking what he'll have. As seriously as though the money were his own.

And now up the stairs. She pulls herself up the wooden banisters hand over hand. She must stretch her knee up to her shoulder so as not to delay. The man with the loudest voice calls out across the course. Somewhere outside she can hear the Bold Boys denden deren the start. They walk across the bar and out through the doorway. She can see nothing. Only if she droops her head to where feet stand with feet, down step after step. Or if she leans right back and looks up to the inside-out roof that lets in no sky. She is too small, a flower among the forest.

The man with the voice draws one long word out across the course. It is a word with a thousand syllables screechy and pulled through his nose. The crowd begin to join him muffling out names of place and colour and unlikely title.

She lifts back her head to look for the bird. She knows he is here somewhere, huge and still, his head turned in profile, his wings spanned over painted flames that rise like feathers from his feet. Then she remembers. He is on the other side of the roof, the bit that slopes like a wooden fringe, where he can see the fences bend and the horses roll slowly across the grass.

The woman on the step below her wears bright red shoes, with heels as long as scarlet pencils. She begins to bounce now, her dress flouncing slightly and her feet clicking up and down again. She stops for a moment then starts again. This time she lifts one foot altogether from the ground. There are scratches on the sole of her shoes and a name in gold that is beginning to fade. She recognises letters that are in her own name and shuffles to the edge of the step to take a closer look. The foot starts to come back to the ground heel first. This time it doesn't return to its own step. This time it reaches in the air and then drops landing on the step above, where her white sandals perch waiting on the edge. It is like a sword flung from a height onto her toes. She calls out but her voice is silent among the urging and the pleading.

'Go on, ye good thing. Go on.'

She cannot reach for her leg because her foot is trapped beneath the sword. She is pinned to the step. The tears pop out by themselves and roll like rain down a windscreen. A pain pushes down from her stomach and she screams. She knows what is about to happen. The woman moves her heel away and she is free. But it is too late. She lowers her head, gulping at her sobs. She watches the water trickle down the inside of her legs, down, down, it goes staining the hem of her upturned sock. She opens her legs and lets the rest fall down in little splashes, darkening the concrete with its pool.

The roar of the crowd cuts to silence just as the last dribble drops. People begin to reverse themselves and then turn towards her to go back to the bar. The woman in the red shoes looks at her, then at the pool, then back at her. Her rosebud tightens in disgust.

Afterwards she clutches her chocolate like a staff and walks through the crowds to the green outside. She can hear her father laugh loudly behind her.

'Stay on your tree-seat, I'll be out in ten minutes. Good girl.'

She walks on feet she must keep soft and sneaky, laying one before the other as though it were a game. She is unheeded by the stragglers and the dealers. She keeps her head down watching the frozen splashes on her sandals and the dent so deep that it is almost a hole. Her thighs smack kisses off each other rubbing the rash that is beginning to rise. Between them she feels her knickers dry hard and crisp, like knives cut into butter.

And in her little head just for a while she forgets her name and this place through which she walks. Though somewhere before her she knows there's a little black man waiting to be unstuck. And behind her the Bold Boys are folding instruments silver and gold into themselves and watching her from a height wade slowly away from the wooden house, across the excellent grass.

BRIDIE'S WEDDING

CHRISTINE DWYER HICKEY

Brim to brim across the hall table, hats lie like puddings on a shop shelf. Behind them are corsages, placed so carefully that only Kay could be responsible. On the floor boxes queue and wait for a vacant space to be found. Each one wears a tight skin of printed paper and a little tag of identification. But she is not tempted, not today, to slip a fingernail where it should not be and tear away a secret spot. No, today she has urgent news. More urgent even than Bridie's wedding. She must find Mother. But first she must find a place for her schoolbag.

She turns out of the hall and into the parlour and now the flowers have arrived and looking as if they've always been growing quietly there and plotting a sly and sudden debut. Kay's foot swings from a ladder and her hand presses a frame of blooms around the mirror. Sheila leans on the end of the ladder, using her weight to keep it steady. 'What are you gawking at?' she says. 'The piano needs polishing.'

'I'm looking for Mother.'

'Can you see her in here? No? Then go. And get that bag out of here.'

Now outside again and in through the second door. Jack makes a table out of boards and Eddie sits, bent over a tin of nails which his fingers tickle through. Bridie stands in the corner pressing starch into best sheets to disguise them as tablecloths.

'What's wrong with Bridie? Is she crying?'

'Mind your own business,' Jack says.

'If you tell anyone about the chocolates, I'll kill you,' Bridie sniffs.

'Tell what?' she asks. But nobody answers. 'How can I tell anyone if I don't know what . . . ?'

'Out,' Bridie and Jack say together. Eddie says nothing but just for a moment his fingers are quiet.

'Can I leave my bag in here, for a while?'

'No.'

And that's how it's been for the bag and her for such a long time. Being shooed from room to room, like a pair of old chickens. And nowhere to go except to the next room, or down to the shops. And it seems to her a little odd that up to now and Bridie's wedding no one even knew what colour it was. And now it was the household pest. It seemed easier just to leave it on her back. But Kay said she'll get a hump. And where's Mother, she wonders, sitting herself at the end of the stairs.

Mr Clifford's voice creeps down behind her. And leaning back she looks upwards where his long legs are growing out of the step at the top, and the chain from his pocket watch makes one silver loop against the dark and his black pinstripe suit. His arms hang by his side, a newspaper flopping from one. 'You can leave the bag in my room,' he says.

I'll have to ask Mother, she says to herself. For already he's gone. Mr Clifford is the opposite to her and her bag. He is the lodger and cannot be upset. She skips down the brown stairs and into the scullery.

Eileen stands at the sink, a cloth in one hand, a small brown chocolate sweet in the other. Carefully she pats it and then lays it back down into its nest at the bottom of the box.

'What are you doing, Eileen?'

'I'm dusting the chocolates.'

'Why?'

'Because I bloody want to.'

'Oh.'

She walks out backwards into the kitchen. 'Oh Mother, you're here.'

'Where else would I be?'

'Eileen is dusting the chocolates . . . '

'Yes.'

Mother stands behind a table laden with pillows of raw meat. Bolsters and cushions, pink and dark red and a funny-shaped one wrapped up in flabby grey fat. So that's why she had to bring Charlie's wages every week down to Costelloe's shop...

Mother rolls her sleeves up slowly and slaps each piece on the bottom before placing it on a dish. She clicks her fingers now and then at a hovering fly as though he were a waiter.

'Such news, Mother. You'll never guess what?'

'Don't tell me *you're* getting married.'

'Oh no. But when I do, I'll have it in a hotel. So you won't have to pay Mr Costelloe one single penny.'

Mother smiles. 'Your news?' she asks.

She takes the schoolbag from her back and slides her hand into the pocket on the front, careful not to graze her knuckles on the catch that hides inside. She hands the note to Mother.

Mother's pinny is a Christmas Card sky, navy blue and flicked over with stars. She wipes the meat stains on its front and takes the note, unfolding it slowly. She sits down then and 'Oh God. That's all I need.'

Sheila comes in behind a box of sherry glasses. So softly she holds it that not one tinkle is uttered. 'What's that? What's she done now?'

Mother lays the note down on her lap and she is so quiet.

'What have you done?' Sheila asks her.

'But nothing, nothing, I can't see the blackboard . . . '

'She needs glasses,' Mother says at last.

'Yes. Nurse says I *have* to.'

'Oh, is that all?' Sheila laughs. 'Sure she can get them on the scheme.'

But she doesn't want them on the scheme. She wants to pay for them. Well, she wants Mother to pay for them. If she gets them on the scheme, everyone will know. Those awful pink frames, that plastic case. Why, it might as well have 'Pauper' printed on it. No, she wants ones like Millicent Green's. Gliding up at the hinge to one small neat diamond. And a special yellow cloth, like a tiny desk duster, folded neatly into a box with a proper Optician's name engraved under the lid. A box that's blue and hard and goes 'clop' when you close it and tries to bite off your hand. If she can't have ringlets bunched in a bow, or a mineral in its own bottle instead of milk from an old whiskey 'baby', well why can't she at least have glasses like Milly Green's?

And her heart has a tantrum while she waits for the verdict.

'Mother,' says Sheila, 'she can get them for nothing. You won't have to pay. Do you hear what I'm saying?'

But Mother stands up and her lips squeeze in tight. 'No child of mine . . . '

And that's all she needs to hear.

She hugs Mother then and whispers a thank you and her face feels a sting from the nappy pins Mother still wears on the breast of her apron. Although there's no babies. Not since she's grown so tall.

'I'll polish the piano now,' she says, running off.

'Your bag,' Mother says.

'Oh Mr Clifford said I could leave it in his room. Is that all right?'

'Yes, and ask him if he could have his tea on a tray. Just for tonight.'

She knocks at his door and waits for his answer. Above her the skylight is ruby and blue. Her eyes stay on it even after the 'Yes. Come on in.' His dressing gown sways on the back of the door and then stays there behind it peeping out with its sleeve.

'My bag,' she says.

He points to a space beside where he stands. A space that seems a long way off. She crosses the room careful not to look around her. But even so it seems so different from when it was Mother's room, before Father died. And Mr Clifford moved in. She places the bag on the ground beside him and slowly he pushes it under the bed with his foot. His hand comes down then and pats her head, one, two, and three times. Then it moves, looking for somewhere to land. It hesitates and then settles on her shoulder. 'Pretty thing,' he says, 'pretty dress.' He smiles at her with all his teeth, but behind his gilt glasses, his eyes stay quite still. She runs towards the door.

'Mother says tea on a tray again.'

Downstairs in the hallway Sheila is waiting.

'Mr Clifford thinks my uniform's pretty. Don't you think that's funny?'

But Sheila doesn't answer her. She pushes her though, straight into the parlour, and Kay looks up slowly from the list in her hand.

'Tell her you don't want them. Tell her you don't mind.'

'Don't mind what?'

'You know very well what. The glasses,' and then, 'Do you know how long I was paying into Cassidy's club to get my outfit for tomorrow?'

She doesn't know. She knows, however, that it's best to keep silent when Sheila is angry. Best to say nothing. To think instead of the box that goes clop, or the skylight's glass with the light pushing through.

'She can't afford it,' Sheila says, pinching her arm.

'Owww . . .'

'Oh leave her be,' Kay says. 'What difference does it make now?'

Sheila goes out and slams the door and the cards on the mantelpiece shudder with relief.

'Kay? What am I not to tell about the chocolates?'

'The chocolates? Mr Clifford's chocolates? Oh there's nothing to tell.'

'Has it something to do with Eddie?' she asks. Because all secret things have Eddie behind them.

'Forget about the chocolates. Just don't eat any tomorrow.'

'Ah Kay, why?'

'Because there won't be enough to go round.'

'Oh. So why did they make Bridie cry?'

'Who knows? Weddings make people cry.'

'Then why do they have them?'

Kay smiles.

Bridie sits on the window sill and sips hot milk and pepper. Sheila kneels by her side. From beneath the bedclothes she peeps out at them. The streetlamp strokes orange onto their long white nighties and again across the curlers bumped tightly over their heads. Their whispers stay with them over there by the window but the odd one strays across the room and delicious it is when it's caught. Bridie is afraid of something, something to do with Joe. But who on earth would be scared of Joe? His swinging smile and adam's apple like a bouncing ball. And Sheila is thrilled by the same something. So what could it be? It had to do with being nude. Milly says when you get married you *have* to go nude. But Bridie would never do that. Why even in here, in front of her sisters, she would undress herself as if she was an orange in a circus. An orange that unpeels itself under a tent. Fancy being afraid of Joe. Oul Joe . . .

Meat sweat sneaks up the stairs and wakes her. Oh and the smell of cooking so early makes her feel funny; half-queasy, half-hungry. She opens her eyes and the room is alive. With crisp dress cloth and perfume hissing and stockings slapping into place. And Bridie's face like a small white turnip through the mirror and then changing slowly with each sweep of colour into a bride for Joe.

'I'm burstin',' she says to anyone who is listening and Sheila says, 'You'll have to wait. *If* you don't mind. Mr Clifford is in there.'

But she doesn't mind. She lies back nursing the urge and imagines what it will be like to sleep alone. Now that Bridie is almost gone.

Eileen says, 'Quick, he's finished,' and they all stop to listen to the cough that he gives each time he comes out of the bathroom.

He's left the smell of himself inside so she holds her nose and tries not to breathe. He's left the heat of himself as well around the rim of the toilet seat. And some dead black hairs stuck in the foam of his shaving soap. She washes her face and looks into the mirror. She makes two circles from her fingers and places them over her eyes. Just to get an idea of what she'll be like . . .

Back in the bedroom Kay helps her to dress. Guiding her frock down over her arms and playing the skirt until it stands stiff and wide. There are petticoats underneath that push it into shape and above a thin skin of peach organza with roses that you can see right through. Kay ties her sash and flicks out the bow, then slowly turns her towards the mirror.

'Now,' she says, 'what do you see?'

'Oh Kay . . . it's so lovely.'

And then looking again, 'Do you know? It's the image of that frock Eileen once had. You know the one in the picture that time at the Dress Dance?'

'Well, there you are,' says Kay. 'Isn't that a coincidence?'

Eddie says he'll walk back from North William St Church, because there isn't enough room in the car. But there is. Right beside her. She tries to tell him. But he doesn't seem to hear.

And even though he walks away, his hands in his pockets and his eyes supervising his steps, she still sits the same way, her dress bunched up into a hump. So that Eddie's space stays vacant all the way home.

Inside the house now and so many people. They all seem to know her, but she only knows some. Jack comes up the brown stairs, a tray over his head, shouting 'Load coming through' again and again. And all the old Aunts laugh and say he's a scream. There's sherry and port wine for each of the ladies and stout for the men and whiskey as well. And each glass grows its own deep colour from stem up to brim. Bridie's cheeks are stained with prints of strange kisses and Joe stands by her side shaking all hands and giggling out of his freshly scrubbed face. The tray with the meat comes up and Mr Costelloe looks down at it, grinning approval as proud as a father. And everyone says that her dress is so pretty and twirl after twirl is called for until she is dizzy. Funny though, Mr Clifford says nothing at all.

And she looks around bursting with pride at the stacks of strange crockery on the sideboard. Oh and if only Milly would believe that they own every piece of it . . .

And the table that Jack made is now a whole village with Bridie's best sheets the snow on its ground. Platters of meat lie low at its centre, the square around which all else has been built. There's mountains of bread, buttered and sliced, and big fat tomatoes heaped into hills. Skinned scallions, cleaner than she's ever seen, sprout like trees from pint glasses. And lettuce leaves lie in hammock layers on top of four plates that stand at each corner. Small pots of thick mustard squat shoulder to shoulder. And butter tubs face them across the way. And now at last it's time to eat, now the dishes of little beady potatoes are coming, their flaky new skin threatening to shed.

Charlie picks up one of Mrs Dolan's knives and spanks a glass until silence falls. 'Now,' he says, his face all red. 'If you'll all please help yourselves . . . '

She walks across to the window and peeps through its curtain. And why is Milly so late? Beneath her is the smaller table. Glass bowls, trifle bursting out from their rims like a fat lady's thigh bursts out from her stocking top and pudgy sponge buns lie back and wait along cake-stands out for the day from the Boston Bakery. The box of chocolates takes up most of the space. Row after row of matt brown jewels. And Mrs Dolan is beside her saying, 'Go on. Take one. Your tongue's hanging out.'

She reaches across and then remembers Kay. 'No. I'll wait. It's all right.'

Mrs Dolan starts to insist. But then Millicent Green walks right into the room and she forgets the chocolates, every last one.

'Oh Milly. Hello. I thought you'd never get here.'

'Mother said I must wait. Seeing as I wasn't *really* invited.'

'Yes, you were so.'

'Well, not to the whole thing.'

Milly looks cross so she says, 'Your dress is gorgeous,' and then, 'Do you like mine?' positioning herself for yet another twirl.

'Not bad for a cut-off.'

'What do you mean . . . ?'

'Hmmm,' Milly says, 'my mother is a dressmaker. Don't forget.' And then walks away to peep through the adults and the table behind them. She comes back in a minute with, 'I see you have our china.'

'Oh. Well, thanks for the loan.'

'Oh, don't mention it. It's not our best set.'

Milly is being so mean, she might not tell her about the glasses. Just arrive in with them as though they don't matter. Creak open the box and slowly take them out. Hawing the lenses and dusting them over first before inspecting them against the light. Yes, Millie can *just* wait.

Downstairs in the kitchen Mother fits dessert dishes into each other.

'Where's Eddie?' she asks.

'Oh he wanted to walk.'

Mother looks over at the clock on the wall and frowns.

'I see Granny Green has arrived,' Eileen says, pushing past her.

'Her name is Millicent,' she answers back.

She walks out to the scullery and Sheila is whispering to Lily Fossett.

'Bridie put them under the sofa, you see. To keep them safe. And you never guess what that drunken blaggard did?'

'No, what?'

'Fell asleep on the sofa. And peed in his trousers. And it dribbled down through the cushions. The chocolates were destroyed.'

'Oh my God. Did you throw them out?'

'No. We didn't dare. After Mr Clifford buying them. Of all people . . . Eileen washed them. They're upstairs on the sweet table. Just you make sure you don't eat any. And here. Promise you won't tell.'

'Don't be so silly. As if . . . '

She walks up the stairs and her face is on fire. How could he? The chocolates. Mr Clifford's chocolates. Poor Mother . . .

Millicent is standing in the hall. 'This is so boring,' she says. 'They're all half piddley-eyed in there. I'm sorry I came.'

'Why don't you go in and have a few chocolates?'

'Where?' Milly brightens up.

'Are you going to give us an oul song?' Mrs Clancy asks and then turning to her husband, 'She's a great little one on the pian-o.'

But Mrs Clancy is only saying it. Just because she knows she's heard what she'd really been saying. About her new glasses and her a disgrace her mother being a poor 'Wida-woman' and having to take in a lodger just to make ends meet.

'I don't know . . . '

'Ah come on. What about "All for Marie's Wedding"? I've heard you play that before. You do a lovely job on it altogether.'

Charlie walks in then and Mrs Clancy hooks on to his elbow.

'Tell her, Charlie. Tell her to play "All for Marie's Wedding".'

'Yes,' he says. 'Go on. That's your special song.'

'I'll have to get my music . . . '

'Go on then. We'll wait. Promise. Where is it?'

'In my schoolbag.'

No colour comes through on the skylight, now that it's dark. She knocks at the door and slowly she opens it. The shaft from the landing makes a path for her to follow. Her hand pokes under the candlewick spread, and it rubs its gentle fleece against her arm. There she feels the bag and slides it to her.

She hears a thud then and the shaft from the landing slithers off.

And everything moves so slowly, it's almost as if it's not moving at all, as if it's not happening. There are hands, she knows, that lift her up from the side of the bed. And at first she think it's someone looking for another twirl. But then she feels herself flop onto the mattress and bounce softly before being flipped over onto her back.

And then she sees him. So that's who it is. There at the end of that outstretched arm. That's his large hand pushing her small hands away. And pulling at her dress too, and tearing its roses that you can see right through. His second hand is a separate animal nibbling at the buttons in his trousers fly. His face is growing nearer and keeps saying shh, shh. Even though her screams are no more than a catch in her throat.

And then her hands go all quiet on her and lie dead by her side And why oh why would they not move? He is taking something out of his trousers now. And one knee is up on the bed and now the other is copying it. And everything so black that she cannot see. She can hear though, the shh shh and shh

shh. And downstairs too the cheering and laughter and Charlie speaking thickly the words that he's practised all week. But her breath gets so tight that the sounds fade away. And she is going to faint . . . just about to go when . . .

Suddenly they move again, her sleeping hands. And like two little birds they curl themselves inwards and tighten for a moment before they fly upward and . . .

PUNCH straight up, each taking a lens of his glasses. SMASH they both go into an instant spider's web. And he falls backwards and stumbles to the floor.

Her legs take her somehow over to the door and as it swings towards her the dressing-gown scrapes her face and brings her scream back to her. As though it had been only hiding.

There's singing downstairs and feet bangbanging on the parlour floor. Eddie sits hunched in a corner of the hall. He looks slowly up at her but then his elbow slips and his head falls back down.

She wants to tell him. To run down and shake him, to make her screams turn into words. She wants him to bash Mr Clifford before he sneaks out the back way. For already she can hear him gather his things. Eddie will get him. Eddie is the one. Sheila might kill her – the price of the glasses. And now the lodger's money gone. What about Kay? Oh look at her dress. Her lovely organza . . . Oh Kay . . . And Mother. What would Mother say? What does she say again when she brings tales from school? 'Well, you must have deserved it.' Yes that's what she says.

'Eddie,' she shouts and her feet start to move. One step then two . . . But the song from the parlour makes them stop:

Step we gaily on we go,

Heel for heel and toe for toe.

Arm in arm and row on row . . .

They are singing her song. Her special song. They started without her. As if she wasn't there. But it doesn't sound right. Something is wrong.

She sits down on the stairs and it comes to her then. Yes, that's it. They have changed the words. Instead of 'All for Marie's Wedding' they were singing 'All for Bridie's'.

One word and now it was a different song.

1994

THE LAST SEASON

MICHAEL BOWLER

*I remember certain mornings between spring and summer,
after the long runs in the woods, after the winter training,
when I experienced an extraordinary feeling of
completion . . . an exaltation. I burned with impatience to
throw my strength into the battles of the home straight.
They would say to me: it's peak form. I know now that it
had another name – le bonheur. You have never been truly
young if you have not known such moments. But one day
the time comes when your best form will never return and
on rather a sad note you leave the games of your youth forever.
Yet you have achieved some fulfilment. Sport teaches us to love
life passionately and to accept it as it is without cheating.*

– Michel Clare

When the evenings began to draw in I got that feeling. The
dread of darkness. Steeling my mind to face another winter's
training. Imagining relentless rains as I warmed up in the
soft September sun. I could feel the sweat oozing from my
forehead as I flicked my legs at the end of the warm up. The
crispness wasn't there. The last race of a long season. I felt
flat and adrenalin-dry and I completed a few strides. Heavy

legs and heavier heart.

The sharp crack of the starting gun made me pause. The 1500M field was away. I watched the initial burst down the back straight. The aristocrats of running. I felt a pang of nostalgia. It was once my event, in the seasons of my prime. When the speed was in my legs; I could change gear in a couple of strides.

I heard the timekeeper shout out the lap times 58, 59, 60 . . . I gave Simon a shout; we'd travelled up to the Palace together. He'd sent off the entries and talked me into a Ten K. It was an open meeting and the standard stretched like the field in the second lap. Four had broken away by the third lap with Simon tucked in at the leader's shoulder. He looked comfortable with that effortless bouncing style.

The sinking sun sliced through the four figures as they took the bell. The red vest Simon was wearing flamed for an instant, fusing with the fire in his face. I watched him closely as they came round, knowing he didn't have a fast finish. I gave him another shout, seeing the suffering on the face of the leader. He seemed to incline his head, then he was off on an extended kick. The surprise move at 300M opened a short gap but the other three quickly recovered. I felt a slight surge of adrenalin for Simon as he hit the home straight. The gap squeezed as he began to tie up but he pumped his arms to carry his legs through the tape. The winner.

The next race was the Ten K and I jogged across to the start. Simon was just lifting his head; there was a glazed look in his eyes. I knew the feeling well: the whirling head, the rapid rasp in the throat and the lactic in the legs. But the flying feeling as you kicked for home was worth all the puny pain at the end. I said, 'Great run, Simon,' as I sat down to put on my spikes. Simon found his legs before he found his voice.

'Thanks Kieran. It was bloody hard work.'

I laughed lightly. 'I know, knew rather.'

Simon smiled. 'Go on, you've still got it, old boy.'

I got up, laughing, and he called after me, 'Have a good one.'

I had time for three strides before the red-coated starter called us to the line. It was a big field and I found a place well away from the inside lane. On your marks . . . the gun raised the runners from their crouches. Meditation in motion. After a desperate lunge for the bend the field settled down to a relaxed rhythm. I dropped off the pace and switched off. Steady state running for twenty-five laps. Concentration became crucial as the laps peeled away. I tried not to notice the lap markers as we came round each time. Years of conditioning made me divide the distance into miles. Feeling free and fluid after a mile. Digging in at two miles as the pace quickened. Surge upon surge down the back straight with the slight breeze. The field finally falling away in total disintegration.

At Five K that sinking feeling that you had to do it all again. Only twice as hard. Running into oxygen debt, your legs going lazy with lactic. The purifying pain that raises the runner above automatons. Christ! The bloody agony! Another burst down the back straight. The leader trying to break away. Stay with it. My lungs labouring. Legs dying under me. I could feel the stinging sweat rolling down my cheeks like bitter tears. A haze before my eyes as we finish another lap.

Was that eight? Can't go through it again! The pain barrier is the figment of a masochist imagination. Must be six? I wiped away the sweat with the back of my right hand. Another miserable mile. Then a lousy lap . . . and . . . the bell. Another savage surge. The remainder of the field cracks. Only three through the figment; the trailing pack pale fragments in the setting sun. Going down . . . gold, silver and bronze. Cold concentration on the two front runners. Every metre mattered now. The pace seemed to settle into a tactical tempo. Waiting for the last lap. I forged to the front on the home straight. Token try. The bell . . . The catalyst setting up the supreme sacrifice. Like a pageant of pain the three runners carried the colours and cross of the crowd. Sharing pride and pain 300M from Calvary. Shadows shortening around the arena. A freshening breeze across the brow. I held the lead at 200M, feeling a fleeting elation. They were on my shoulder. Poised . . . I couldn't lift my knees as they pushed past, engaged in their own private battle. Off the last bend . . . they were gone, into gold and silver. I tried again down the home straight. Leaden legs driven by iron will. It wasn't there. Either the legs or the will had wilted. The finishing line. Home. Calvary conquered. Leaning over the steeplechase barrier. Feeling sick, faint, sad. The tragic trinity. Someone put a palm in my hand.

'Well run.'

Palm. Peace. I shook the hand weakly. The winners.

My legs wobbled when I tried to walk again. The sweat was cold in the small of my back. Simon came over and handed me my tracksuit.

'You really took them on in the last lap, Kieran.'

'Well, to tell the truth I was tying up at the bell,' I admitted.

'Your reserves must be well in the black then.'

We were interrupted by the results being announced. Name and time flashed onto the giant scoreboard. Bright bronze. Fading light flung from the imminent night sky.

Simon warmed down with me even though he'd already jogged a mile. I felt the lactic lighten in my legs as we finished. A quick shower and we were on the road. I relaxed while Simon took the wheel. Talking of training and times. Mileage and memories.

He was bound for Israel in October. The simple socialist alternative to the American scholarship system. It was a letter in *Runners Review* inviting athletes to Israel that prompted him. To work six hours a day in a kibbutz and to train in the sunlit citrus groves. Imagine. Idyllic days in December working on the land, Holy Land, lapped by the Sea of Galilee. Soft breezes from the hills fanning your face as you ran. In the evening of my athletic life. One more Everest to climb. The marathon. The mountain in my mind. When I read the international fixture list in the *Review* the dream began. 'The outstanding event of the Israeli athletic calendar is the Sea of Galilee International Marathon around the holy and historic lake on December 20th!' I realised Israel wasn't alien; outside Ireland it was the first land in my living memory.

Was not Jerusalem the city state I was searching for in the agony of exile. The ephemeral Peace I almost touched in my twenties. In the long walks through a little Kerry town. Enclosed in a verdant valley. The summer sun laid to rest. A scattered reflection in the river. Shadows fading from the hills.

Across the lonely road where my father was killed. A silence falling over the night.

It was past midnight when we got home both tired and troubled with our own thoughts. On the second Saturday in October Simon flew to Tel Aviv. We went for a pint with a few of the middle-distance squad before he left. I felt a certain sadness as we said good-bye to my training partner. Although it was six years since the Yom Kippur War the Middle East was still ravelled in a colonial contradiction.

In November I began the twenty-mile runs every Sunday morning. The first ten miles through the little village of Wakering were relaxed, my breath condensed in the crisp air. At fifteen the tingling in the thighs as the distance told. The last five miles with legs like lead; dead to the world for the rest of the day. Slumped in front of the telly watching the Big Match and drinking litres of orange juice.

Staying in every weekend; waiting for a letter from Simon. Taking my running gear to the launderette on Friday night. Shopping for the week on Saturday. Sometimes feeling restless and lonely in the weekend shopping crowd. Out of this mood I began to dabble in writing. During my Wednesday ten I got the feeling for the first vignette. It was a skinning cold night; I pushed the pace from the beginning to get warm. After five miles my mind was floating half-way between Bethlehem and Beenatee, a hill of home. I stole a Christmas scene from my childhood. Buried deep to build a personal pyre to my father. A reflection of his light. A guilt offering that I didn't believe in his everlasting life.

One Saturday I ran into Yussuf in the library. He was a

history teacher I used to share digs with when I first arrived in this town. I had picked out four books on the Middle East. Over a cup of coffee in the café I told him I was thinking of going to Israel for a race.

'Kieran my friend, Israel is a reality even for an Arab historian. Go by all means with your eyes and mind open. You're ready to suffer for your race. But think as you run: is your agony anything compared to the pain of the Palestinians?'

I didn't respond for a moment. I drained my coffee cup.

'Of course I'll try to understand, Yussuf.'

'Palestine is people as well as land. Subject to suffering without a home, scarcely a hope.'

'But Yussuf, you dreamed yourself free in Egypt. You once told me that instead of being a teacher you could have been tending a flock on the banks of the Nile.'

'Personally I think it would be more meaningful than teaching history to ignorant amnesiacs!

Seriously, I believe the Palestinians will have a state some day and in the meantime I feel that I can learn more by travelling.'

'*Asalaam aleikum*, Kieran, Peace be upon thee.' Yussuf gave his blessing on my journey. As we parted I said I'd send him a card from 'Palestine' and he laughed and shook my hand.

After an early afternoon five miles I settled down to read. *Green March, Black September*, the story of the Palestinian Arabs. I became so engrossed in the tragic story that I missed Man United on Match of the Day. The longing in their literature, the pain in their poetry . . .

Write down,
I am an Arab
I am a name without a title,
Steadfast in a frenzied world
My roots sink deep
Beyond the ages,
Beyond time.

I lay awake a long time; the night turned and my mind found succour in sleep.

Next morning I started my last long run in a grey mist. Going through the first ten miles in 65 minutes with a cold wind against me. I tried to keep the rhythm going along the seafront, the wind wild in my hair. I vowed to visit the barber as a gust nearly took me off my feet. The last three miles dragged and the little incline on the Boulevard became as hard as a hill. Once I cleared the last summit my mind had drifted to the shores of Galilee.

The elation of the run lingered into Monday. A weak winter sun glinted on the grass in Priory Park. A green prism through a film of frost. I seemed to flow over a forest. My mind cleared away the offal of the office. The naked trees trembling in a shadow. A cooling cloud across my wet brow. Into the sun for the second lap. Frozen faces filing from a tower block. Turning collars and noses up. I float across their path; beyond the life of concrete creatures. The grass softens under my feet and I find myself in its silence. I faintly hear my breathing, feel my footsteps. My mind and my body are suspended. One. Time better spent, in pubs and clubs. Disco here and disco there. Disco nowhere. The moment when running is simply a sacrifice. As close to the sacred silence of the soul as I could ever get.

After that five miles in the forest of my dreams the week was denuded of daylight. By Saturday I could write 100 miles for the week in my diary and my mind was ready for the marathon.

Christmas crowds rushed in and out of shops. Tarnished tinsel on a Christmas tree growing out of the hardness of the High Street. I got caught up in the mercenary madness as I bought an instamatic in Boots. As I was buffeted by the hordes I wondered would there be peace on the West Bank, in Bethlehem.

My last day in the office was interminable. The afternoon dragged; a dreary mist fell across the window. Passing time over a tea-cup. Later packing my travelling bag with T-shirts and jeans. The night before flying out I was going to spend at Aunt Áine's in London. The mist had multiplied when I finally caught the train at five.

Snatches of Christmas conversation on the Underground. Glossy ads glorifying plastic people. I read the meaningless messages to avoid the insolent eyes of a scut of skinheads. The rain had ceased when I reached Muswell Hill. The night was quiet, the streets bleak. Only one old man shuffled past me as I walked to my aunt's. He held a carrier bag in one hand. He was looking in doorways, searching for a home. So this was the streets of London. The last loneliness. The longest. Aunt Áine had kept a dinner for me but I could only pick at it. I felt tired and ventured to bed at ten. I lay awake listening to the late-night trains. The endless journeying.

I travelled in a dream during the night, a sadness shrouding my subconscious. I witnessed myself in stone silence staring for the last time through the front window at home. Rain-clouds ebbing away the restless evening. The hills huddled on the horizon, defining darkness. The rain comes pelting down.

I look at the clock on the mantelpiece; the one made in China. The time is twenty past nine. There is no knowing whether it is morning or night. But I'm leaving. My mother's face is drenched with tears. I reach out but can't find her hand. I board the morning bus. Passing through the soft shadow of the hills and into the nowhere of neon.

Another morning. Sounds seeping into my room. A child's voice; inarticulate tears. A train catching the echo of a tremor at the bedroom window. I drew the curtains across the day. Rain-faded light found the time on my watch.

I left in good time for Heathrow. I had to be there by midday although the flight wasn't until two o'clock. Israeli security had me opening my carefully packed bag. They didn't quite understand my pronunciation of kibbutz Ginossar as I explained the reason for my trip. My Hebrew was hairy. I ended up discussing the merits of my NIKE ELITE racers with one of them who did a bit of running. After moping around the concourse the flight was finally called. I found a seat on the last coach across the tarmac.

I glanced once more at the grey sky and couldn't wait to leave London. Within ten minutes we were in the air. EL AL: To the skies.

BIOGRAPHICAL NOTES

DAMIEN ENRIGHT: Born in Cahirciveen, County Kerry. Since 1958 worked in many jobs in Ireland and all over Europe. Returned to Ireland in 1989 to 'get down to work.' Writes on nature for the *Cork Examiner* and has also been broadcast by RTE and the BBC. At present writing one fiction and two non-fiction books.

MAURA TREACY: Born in County Kilkenny. Has had many stories in the *Irish Press* 'New Irish Writing' and in anthologies. In 1977 Poolbeg Press published her collection, *Sixpence in Her Shoe* and in 1981 her first novel *Scenes from a Country Wedding*.

GILLMAN NOONAN: Born in Kanturk, County Cork. Had his first and many subsequent stories published in the *Irish Press* 'New Irish Writing' and Poolbeg Press published his first two collections, *A Sexual Relationship* in 1976 and *Friends and Occasional Lovers* in 1982.

MICHAEL COADY: Born in Carrick-on-Suir, County Tipperary. His first poems and stories were published in the *Irish Press* 'New Irish Writing'. He won the Patrick Kavanagh Award in 1979 and was a prizewinner in the RTE Francis MacManus short story competitions in 1987 and 1993.

BARBARA McKEON: Born in Dublin. Since her Powers Gold Label story in 1977 she has published and broadcast many more stories and has had plays on RTE radio and television. She worked with the United Nations in New York for two years.

ANNIE ARNOLD: Born in Scotland, she was brought to Ireland at an early age. She taught Irish in Donegal, where she now lives. Her stories and plays in Irish have won Oireachtas awards.

EDWARD O'RIORDAN: Born in Cork, his first stories were published in the *Irish Press* 'New Irish Writing'.

MARY LELAND: Born in Cork, she has worked on the *Cork Examiner* and as a production assistant in RTE. Since her 1980 Powers Gold Label story she has published two widely acclaimed novels and a short story collection.

NESTA TUOMEY: Born in Dublin, she has had plays and stories on RTE radio and the BBC, and her stories have been published in many magazines.

MÁIRÍN O'CONNOR: Born in Dublin, her stories appeared in the Maxwell House anthologies and in *Threshold*. An art teacher, she has written many articles on the aubject.

JIM McGOWAN: born and lives in Dublin, where he is a member of the Inkwell Writers' Club. He has won awards in a number of short story competitions and has also had a story published in *Stand* magazine.

JOHN McDONNELL: Born in County Louth, he had a distinguished career in journalism and for some years before his death was editor of *Ireland's Own*. He wrote many stories, articles and TV scripts, and his plays were performed at the Abbey and Olympia theatres.

AIDAN MATHEWS: Born in Dublin, his first collection of stories was published in the year of his Powers Gold Label Award. Since then he has published a second collection and a novel, and is one of Ireland's most highly regarded contemporary writers.

PHIL FEIGHAN: Born in County Galway, she graduated with a degree in European Studies from the University of Limerick. She has had stories published in Ireland, the UK and USA and in 1990 won an Ian St James Award.

CATHERINE COAKLEY: Born in Cork, she won a Hennessy Literary Award in 1981 and her stories have been published in Ireland.

MARY McENROY: Born in County Leitrim, she is a Science graduate of Galway University. Has written little because of her teaching duties and 'dabbling in art'.

LIZ McMANUS: Born in Montreal, she grew up in Ireland and is now a TD for the Democratic Left party and a Minister of State. She won a Hennessy Award in 1981 and has published a novel, *Acts of Subversion*.

MARY O'DONNELL: Born in County Monaghan, she is a graduate of St Patrick's College, Maynooth. She has published two collections of poetry, a collection of short stories and a highly praised novel, *The Light-Makers*.

MARIE HANNIGAN: Born in London, she has lived in County Donegal since the age of two. She has had stories in the *Donegal Democrat* and the *Sunday Tribune*.

CHRISTINE DWYER HICKEY: Born in Dublin, she was runner-up in the 1993 *Observer Short Story Competition*. She has published one novel, *The Dancer*.

MICHAEL BOWLER: Born in Cahirciveen, County Kerry, he works in Essex as a customs officer. He had a novel, *Destiny of Dreams*, published in 1990 and won the *Irish Post*/B & I short story competition in 1993.